To my brother, Samuel C. Griffin,
and all of those who are smiling
on us from above.

LOVE LIKE SKY

LESLIE C. YOUNGBLOOD

SCHOLASTIC INC.

ISBN 978-1-338-64488-3

12 11 10 9 8 7 6 5 4 3 2 1   20 21 22 23 24 25

Printed in the U.S.A.   23

First Scholastic printing, January 2020

This book is set in New Caledonia Medium/Monotype.
Designed by Marci Senders

1.

THE WHOLE SHEBANG

"Ooh, watch me, watch me. Ooh, watch me, watch me," I sang as I finished the Nae Nae, and Peaches clapped. No one was hardly even doing that dance anymore, or the Dougie, but Peaches still liked for me to do 'em. They were her favorites.

"Dance some more, G-baby," Peaches yelled.

"Let me catch my breath first. That was the third time." I flopped down next to her on my bed, worn out.

Being a big sister was hard work. I was dancing the Nae Nae and the Dougie darn near every day. Sorta like I was on Grandma Sugar's favorite show, *Dancing with the Stars*, except I was dancing in pajamas and my bare feet.

And if all that wasn't enough, I let Peaches sleep in my

room, when she had her very *own*. She only ever wanted to go in her room to feed her goldfish, Girl. Guess I can't blame her, my room was pretty spiffy. I picked out everything in my favorite color—lilac, which is like purple with milk in it.

It's not like I had much else to do since Mama got remarried and we moved out here to Snellville, Georgia. It don't even sound like a place kids should live unless they want to collect bugs. When we were in Atlanta, my best friend, Nikki, and I went to the mall every weekend. There were more singers, rappers, and other famous people at Lenox mall during Christmas than I could name. But not one in Snaily Snellville.

Like Nikki always said: "Zip. Zero. Zilch."

I thought one cool thing about Mama marrying our new stepdaddy, Frank, and moving us out here would be that I'd have a big sister; that's something that even Nikki doesn't have. Her situation isn't as bad as all that, though, because she has a big brother, Jevon. Sure, he teases her and makes her do his housework, but Nikki can still go to him if she needs help. Even though Mama says I can always talk to her, she means Mama stuff, like if someone is bullying me, or if a teacher is mean. Not like how to kiss a boy, or when it's time to sneak a few cotton balls in my bra, 'cause Nikki says I'm flat as a pancake.

It don't even seem like we got a spanking-new big step-sister right across the hall. We've been together in our new house for six months, and she's never invited me into her room—never even seen her door open all the way. She left it cracked once, just enough for me to see a zillion cheer-leading and gymnastics trophies in there.

"Look, G-baby, I'm jumping like Tangie!" Peaches hopped up and down, using my other bed as a trampoline. Funny thing is that neither one of us had ever seen Tangie jump in real life, just in videos Frank liked to show us sometimes.

"Stop that before you break your neck. And you're making too much noise."

"Can't nobody hear me," she said. "Can I ask you somethin', G-baby?"

"What?"

"Do you think Tangie don't like us 'cause her real sister's in heaven?"

That question almost knocked me off the bed. Took me a minute to figure out what to say, since I'm supposed to have all the answers. That's what it means to be a big sister, and why I want one of my very own. I'd have to share her with Peaches, like my room, but that's fine with me.

"Remember when we first met Frank and you cried because he wasn't Daddy?"

"Uh-huh."

"Well, Tangie might feel a little like that. She doesn't intentionally *not* like us, but she misses her own sister."

"Will she like us one day?"

"Maybe. It might take longer than it took for us to like Frank."

"Why?"

"Umm, 'cause she's a teenager, and like Mama says, 'she has a mind of her own.'"

"We share minds, G-baby?"

"No, everybody got their separate minds . . . but when you get to be a teenager it works differently."

"You'll be a teenager soon?"

"Yep, in two years, I'll be thirteen."

"Will you have a mind of your own, too?"

"I guess."

"You'll still love me?"

"Not if you keep jumping on the bed, I won't," I said, trying to sound serious.

A second later she crash-landed on the floor and made a huge bang, because she's chunky for six. I'm kinda tall and skinny, what Mama calls "a beanpole." The school nurse said I was fifty-three inches, that's almost five feet. Mama says I'm bound to sprout up past that at any moment.

You don't have to study long to tell we're sisters. We both got Mama's dark brown eyes and dime-size dimples, but Mama said we're "double fudge-dipped," like our *real* daddy.

Just then, Mama opened the door and stepped into my room. Last night, we put gel on Mama's hair, then twirled it around spongy rods. After that she covered it with a silk scarf. Now her hair was big and curly around her face, and it made her look like an angel.

She had on pink lip gloss, and her eyelashes were as long as a baby doll's. Frank calls Mama his "cinnamon beauty."

"G-baby, Peaches, what are you two doing in here?"

"Nuttin'," Peaches fibbed, scrambling up off the floor.

"Too loud to be nuttin'. You two behave yourself. Frank and I are getting ready to leave." Mama kissed me on the cheek, then Peaches.

I sniffed. "Red Door!"

"You are a little bloodhound." Mama kissed me again. She has a dresser full of fancy perfume bottles. I can always tell which one she's wearing.

Peaches hugged Mama. "I knew it, too."

"No, you didn't," I said. Peaches is always trying to get in on something.

"Did so!"

"Fooling with you two gonna make us late for our date night," Mama said, as she tickled Peaches.

Mama didn't start that date-night business until she read President Obama and the First Lady had 'em. When Mama explained it, she said they're like "mini honeymoons." Now, once a month, sometimes twice, she and Frank get dressed up, and go out to dinner and a movie. Sometimes they even go dancing.

Mama calls those nights "the whole shebang." But I bet when Malia and Sasha lived in the White House, they weren't stuck in their rooms while their parents were out doing "the whole shebang." I wondered if, when Malia was a little girl, did she ever want a big sister?

"Katrina . . ." Frank called, his keys jingling as he jogged up the steps. His voice is deeper than Daddy's. Grandma Sugar said he sounds like Barry White. Frank used to be a marine and likes to be on time for *everything*.

A few seconds later he was at the door dressed in his favorite navy-blue sports jacket and tan pants. He'd shaved and was in shape like a soldier, unlike Daddy who'd slap his belly and say, "This here is evidence of good living."

"If you two behave yourselves, we might bring home doggie bags," Frank said.

Peaches's eyes lit up. "Chocolate cake?"

"That's your favorite, isn't it?" Frank said.

"G-baby's, too." Peaches pointed at me.

Frank held up two fingers. "Couple doggie bags it is." He palmed my head and then Peaches's.

That's his way of hugging us.

"We're leaving, Tangie," he shouted on his way downstairs.

"Yeah, okay!" she yelled without opening her door.

"We'll be home before midnight." Mama blew us kisses and walked out the door.

I folded my arms. "Mama?"

"Yes, G-baby?" She stepped back in.

My words stuck in my throat.

"What is it, honey?"

"You think if you and Daddy had date nights, you'd still be married?" I asked. Mama and Daddy divorced three years ago. She and Frank have been married close to one.

Mama unfolded my arms. "Oh, sweetie. It wasn't one thing that could have fixed your daddy and me. If it was, we would've done it. Understand?"

"Yeah, I guess."

"But grown-ups who've been married before learn from mistakes and try to get it right the next time."

"Is Daddy coming to see us soon like you said, Mama?" Peaches asked.

Now I really felt bad for saying anything. Sometimes most of my dancing was to make Peaches get used to the fact that we were in what Mama called a "blended family" and there I had to go talking about Daddy.

"I'm sure he will, baby."

I glanced at Mama's hands to make sure she wasn't crossing her fingers behind her back.

Mama planted a kiss on Peaches's forehead, then gave me a big hug. I sniffed her perfume and wasn't sure it was Red Door. She could be fibbing about Daddy calling, too.

When Mama and Daddy first tried to explain it, Mama said sometimes grown-ups "fall out of love." The best I can figure it: love is just a big old bed. When you're not happy, you fall out of it.

When I heard Frank toot his horn twice, I ran to the window and watched them drive off. Frank's minivan was the only thing moving outside. Some houses had lights on, but there was no other sign anyone was home, not even a dog barking. When we lived in College Park in Atlanta, if you stared outside long enough, you were bound to see someone opening a window, closing a curtain, or coming out to sit on the porch. This whole entire neighborhood seemed to have an eight o'clock curfew.

As I stood there, I plotted how I could get Tangie out of her room.

"Think he'll call tonight?" Peaches asked.

"I doubt it," I snapped, though I didn't mean to. "Who knows, maybe."

"G-baby?"

"Yeah?"

"Do you still love Daddy?"

"Of course. That's a silly question," I said as quickly as I could.

Peaches went back to jumping on my bed. All the jumping made her ponytails come loose. She had two thick puffs of hair on both sides of her head, with butterfly barrettes hanging on.

Before I could work out anything close to a way to talk to Tangie, she called "Dinner!" from downstairs.

As soon as we sat down, Tangie slid our plates in front of us. Tonight, it was chicken nuggets, mac and cheese, and sweet peas.

Tangie stood next to me filling my glass with apple juice like I couldn't do it myself. Her hair was in a million tiny braids she'd put up in a messy bun to hide the braids that were unraveling. And like cool girls on TV, her long T-shirt was hanging off one shoulder and had *Georgia National Cheerleading Competition* written on the front.

I closed my eyes and leaned over the plate. "Mmmm, this smells so good. I love peas."

"G-baby, you said before that you don't like—"

I kicked Peaches's foot hard enough so she'd stop talking. She wrinkled up her face and chomped down on a nugget.

Tangie didn't say a word as she dropped napkins on the glass tabletop.

"Tangie?" I asked.

For the first time that night, she looked at me. Tangie's hair and eyes were sandy brown like Frank's, but she had a face full of teeny-weeny freckles.

"Yeah?"

"Uh . . . can you teach me to cook like you?"

She sighed. "Open a can of peas. Pour them in a pot.

Get some frozen nuggets, put them inside the stove. Turn the thing on. And voilà! You're cooking."

"Well, you made the peas taste delicious. Better than Mama's." I bit my lip.

I hadn't even tasted half a pea, too scared she'd say something and my mouth would be full.

Peaches's eyes widened. "Nobody cooks better than Mama."

Tangie turned to leave but paused to uncuff her sweats.

"Pink!" Peaches shouted when she saw the word printed on Tangie's backside. "Oooh, your daddy said not to wear them pants."

I almost choked on the peas I'd finally shoveled into my mouth. Peaches didn't know when to shut up. I squinted my eyes so tight at her she was only a head. "Frank only said she can't wear 'em out the house," I corrected.

What he'd really said: "No daughter of mine is walking around with big letters across her butt. Just like she isn't going out with no octopus college boy."

Tangie ignored her, and Peaches knew better than to glance my way.

I had a feeling why Frank called the college boy "an octopus," and it wasn't good. He might be like that boy at my old school who got sent to the principal's office for pinching girls on the behind.

On her way out the kitchen, she ordered, "Before you two come upstairs, I want the table cleaned off and the dishes put in the dishwasher." Then she glared at me. "And could you keep your sister quiet and not work my nerves for a change?"

9

"Yes, ma'am."

"Don't 'ma'am' me. I'm not one hundred," she snapped.

An hour later, Peaches tired out and fell asleep, but I was still wide-awake. If Tangie's music wasn't loud, and Peaches wasn't jumping around, all I heard was crickets. I lay there in bed looking up at the ceiling, wondering how many lonely crickets were out there rubbing their wings together. Then, along with crickets, I heard voices outside.

I got up and flew to the window. In the corner of our porch I saw Tangie talking to a boy.

Octopus.

2.

LOVE LIKE SKY

I once heard Tangie giggling about a boy named Marshall to her best friend, Valerie, so I guessed he must be the octopus. She'd snuck those Pink sweats out in her purse when Frank made her take us to the mall with her and Valerie. Valerie kept an eye on Peaches and me while Tangie changed in the bathroom. I got two dollars, and Peaches got fifty cents, for keeping our mouths shut.

"You don't have to pay me, Tangie. I'm not a tattletale," I'd said, standing in front of Chick-fil-A.

"Well, you look like one," Tangie had said, and she and Valerie laughed.

When I put that out of my mind, it hit me: this was my chance to prove her wrong. If Frank caught Octopus at our house, he would ground Tangie for life and then some. I had to keep watch for her.

Trying to get another glimpse, I bumped my head against the pane.

I bit my lip and leaned back. Then the front door opened. I peeped out again, and they'd gone.

"Peaches?" I called real low. *Good, still asleep.* I tiptoed over to the window.

The first step in being sisters, even stepsisters, was not to be a tattletale. This was my chance to show Tangie all her secrets would be safe with me without her paying me a dime. Even as I thought about that, though, butterflies went fluttering in my stomach like when I had to give my speech about Shirley Chisholm in front of the whole class.

I inched into the hall and stood at the top of the stairs. I couldn't hear anything. Holding my breath and tiptoeing, I crept down the first step, then the second and third.

"Where is your car?" I heard Tangie say.

"Around the corner. You sure you can't leave for an hour?"

"Nada chance. The older one is talking about cooking. Nothing but a house fire waiting to happen."

"I'm not," I said under my breath, glad Peaches didn't hear Tangie's meanness.

"But they're sleeping," he said in his library voice.

Please don't check. Please. I squeezed my eyes shut.

"If they weren't, the chubby one would be shaking the floors. But I can't leave them here alone."

"Not even for me? C'mon, please. We won't be gone long."

"I can't risk it."

"Y'all out here in the 'burbs. How risky can that be?"

"They're little kids. Think about it."

"You're right. My bad. But I can only stay a sec. Meeting up with my roomie and a few others to lock down some plans."

"So you're going through with it?"

"Have you heard anything on the news or social media about Roderick Thomas?"

"Nothing."

"See. Told ya. That's what I'm talking 'bout." Each of Marshall's words sounded like exclamation points. "Media and social sites only get riled up when somebody is killed. What about the everyday violations of black people? Rod's like the second one harassed this month."

"No lawyer, huh?" Tangie asked.

"Tee, we talked about that." Marshall sighed. "Not everybody can lawyer up. This is real life, not *Law and Order*. But what we can do is march, obstruct traffic, whatever we need to at the very spot the police stopped him. When it happens to any of them, it happens to me. I can't just sit back." He must have hit his fist into his palm because it sounded like someone catching a baseball in a mitt. "I can't."

His voice was low and heavy with sadness. I felt like an intruder for eavesdropping, but Frank wouldn't care how his voice sounded if he caught him in the living room.

I'd leaned forward a bit more to hear Tangie because her voice was even lower, like when Mama comes in to tell Peaches and me good night.

"I know we've gotta do something. But blocking traffic? That's what the mayor wouldn't allow during the Ferguson protest downtown. Trying to cross that barricade got protesters arrested. My dad and I were there."

"Can't barricade what they don't know. And if some of us get thrown in jail, better for this than for no reason at all."

My stomach twisted when he said that. I'd heard Frank tell Mama that he and Tangie were at one of the Ferguson protests. He said it was the closest he'd been to going to jail since he was in his teens. When I saw Michael Brown's picture on TV, I asked Mama could I go, too. But she said that I was too little. But every time she'd see his picture she'd say, "Bless his mama, Lord. Bless his mama."

"Count me in, Marshall. I mean, I can make posters, whatever you need me to do. I just can't go tonight. But for the protest, I want to be there."

"Not happening for about two weeks or so. Thinking about gathering in the evening. How are you going to get away?"

"I'll come up with something. If he could just get to know you, then he'd see what you're all about."

He laughed quietly. "Yeah, he'd see I'm all about you."

She said something soft back, and they moved away from the stairs. I heard whispering and then . . . smacking. Loud smacking.

Kissing. They're kissing.

To get to my room, I had to go for it now. I got as low as a turtle and crept back.

Nikki. I wanted to tell Nikki but knew better. The first

time she got mad at me, she'd go tell anyone who looked her way.

This was my first real little sister test, and I had to ace it.

Then a light flashed in my window. I raced to check it out. If it were Mama and Frank, nothing would stop me from leaping down those steps like a super ninja to warn Tangie.

"Whew!" I said when two taillights lit the street. I made it my business to stand in that window like a scarecrow. After a few minutes, I put my elbows on the windowsill and rested my head in my hands.

Everything was quiet.

Minutes later, our front door opened.

Please don't leave. I could be a lookout for her, but I couldn't cover for Tangie if there was no Tangie in the house.

Marshall was standing closer to the light this time. He was almost taller than Daddy and had on a hoodie with jeans. I squinted hard to see if his jeans were all the way up, no underwear showing. If they were sagging, Frank wouldn't like him for sure, and neither would Mama. They didn't mind hoodies, especially after what happened to Trayvon Martin. But Frank says, "There's no reason on God's green earth a boy should walk down the street with his boxers hanging out."

Marshall bent down and hugged Tangie, who was a little taller than I was. Spying on them wasn't even on my mind anymore. I stretched my neck to see down the street, still keeping an eye out for Mama and Frank. If Frank caught

Marshall here, he'd be so mad at him that he'd never get to know what Marshall was all about. Well, it wasn't like I knew what he was all about, either. But anybody who wanted to stand up for people couldn't be all bad. Plus, if Tangie thought he was worth the risk of getting grounded, so did I.

My thoughts went back to Mama. She'd said that she and Frank were doing the "whole shebang." But what if, for whatever reason, they only did a half shebang? They could be home early.

When I looked at Tangie and Marshall again, he was walking down the street. I jumped back from the window and sat on my bed, listening. The door closed. Moments later, Tangie rushed up the stairs and her door slammed.

That woke Peaches. Just my luck, she picked up where she'd left off, like she hadn't been sleeping at all. "Let's play Beauty Shop."

"Did you dream about that or something?"

"C'mon, G-baby, it'll be time to go to bed for real soon." Peaches went to my dresser and snatched up my comb and brush.

"Just for a little while."

I undid my two French braids and let loose what Grandma Sugar called "a gloriously wild bush of hair." Next to my dresser Peaches pulled up a chair, and I flopped in it while she stood on a plastic crate behind me.

As Peaches tugged the comb through my hair, I thought about Tangie. If I could get her to trust me and talk about Marshall, then I could ask her what to do about a boy, too— Kept Back Kevin Jenkins. He used to always hang around us at my old school, Sweet Apple Elementary. Nikki said it was because he liked me. I'd never say it to Nikki, but I thought he was cute. His eyes were two different shades of brown, and his eyelashes were longer than mine. And he never made a girl cry like some of the other boys.

What if he did like me? What was I supposed to do? My brain was pounding.

I leaned back, and Peaches scrubbed her stubby fingers on my scalp. One thing was for certain, I could think until my brain exploded, but I wasn't gonna figure it out alone.

I needed help from a *real, experienced* teenager, not Know-It-All Nikki, who was just like me and never even kissed a boy.

"Ouch, Peaches! That hurts."

"Sorry."

Peaches pulled and twisted my hair for what seemed like hours before an idea hit me. I remembered Tangie's loose braids and figured she'd been trying to take them out. I sprung up in the chair.

"G-baby, water is dripping everywhere!" Peaches shouted.

I pretended to take a towel and wrap it around my head. "I got something better we can do," I said.

"What?" Peaches forgot about the make-believe water.

"Let's ask Tangie if she needs help with her braids."

"Okay," Peaches sang, hopping off the crate, then heading for the door.

As soon as we opened our bedroom door, I heard Drake's voice belting out of Tangie's room like he was having a concert in there. Peaches and I stood in front of her door like we were about to see the Wizard of Oz.

"She might be a little nicer to you, Peaches." I eased her toward the door. "Knock and ask if we can help take out her braids."

"Okay," she repeated, and gave the door three good knocks. We waited for a minute. Drake was on full blast, so she knocked again.

"What?!" Tangie turned down the music.

I elbowed Peaches.

"Can you play Beauty Shop with us?"

"That's not what you were supposed to ask," I whispered.

When Tangie opened the door, I snapped to attention like Frank showed us he used to do in the marines.

"She means, do you need any help taking out your braids?"

"No, thank you. Val's gonna do it."

I stared right at her. "I'm really good at it. I used to help my mama take her's out all the time," I said, hoping Peaches kept her mouth shut. I imagined helping Tangie and letting her know I saw Marshall and that her secret was safe with me. I just needed that time with her.

"Val's got it. Anything else?"

When I hadn't answered in three seconds, she shut the door.

Peaches's smile dropped as she walked away. "She hates us."

I put my arm around her shoulders and eased her back to my side.

I didn't say anything to Peaches as we returned to my room, but all I could think was maybe Tangie does hate us.

* * *

Peaches checked on Girl. I'd seen her watching Girl and wondered what she was thinking. But little girls need to have private thoughts, too, so I didn't ask, and I went to my room. Minutes later, Peaches hopped on *her* bed and I closed my eyes, pretending I was sleeping. I thought I'd fooled her. No sooner than I was drifting off Peaches called, "G-baby?"

I cracked my eyes open. "What is it?"

"It's about Girl."

"What about her?

"Does . . . ?"

"Does what?"

"Does Girl have to die?"

"Someday, Peaches. Everything has to someday."

"Even if I take *real* good care of her for always?"

"Yeah, even then. But the better you do that, the longer she'll live."

"Oh, okay."

She fumbled with the tiny stethoscope around Nurse Barbie's neck for a minute or two.

"G-baby?"

"Yeah."

"Daddy got Girl so we wouldn't miss him so much, huh?"

"No. He bought it 'cause Mama wouldn't let you have a rabbit, remember?"

Actually, Peaches was onto something, but I didn't want her believing Girl was some sorta replacement for our daddy.

"Do you think Daddy still loves us?"

Now I felt really guilty for talking about Daddy to Mama.

"You just asked me that a little while ago."

"No, I didn't. I asked did *you* still love Daddy. That ain't the same."

"Well, the answer is the same. Of course Daddy still loves us."

"How I know you're not lying?"

"What Mama say about that word?"

"Sorry . . . You might been fibbin' or telling a story. Like you were telling Tangie that Mama had braids, 'member?"

"Yes, I *remember*."

"Mama don't like her hair braided because she said they pull her brains out."

"She don't say that."

"Well, something like that."

"I'm trying to get Tangie to like us, so I was fibbin' to be nice. That's okay sometimes."

"Like when someone gives us a Christmas present we don't like and we have to say we do?"

"Yeah, that's close. But I don't have to fib about Daddy. We talked to him a few days ago, right?"

"It was eight. I counted backwards."

I sighed. "Okay, eight. That's not that long."

"Yeah. But he got a new wife."

"I know. We were flower girls, just like at Mama's wedding. That means he loves us, too."

She took a deep breath. "What if he runs out of love? You know, give it all away to her and don't have none left for us?"

20

"That won't happen, Peaches."

"How you know?"

"'Cause love don't run out like that."

"Like what?"

"Like gasoline. Love ain't like that."

"How is it then?" she asked, turning on her stomach to face me.

I'd been working on that question since she asked me the first time, and I still was tuning up my answer.

"Well?" Peaches nudged.

"It's like sky. If you keep driving and driving, gas will run out, right?"

"That's why we gotta go to the gas station." She flung her covers back and jumped into my bed.

"Yep. But have you ever seen the sky run out? No matter how far we go?"

"No, when we look up, there it is."

"Well, that's the kind of love Daddy and Mama have for us, Peaches—love like sky."

"It never ends?"

"Never."

Moments later, she had fallen back asleep and was hogging most of my bed.

That answer was good enough for Peaches, and I believed it, too, sorta. Daddy hadn't been calling as much as he used to, but I didn't want to worry Peaches. I figured the best thing to do was love her that much more in case Daddy's new wife made his love run out just a little.

3.

SNOOP TATTLER

The smell of Mama's biscuits woke me the next morning. When I opened my eyes, Peaches wasn't in bed with me or in my other bed.

"Peaches?" I jabbed my feet into my stuffed-animal slippers. Peaches's pandas and my koalas were supposed to be Christmas gifts from Daddy. But I bet his new wife, Millicent Parker, aka Millipede, bought them. Daddy probably didn't have time, which was one thing he and Mama used to argue about. I hated the slippers even more, knowing that Millipede bought them. Plus, who wants a big-eyed koala staring up at you all the time? I hurried into the hall. Peaches's door was open, as usual, but I didn't expect to see Tangie's like that. It wasn't cracked open, it was *wiiiide* open. And she wasn't even in there.

I tried to shift my koalas into reverse. But they kept stepping at full-speed to Tangie's room.

Glancing down the hall, I didn't see any sign of her. So I tiptoed in. A few steps, then a few more. Next thing you know, I was all the way in.

It was childish, but I imagined music playing as balloons and confetti rained from the ceiling. It was kinda like when Charlie got that Golden Ticket. Tangie's room was beautiful. There was a bookcase built into her wall filled with trophies. There was a poster of Gabby Douglas and Simone Biles as they twirled in midair. At the bottom of the poster were the words *Gymnasts Don't Defy Gravity . . . They Defeat It.*

Above Tangie's bed were clouds of pom-poms. I wondered how long it had taken Frank to put them up, and would he ever love Peaches and me enough to do something like that?

On the dresser were pictures of Tangie's sister, Morgan, and their mama. From what I could piece together about Tangie's mama, she lived in Houston. I heard Frank telling Mama that she blames herself for what happened to Tangie's sister and spent a year not saying a word, not even to Tangie. Mama just shook her head and said, "Some hurt only God Himself can heal."

Along with the pictures, different flavors of lip gloss were sitting on it: Chocolate Fudge, Strawberry Gumdrop, Orange Sherbet Surprise. She had as many kinds of lip gloss as Mama had fancy perfume bottles.

I didn't touch the lip gloss, but I picked up the picture

of Morgan—she had died in the car crash. When Frank and Tangie took Morgan flowers last month, Mama said she'd been in heaven almost five years. She looked so much like Tangie, except without freckles. I held the picture closer. I'd never seen anyone up close younger than me who was dead. My lips quivered. Morgan looked the same age as Peaches.

"What are you doing snooping in my room?"

I froze, like not moving would make me invisible, but not before the picture crashed to the floor.

"Oh my God!" Tangie shouted and rushed to pick it up. "The glass . . . it's cracked." She cradled the picture in her hands.

"I'm sorry. . . . I'm so . . . so sorry."

Tangie rubbed her thumb across the frame, then pressed it to her chest.

"There's money in my bank. I can—"

"Are you serious? I don't want your money!" When she glanced up at me, her eyes were teary. "Answer me! What are you doing in here?"

"Your door was open. I came in to tell you that breakfast was ready."

"Don't lie. Your mom sent me up here to tell *you* to come down. If you're a snooper, just say it. I knew I was right not to trust you. You said you weren't a tattletale, but you're worse." She wrinkled her brows like Mama when she was concentrating real hard or mad. "I know what you are. . . . I know exactly what you are. . . . You're a snoop tattler. I'll get my dad to put a lock on my door like he's been promising since you two gremlins moved in here.

Matter of fact, I bet you've been tattling to him about my every move. Haven't you? What is he doing? Paying you a few dollars to keep your big, floppy ears open, Snoop Tattler?"

"Stop calling me that. I don't have big ears. And I'm not a snoop tattler! I'm not. And I wouldn't burn down the hou—" My hand couldn't get to my lips fast enough.

"Oooh, I knew it." I got chills as her eyes laser beamed on me and her voice lowered. "Last night. You saw him, didn't you?"

"Saw who?"

"Don't play dumb, Snoop Tattler. He told me he saw someone peeking out. Now you think you can blackmail me? Come into my room whenever you want?"

"No, I would never do that. I wouldn't! I didn't mean to see him."

"So it's true."

"I didn't mean to. I didn't. I'm not a snoop tattler." I widened my eyes, hoping that would keep the tears in.

"What you call it then?" she asked. She was still cradling the picture of Morgan, which made me feel worse because she held on to it like Morgan was right there in her arms.

"I'm sorry. I've never seen that picture of Morgan before. I didn't touch anything else."

I held up my hands like Daddy would do when he was trying to convince Mama he hadn't eaten the last piece of cake.

"Well, you've seen it. And you almost shattered it to pieces, too," she said. Her voice cracked some. "You've done enough. There's the door. And put your hands down."

Then she whispered, "And you better not breathe a word to anyone about Marshall and what we were talking about. I mean *anyone*. You hear me?"

"Yes, ma'am." As soon as I said it, I wanted to turn to slime.

"Ugh. What did I tell you about that? I'm not your mama. Don't be a snoop tattler and a suck-up rolled into one."

How could I have been so stupid? I eased backward until I was at the edge of her doorway. Tangie sat the picture back on her dresser.

"She looks just like you. She's real pretty. I mean, *was* real pretty." I wanted to chop my tongue off. I dug my nails into my palms, preparing myself for more of Tangie's stinging words.

"Are you done yet?"

"I didn't mean to drop the picture, and I promise—"

The door clicked shut. I stood there with the eyes of my koalas staring up at me. They knew just like I knew: my chances of getting closer to Tangie were just like seeing someone famous at the Snellville mall: Zip. Zero. Zilch. I needed help, and quick.

I ran to my room and dove face-first onto my bed. I was glad that Nikki hadn't heard Tangie call me "Snoop Tattler." Nikki would wear it out for sure.

Now because of me being a snooper, I'd never have a big sister to tell me anything.

And I could forget about ever knowing if Kevin Jenkins liked me or not.

I buried my face in my pillow and soaked it with tears.

All I wanted to do was get Tangie to like me, and I ended up making her hate me more. The more I cried about it, the more I felt like a huge potato head. I needed to think. Daddy said if he sat around and twiddled his thumbs and waited for people to want to buy a car, he'd be belly-up. What was his word? Pro. Pro. Proaction?

Proactive. That was it! It was time to bring in the getting-out-of-a-jam expert. I sat up, wiped my eyes with the back of my hands, picked up my cell phone and called Know-It-All Nikki.

"What up?" Nikki answered on the first ring. She was always on her phone. Mama got me the kind with limited minutes and no internet. I made sure I didn't sound like I'd been crying. Nikki might say something about me being a "crybaby" and we'd argue.

"Need your help."

"What else is new."

"Anyway," I said. I hurried up and told Nikki what was going on. I left out Tangie calling me Snoop Tattler and everything about Marshall.

"You need to get over here, and fast. She's probably hating you more every split second."

"My mom put me on break from coming over there since we argued so much last time."

"Uggh. That was a week ago. She's probably forgotten. This is what you do: Clean up without being told. Take your shower without being told. When you do stuff like that, grown-ups like to reward you," Nikki said, popping her gum.

"Proactive."

"Pro-whatever. Do I have to think of everything? You know what, don't ask to spend the night. See if you can come over for the afternoon."

"I'm on it!"

After that we hung up, I hit the shower, dressed, and ran downstairs.

"Top of the morning to you," Frank said, and pretended to tip his top hat.

"And a good rest of the morning to you," I said, and tipped mine. He liked teaching me different ways to say the same thing—good morning.

Peaches was so busy swirling strawberry syrup on her biscuits she didn't even look up.

Mama kissed my cheek. "Good morning, baby. What kept you?"

"Shower."

Mama raised her eyebrows. "Wow, you're getting your-self together early this morning."

"Yes, ma'am," I said.

"Turkey bacon or sausage?" Mama asked, plonking a scoop of grits on my plate. Mama used to cook *regular* bacon till she learned Tangie wouldn't eat it. She still eats like a gymnast, even though I heard Frank say that she hasn't been on a team in two years.

"Bacon, please."

"Coming right up."

"Think I can go over to Nikki's today, Mama?" That didn't come out the way I was thinking, but I didn't have time for beating around the bush.

"Well, I doubt you'll want to when you hear what I

have to say. I was waiting for you to come down so I could talk to you and Peaches." Mama cinched the belt on her silk robe that replaced her old terrycloth one Daddy had helped me pick out years ago.

"Let me give you ladies some time. I'll be home around six, good-looking." Before Frank waved good-bye to us, he kissed Mama's lips and both of her cheeks. "See you this evening, Tee," he shouted upstairs to Tangie, then he clanked out the door with all his telephone line repair tools.

Mama walked to the door and kissed him again. A loud smack like Tangie and Marshall. I decided I'd better put Tangie's kiss out of my mind because Mama had a way of peering right into my brain.

When she returned, Mama was smiling brighter than neon fingernail polish.

I pushed my plate back a little. "What about Nikki's, Mama?"

She raised her eyebrows at me, and I knew I'd gone a little too far.

"Didn't I say I had something to talk to you two about?" She grabbed a pan out of the oven, set it on top of the stove, and then faced us. "Your daddy called this morning."

Peaches almost choked on her biscuit. "Why didn't you let us talk to him, Mama?"

"He was supposed to call last week," I said, and mashed my grits with my fork.

"You know your daddy's schedule, G-baby. What matters is he's calling now."

"'Member, G-baby? It's just like you said. You told me he'd call, 'member?"

"Yeah, I remember."

"Don't you want to know what he said?" Mama asked.

"That he'd call back later?"

It wasn't thinking about Tangie that made me sad now, but Daddy's new life that didn't include us as much as he'd promised.

"He said he wants to come and pick you two up."

"Just Daddy, or Daddy and Millicent?" I said but thought, Millipede. My plan to get over to Nikki's might be worth putting off to spend time with Daddy, but not Daddy and *her*.

Daddy moved with Millicent to Charlotte right after he and Mama got divorced. There must be a time a man and woman are supposed to wait before moving out of town together, because Mama told Nikki's mom that Daddy was living in sin. The summer after he moved, he'd come get us every other weekend, and we'd stay at a Comfort Inn with cable, free breakfast, and an indoor pool. I hated the pool because it was filled with happy kids, who had their mama and daddy with them, splashing around. Peaches doesn't remember it, but I do. Even now, when I see a Comfort Inn, my stomach gets queasy like I'm losing Daddy all over again.

He came back to Georgia 'cause he *said* he missed us too much, though I can't really tell it.

"Now G-baby. Millicent is his family, too. Just like Frank and Tangie are ours."

"When's he coming?" Peaches shouted.

"In a little while. He wants you two to pack for over-night."

30

Peaches lit up like a Fourth of July sparkler.

"C'mon, G-baby. Let's get ready. C'mon."

"I'm not going. I want to visit Nikki, not Daddy and his *girlfriend*."

Mama frowned at me. "G-baby! You know good and darn well they are married."

"I'm just not going over there. . . ."

"But you said you still loved Daddy." Peaches stabbed her biscuit with her fork. I wished I could remind her about those eight days without a word from him. She was ready to jump in his arms like he'd only stayed out of touch for eight hours.

"That don't have nothing to do with nothing," I said.

Mama tussled Peaches's hair. "Go on upstairs. We'll be up in a minute."

"You going to come with me to see Daddy, G-baby?"

When I didn't answer, Peaches turned and waddled upstairs. Mama sat next to me.

"Now that it's just us, young lady, tell me what this is all about."

"I don't want to go, that's all. I never get to see Nikki since we moved out here."

"Pick up that lip right now. If you two didn't fuss so much, you'd see more of her. School hasn't even been out that long. But you know darn well that's not what I'm talking about. Why are you so angry at your daddy and Millicent?"

"She's why he's not coming around like he promised."

Mama closed her eyes for a few seconds, then she wiped her hands over her face like a handkerchief. When she sighed a strand of hair curled up.

"It doesn't matter, Mama. I don't want to go. I want to go to Nikki's. Why we gotta jump when he's ready? What about the times we waited on him and he didn't come? I bet he doesn't keep Ms. Millicent Parker waiting for nothing. She's his 'best girl' now."

"Watch your tone, G-baby. Her name is Millicent Matthews since the wedding. Your daddy moved back here to try to make up for some things. He and Millicent have been getting settled in. We have to work with them, okay?"

"Whatever" sat right there on my tongue, but I knew if I said it, Mama would slap the taste right out of my mouth. "Peaches wants to go," I decided on.

"That's right, and you know she won't go if you won't."

I dropped my head and thought about how much she missed Daddy. "I'll get ready."

Mama pinched my cheek. "Peaches is lucky to have a big sister like you."

I nodded as "lucky to have a big sister," "lucky to have a big sister" ping-ponged in my head, leading me right to Tangie's door.

4.

SWEAR TO JOSH

Once upstairs, I could see Peaches was in her room, opening drawers and stuffing everything she owned into her overnight bag.

I eased in front of Tangie's door, practicing different ways to apologize, then it opened.

"What are you doing by my door?"

"I wasn't trying to listen in on you," I said, and put up my hands, like I'd been busted.

"What's up with the hands?" she asked as I dropped them.

"It's what my daddy does sometimes."

"It's not what *girls* do."

If my tongue wasn't a brick, I would've been fast enough to ask her what girls did do.

"Hello? What do you want?" she asked, tucking some braids behind her ears.

"Just wanted to apologize for before."

"You already did. I'm not buying it, Georgiana. What else?"

"You can call me 'Georgie.' It kinda sounds like Tangie."

"I'll call you Georgie, G-baby," Peaches said, going from her room back into mine.

Probably wasn't the best time to ask her not to call me "Georgiana," but I didn't like it, only Georgie or G-baby. Georgiana sounded like a teacher's pet. Mama said I got the name G-baby because I'd run to Daddy for every little thing. He'd swoop me up and say, "What's wrong with George's baby?" Peaches's real name is Patrice, but Mama loved Libby's sliced peaches when she was pregnant with her, so that's how she got her nickname. I didn't mind G-baby, but Georgie sounded like an *almost* teenager.

"I got the name for you and you know what it is?" Then she mouthed in slow-motion, "Snoop Tattler."

"I'm not a tattletale. I won't say anything. Swear to *Josh*."

"What?"

"I mean, I swear to God."

I flinched like a lightning bolt, or, worse yet, Grandma Sugar, was about to strike me for using the Lord's name in vain. But I needed Tangie to believe me. I zipped my lips like I was five. That dorky move made me want to crawl underneath my koalas.

Tangie's cell rang. "Just a sec, Val," she said. Right

before I turned to walk away, she grabbed my arm. "Just be sure to keep your mouth shut, Georgiana, Georgie, G-baby, whatever your name is. If you blab, you're gonna wish you weren't any of them."

A baseball-size lump sat in my throat, and I could barely respond. Tangie's door shut so hard it almost blew me to my room, which is just where I needed to be to figure how to get to Nikki's. I went and combed Peaches's hair, and we got ready to go to Daddy's. After putting on her favorite Princess Frog short set, somehow Peaches fell asleep, and I watched Tangie's door like it was the entrance to Willy Wonka's factory.

About an hour later, Daddy's car pulled up. Even though they'd been divorced for a while, hearing Daddy ringing the doorbell was odd. It used to be that whenever I'd hear his car, either I'd run to the door or Mama would. Or I'd listen to his keys bang against the doorknob. I wouldn't move a muscle until he'd say, "Daddy's home," and then I'd take off.

Mama would put her hands on her hips. "You gonna break your back letting that big girl jump on you like that. You know what the doctor said."

Peaches was still a baby, so Daddy would scoop her right up. He'd wink at Mama. "I got room for one more." She'd wave her hand like she was shooing a fly.

I pushed that out of my mind and walked to the top of the stairs to listen.

"Come on in," Mama said.

"Good to see you," Daddy replied.

"Sales okay?"

"It's up and down. People always going to need a car sooner or later. How's it going at Aetna?"

"Folks always going to need insurance, sooner or later."

They laughed. I loved the familiar sound of it. I used to fall asleep to it as they watched *The Late Show*. But those times happened before the shouting and slamming doors. If divorce made them laugh together again, it had to be better than them being married, I guess.

"G-baby . . . Peaches . . . your daddy is here. Get your bags together and come downstairs."

Peaches was still out cold. It was sorta strange that the news about Daddy didn't keep her bouncing around, but I figured that Mama's big breakfast must have caught up with her.

"Hey, Daddy's here," I told her.

She yawned and rubbed her eyes. "Okayyy. Is he coming up?"

"No, silly. This isn't his house. We gotta go downstairs. Go wash your face. You got sleep in your eyes. I'll get our bags."

Peaches's excitement seemed to have gone down the drain. She walked to the bathroom as if I were making her brush her teeth to get ready for bed.

"G-baby, what's keeping you two?" Mama asked on her way upstairs. "You okay, Peaches? I thought you would have met your daddy at the curb."

Mama eyeballed me.

"I didn't say nothing, Mama. I did her hair and everything. She's just tired."

Peaches fastened a barrette. "I'm not tired. I'm ready."
Mama put the back of her hand on Peaches's forehead.
"You're a little warm."

"I feel good, Mama."

"I'll call and make sure your daddy takes your temperature later today."

I touched my forehead with the back of my hand.

"Don't you even try it," Mama said.

Once we got downstairs, Peaches shrieked, "Daddy!"
loud enough to make the house rattle.

I bet Millipede was waiting in the car with that cheesy
too-white grin of hers. The only thing that wasn't perfect
about her smile was that it belonged to her, and so did my
daddy.

"Am I imagining things, or did you turn into a super-
model when your daddy wasn't looking?" Daddy said as he
hugged me. I breathed in his Drakkar Noir but didn't enjoy
it as much when I thought of Millipede buying it instead
of Mama.

I kept my hands at my side, but I wanted to wrap them
around him tighter than I ever had. Daddy's hair and beard
were what he called "fresh-out-the-barber-chair neat."
I was happy he had on jeans and a Falcons T-shirt. He
never stopped by his dealership with jeans on, even when
it wasn't open.

For a few months, Mama and Daddy got "separated,"
which Mama said meant, "taking time to remember why
they got married in the first place." Now I know it was
nothing but a dress rehearsal for divorce. Just like when I
was in *The Wiz,* and we had to pretend it was the real show

when it wasn't. Daddy called us right before bedtime, and some nights I'd hear Mama crying in her room when she thought we were asleep. That's what she did a lot until she met Frank, which is one reason why I like him, but I never told anybody that.

One time, Daddy picked us up for what Mama called our "outing." We stopped by the dealership for a "quick minute" and watched TV in his office the entire day. Peaches and I didn't mind because we could peek out Daddy's office window and catch a glimpse of him shaking hands. He'd blow us a kiss if he'd caught our eye, and it sorta made up for him not being there to kiss us good night. When we got home, we told Mama what we'd done. That next morning, she called him and they argued and argued. We haven't been back to the dealership since.

Daddy tickled me, and I put my hands to my stomach. He went for my neck. "Kit-Kat, we better sign this girl up for that top-model show. She could be our meal ticket."

I giggled. "Stop it, Daddy." It wasn't even the tickling or modeling stuff that was making me giddy. He hadn't called Mama "Kit-Kat" in forever, and it sounded real nice.

"I'll have them home by this time tomorrow, Kat." Daddy walked us to the door. Peaches was on one side, and I was on the other.

Mama rushed ahead of us and opened the door. "That's fine."

I squeezed Daddy's hand tighter. "Is Millicent in the car?"

"Nope. It's just Daddy and his girls."

"Really?" I said.

"Scout's honor."

Mama stood at the door and kissed both of us. "Call me before bedtime."

"Okay, Mama," I said, and took off.

As Daddy was struggling getting Peaches into her booster seat, Mama shouted, "Need any help?"

"I got it, Kat! Strap stuck."

"Make sure they stay hydrated, George. Already 'bout seventy-five degrees and it's only eleven o'clock in the morning. Might hit a hundred."

Mama stood rubbing her hands around each other like she was putting on lotion. That's what she does when she's fighting the urge to do something that she doesn't think Daddy can do, anything from cooking spaghetti to giving us medicine.

A few seconds later Mama was waving like we were going to a weeklong summer camp. I waved back, then gazed up, and there was Tangie watching us from the window. I waved, and I thought she waved back, but I couldn't be sure.

"Miss my girls already. Take care of them, George."

"They're in good hands, Kat."

I rolled my eyes at that and wondered how I could get out of his "hands" and over to Nikki's, and how long we'd *really* be Millipede-free.

I swear we hadn't been driving one whole minute, and Peaches was sleeping again. What was with her today?

"Where you taking us?" I asked.

"Out for some fun."

"You haven't come around like you promised. You said we'd see you so much, it would be like you and Mama wasn't divorced."

He reached over and put his hand on my knee. I folded my arms.

"Things have been a little hectic, Georgie. Your mama and I figured that you and Peaches needed time to adjust to your new home, you know?"

Adjust. Not that word again.

"No, I don't know. Why don't you tell me?"

I braced myself. Those words would never fly with Mama or old Daddy, but this was guilty Daddy.

"Time to get used to the Frankster."

I almost didn't answer, surprised that he didn't say anything about my sassiness. "I like when you call him Dr. Frankenstein better."

He chuckled. "I shouldn't have started that. I was being immature."

"So you saying it's Mama's fault you haven't been around?"

"Not at all. I'm going to do better. Starting today. You two getting along with his daughter?"

"So-so," I said, even though it was a disaster. But I didn't need him spouting off to Mama on my behalf. "If we have to get used to Frank, shouldn't you have to be around Tangie?"

"You mean taking her out with us?"

"Yeah, I guess."

"Well, it's not that easy when the kid is older. But that's a good idea. I'll be sure to ask her next time, okay, baby?"

His voice was too soothing, and he called me "baby." Not "Georgie," or "G-baby," but "baby."

Bad news coming right up.

Peaches snorted, and I looked back at her.

"What time did she get to bed last night?" Daddy asked. "She's usually into her second story before we hit our first stop sign."

"She woke up early and had her favorite breakfast."

"Biscuit with extra strawberry syrup?"

I laughed. "A couple. I think it zonked her out."

When Daddy got off the highway, I knew where we were going—Monster Miniature Golf. It was a haunted house for putt-putt, open all year. Daddy wanted to mold one of us into a female Tiger Woods. It was in College Park, which wasn't that far from the Atlanta airport. Whenever we'd see a plane coming in to land, Peaches pointed up to it like it was a pterodactyl. But I really didn't care where we were, or what we were doing, as long as we didn't have to share him.

"Think your sister will be up for some golf?"

"She'll be excited."

Peaches kicked the back of my seat in her sleep. When I peeped over, she opened her eyes.

"You okay?" I asked.

"Yeah."

Seconds later, Daddy pulled into Monster Golf. In the center of the parking lot stood a huge Godzilla with pointy teeth. It would've been more convincing if the pigeons hadn't built a nest on its head.

"We're here!" Daddy said like we'd landed on the moon.

41

Peaches didn't squeal or reach for her seat belt. Daddy hopped out and unbuckled Peaches, then she grabbed his hand and mine.

"Ready for me to beat my girls at putt-putt?"

"You never win, Daddy," Peaches said.

As soon as we opened the doors, a skinny girl with white makeup and lipstick for blood running down the side of her face greeted us.

"You got me shaking in my boots," Daddy said.

She smiled and slid Daddy a flyer showing the summer specials. "Three today?"

"Yes, ma'am," Daddy said. He opened his wallet as she scanned the coupons. "We're in luck, girls. Two-for-one cotton candy."

There were about twenty other people in the place, and Michael Jackson's "Thriller" blasted from the speakers. I was nervous, like that girl in the "Thriller" video, waiting for Millipede to pop up at any second.

But even after four games of putt-putt and a wad of cotton candy, we were safe. That was until Daddy said, "My girls ready for lunch?"

We were walking from the course and back inside the haunted house, where Daddy had to pay the bill. "Monster Mash" was playing for about the fiftieth time.

Peaches raised her hand. "I am."

"Not really," I said, and narrowed my eyes at Daddy.

"Me either," Peaches said.

"Well, Millicent would like to cook lunch for us."

I knew it.

I pounded the artificial grass with my club. "You said this was *our* time."

"Now, baby. It is. It's us right now, right?"

I didn't answer.

"But just like you two need to get used to Frank, I want you to also be comfortable around Millicent."

We checked out and walked toward the exit. Once we got in the car, Peaches talked about hitting the ball in the goblin's mouth for about five minutes before she fell asleep again.

"You know, you gotta give Millicent a chance."

"Okay, Daddy," I said, thinking of Peaches. She'd take time with Daddy any way she could get it. Helping her with that whole "adjusting" thing was like what Grandma Sugar said sometimes: it was wearing on my nerves.

5.

"CAN I GO TO NIKKI'S, *PLEASE?*"

As Daddy drove, the streets and signs became familiar. Chestnut Street, Baker . . . We were in our old neighborhood. Had he read my mind? Was he taking me to see Nikki? Did Mama mention how responsible I'd been that morning?

After a while, we veered down Black Swan Drive and into our old driveway. Daddy parked.

"Surprise!"

I turned toward him. "You know the people who bought our house, Daddy?"

"Yes, siree, Bob."

"Was it Grandma Sugar? Did Sugar buy it?"

"Nope!"

"Who?"

"You're looking at him!"

I undid my seat belt, hoping that what Daddy said wouldn't change. "Really? I thought you and Millipe— Millicent moved out to Decatur. There was a *For Sale* sign in the yard."

"Do you see one now?"

Just like in Snellville there were trees all around, but underneath some of the trees in our old neighborhood were sidewalks with pastel color chalk, bike skid marks, and cracks that we'd say if you stepped on one, "You'll break your mother's back."

"Peaches! Peaches! We get to be in our old rooms! We can see our friends, Peaches. Our friends!"

"We're visiting our used-to-be house?" Peaches asked.

She wasn't moving fast enough, so I jumped out, opened her door, and started unbuckling her seat belt. "We can play at our old house?" I whipped around to Daddy. "Does Mama know?"

"Yes, siree! We wanted to surprise you two."

Whew, that's a relief. Didn't want another dealership situation, or for Daddy to do anything behind Mama's back. That's one rule I learned about divorced parents: unless they tell each other their every move, it's suddenly "behind my back."

As I was getting ready to hug Daddy's neck, who should appear on the porch but Millipede wearing overalls like she was the farmer in the dell. Daddy reached for our hands. Peaches grabbed his, but I folded my arms across my chest as we walked toward Millipede.

She stood on the porch fanning her hands like they were on fire. "You girls have gotten so big," she said.

"I wear a size thirteen shoe now." Peaches wiggled her Big Bird tennis shoes.

"Wow, and what neat sneakers those are. And look at you, Georgiana. I swear, you have grown a mile."

"She's almost taller than Mama," Peaches said.

Millipede smiled. "You two are as pretty as you wanna be." Daddy's eyes fixed on me as we walked into the house.

"Thanks," I said so softly even I barely heard it.

"Is this my house or a soul food kitchen?" Daddy asked.

That made me mad, because he used to say that to Mama. But unlike Mama, who could make a shoe taste good, Millipede couldn't cook worth a dang.

"Were you surprised, Georgiana?" Millipede asked.

"Not really. It's just our *old* house. Our *new* house is bigger and we might get a pool."

I wasn't sure if I was fooling Millipede or not, but I didn't want her to have any part in making me happy. The living room seemed twice as big without our giant couch, bookcases, and our china cabinet that Peaches used to think meant the real place in Asia.

Daddy was quiet, but Millipede kept yapping, her natural hair twisted and flopping around like curly fries.

"Well, we haven't decorated much in the living room or dining room yet. We can get started on your rooms as soon as you like."

"Mama already let us decorate *our* rooms. Not like we'll be living here," I said.

"I want to decorate, G-baby," Peaches said.

"Milli, why don't you take Peaches to wash her hands?" Daddy said.

Peaches held up her hands. "I can do it myself."

"Can I wash mine with you?" Millipede asked.

"Okay," Peaches said.

I started to follow them, but Daddy's hand dropped on my shoulder like a cement block.

"You stay with me for a second." When Peaches and Millipede were down the hall, he lifted up my chin and waited until I met his eyes. "I get that this is hard, Georgie. But you got to try here. Millicent agreed to live in this house because she realized how much it means for me to be able to do this for my girls."

"Mama wanted to stay here."

He removed his hand from my chin and softly rubbed my cheek. I fought back a smile. "You're right. But Frank bought a new house, and just like you said, bigger than this one, and in a top school district, you name it. And he has a daughter who also needs stability. Millicent agreed to this for us. So what you think about trying to be nice to her?"

"Can I go to Nikki's?"

"Is that all you got to say?"

"Can I go to Nikki's, *please*?"

Daddy took my hand, and we sat down on the leather couch. Mama would never let Daddy get a leather couch. She said she didn't know why anyone would want leather sticking to their legs in their own home. Now Daddy had a whole living room full of it.

"Georgie, no one is expecting you to act like Millicent is

your mama. But we raised you to be respectful, so I know you can do better than what you're doing."

I rolled my eyes.

"Peaches is watching you," he said.

"I know. I know. I gotta help her *adjust*."

Daddy put his arms around my shoulders and pulled me closer, the leather ripping from my legs.

"We're all trying to help each other. That's the best any of us can do right now." He kissed my forehead.

"I won't be a smart aleck."

"Promise?"

"Scout's honor," I said, and he wrinkled his brow. "Think I can go to Nikki's before it gets dark?"

"Baby, let's enjoy family time. No Nikki's today. I'll make it a point to invite her out with us next time, though, if you want. So can we agree on that? Fair deal?"

"Fair deal."

Daddy stood up and extended his hand. "Good doing business with you, young lady."

"My pleasure, sir." I shook his hand.

I crossed my fingers behind my back. If Daddy didn't have to keep his word all the time, why should I?

"Georgiana," Millipede said, as she and Peaches breezed into the living room.

As politely as I could, I said, "It's Georgie."

"Sorry . . . Sorry, Georgie. You want to get washed up and come help Peaches and me set the table?"

"Sure!"

Millipede smashed me into her bosom like she was Grandma Sugar. "Thank you, Georgie."

Somebody seeing the way she rocked when she squeezed me would have thought I'd saved her cat from a fire.

I played right along with it. Once she finished rocking me to death, she let me breathe for a minute, and I left to wash my hands. When I got back, she slung her arm over my shoulder and grabbed Peaches's hand, and we went to set the table.

Even though she'd done little to the living room, Millipede had spent a lot of time fixin' up the kitchen. Betty Boop was everywhere. There was a Betty Boop menu board with *Millicent's Kitchen* written on it. Dish towels, salt and pepper shakers, and a rug each had a wide-eyed Betty Boop.

"Wow!" Peaches said.

Millipede spread her arms wide. "You like it?"

Peaches walked around like she was at Six Flags Over Georgia. "Ooooh. Betty Boop?"

"Yep. She's my favorite. When I found out that the character of Betty Boop was stolen from a black woman, Esther Jones, I went a little overboard. Used to have her all over my bedroom. I couldn't put your daddy through that, so here she is."

Peaches poked the Betty Boop figure on top of the cookie jar and watched it wobble. "It's more funner than our kitchen."

I sighed. "'Funner' isn't a word."

"It's funnier than our kitchen."

Millipede turned to me. "You like her, Georgie?"

"She's okay." I wanted to ask Millipede more about Betty Boop, but I stayed focused on downing lunch and checking the time on the Betty Boop clock that had lips in place of numbers.

I put on an extra smile. "Whatever you have in the oven smells tasty."

Peaches rubbed her stomach. "Real yummy."

"I hope you two like it. Found a recipe for it on the internet last night. You girls go on ahead and set the table. I'll get the salad."

Millipede handed me four red plates and four shiny forks. She passed napkins and those indestructible plastic glasses to Peaches. When Millipede took out the salad, I said, "That looks delicious," even though it looked like something that Tangie would eat.

"Whew, good, I worried that I overdid it with the raisins, nuts, cranberries, and apples."

Daddy stood in the living room with his back to us. He had one hand gripping his cell phone to his ear and the other squeezing the back of his neck. That's how Mama talked to him sometimes, too. I guess falling out of love made your neck hurt.

"They're fine. . . . She's fine . . . a little drowsy is all. Putt-putt energized her. . . .We didn't eat there. Getting ready for lunch right now. . . . Yep, they were both surprised. She's coming around. . . . Takes time. Why now? I'll have them call you before bedtime. I don't do this to you. . . . You don't have to remind me about that. Yeah, okay, I'll check it. There's one here. I know how to look after my girls, Katrina."

No more Kit-Kat.

Peaches didn't ask to speak with Mama. She was too

busy folding napkins into pyramids and biting her lip, concentrating on matching the corners.

Once Daddy, Peaches, and I sat down at the table, out came Millipede with her Betty Boop oven mitts, holding what looked like a chunk of the moon with millions of craters.

"If it isn't burnt, I've outdone myself."

I sniffed the air. "Smells scrumptious!"

"Scrumptious," Peaches repeated.

When Daddy eyed me and squinted, I knew I was overdoing it.

Millipede set the dish in the middle of the table. "Thank you, Georgie. Thank you."

Overdoing it or not, I was getting to Nikki's.

We hadn't been eating lunch but ten minutes before Peaches said, "I'm not feeling too good, Daddy."

"What's the matter, Peaches?" Millipede asked.

When did your name become "Daddy"?

"My stomach hurts," Peaches whined, and dropped her fork in the middle of her Tater Tots and Velveeta casserole.

Daddy reached over and gently squeezed her shoulder. "I shouldn't have let you two have so much cotton candy."

A part of me was glad that we didn't have to be Millipede's internet-recipe guinea pigs for dessert.

"Let me take you two up to get you settled," Millipede said.

"I can handle it, Millicent," I offered.

"You just want to take a little nap, huh, Peaches?" She nodded and I took her hand. It felt warmer than usual, probably from all the excitement. "I take care of her all the time at home, Daddy."

"I know you do," he said.

"I'm a little sleepy, too," I fibbed. It seemed like the best escape route.

"Okay. You two go on and rest. I will be up and check on you in a bit," Daddy said.

I took Peaches's hand, and we headed upstairs. We both hooked a left straight to our old room. Two twin beds with light green comforters and a tall chest sat waiting for us. The walls were bare and the knickknacks that made it ours were gone. Though it was our "old" room, it felt as unfamiliar as a new school. It was like when I'd see someone who I used to know in first grade: we were not strangers, but we had to become friends all over again.

Peaches flopped on the bed without taking off her shoes, so I did it for her.

"It's probably just that brick Millicent called a casserole that made your tummy hurt."

"Yeah."

"Daddy's gonna come check on us in a second. Just pretend you're sleeping, okay?"

"Think I wanna go to Mama, G-baby," she mumbled.

"I'll call her later for you, okay? Right now, we need to stay at Daddy's."

"Why? You didn't even want to come."

"Know how I always help you and dance for you?"

"Yeah."

"I need you to help me now. Just pretend you're sleeping. Can you do it?"

She nodded and disappeared under the blanket.

I kicked off my shoes, jumped in the bed, and waited.

Less than ten minutes later, Daddy opened the door.

"G-baby? Peaches?" I peeked at him but didn't stir. Neither did Peaches. He left the door cracked and headed back downstairs. I jumped up, and I did one of the oldest tricks I knew, stuffed two pillows underneath the sheets.

I tiptoed over to Peaches and nudged her shoulder. I didn't need her waking up and freaking out when she hopped in the bed with me and found the pillows.

"I'm going to Nikki's. But you can't tell Daddy, okay?"

"I really feel sick. I wanna go to Mama."

"You'll be okay, Peaches. We'll go home tomorrow and eat Mama's cooking. We'll make up our own dances, too. Wouldn't you like that?"

"Uh-huh. Can we call it 'the Georgie Peaches'?"

"Sure can. Just don't get up. Be a big girl for me."

"You won't stay long."

"No, gotta talk to Nikki about something, and I'll be back. Okay?"

"Okay," she said. I kissed her cheek. She still felt a little warm, so I took the blanket off her. When I got back, I'd tell Daddy to give her some Pepto-Bismol. I'd even take some, too.

With my sandals in my hand, I crept down the rear stairs. The dishwasher was running and Daddy was on the phone. It took me about a full minute to unlock that door, and I turned the knob so quietly I barely made a sound. Once on the porch, I took about another minute to close it, whipped on my sandals, then with Usain Bolt speed, I took off.

6.

SNORING BORING

In less than three minutes I landed right in front of Nikki's porch, and there she stood, her bangs and ponytails looking like her mama just did 'em for Easter Sunday.

"What took you so long?" she said, and popped her gum. "How'd you get here?"

"I'll tell you all that later. But we don't have a lot of time to talk. Tangie—"

"Stay right here. I'll be back in a second. And watch my bike!"

If I was Nikki's best friend, her second best was that bike. Or even vice versa. It was pink with turquoise specks in it. When she couldn't find the color she wanted, her daddy took her new bike to a body shop and had them paint it all her favorite colors. When the sun hit it, it sparkled like glitter and rhinestones. I wished that I wasn't sneaking over, so we could forget all about Millipede playing mama and Tangie hating my guts and just go bike riding like we used to do before I had to move away.

Even if only for a short while, I loved being back in our old neighborhood. It wasn't boring like Snaily Snellville. Kids ran in and out of screen doors, and grown-ups sat on the porch early in the morning until late at night. There was the smell of barbecue, not just fertilizer and cut grass. Then in the middle of the day, the slow ring of the ice-cream truck.

As soon as I sat on the porch, Nikki was back.

"Here, give her these." She handed me a Macy's box. When I opened it, there were gold hoop earrings.

"Where you get these?"

"What's it matter? My mama says they're too old for me. I was gonna give 'em to Jevon, but I don't like his new girlfriend like that. So they're yours. Give them to Tangie. That will let her know you're thinking about her and you got good taste."

"Thanks, this is a start."

"Know what the most important thing is?"

"What?"

"Stay out of her way. Like, don't be a pest. Don't ask her to show you how to do stuff. Don't try to be her bestie. I bet that's what you been doing."

I shrugged. "Sorta."

"I knew it."

As I was thinking about the perfect way to present my

gift to Tangie, a rusty car rattled up, and one of our friends from school, Tammy, got out. The car beeped once and drove off.

"Hi, Georgie," Tammy said.

"Hey," I mumbled, hating that my time with Nikki was interrupted. Tammy didn't have a brother, sister, daddy, or even a stepdaddy, so what help could she be right now? At any moment, I expected to see Daddy turning the corner.

"Thought you were riding your bike over," Tammy said.

"On my way until G-baby showed up. Your mama grilling out?"

Tammy shook her head before wiping the tiny rolls in her neck. "Nah, MARTA called her in. She might have to drive until midnight."

"Bummer," Nikki offered.

Tammy hunched her shoulders. "Used to it. Wanna walk to my house and get some snacks?" Since her mama didn't cook much and left her alone a lot, Tammy's house was like junk food heaven.

"We're kinda in the middle of something," I said.

"G-baby stepsister hates her guts. She needs me to fix it."

"Do you always have to tell everything, Nikki?"

Tammy tilted her chin up before she spoke. "My mama's boyfriend has a daughter. I talk to her sometimes."

"Big whoop," Nikki said.

"Is she older than you?" I was desperate.

"I'm the oldest."

"Then why are you even flapping your gums? She needs help with a big sister," Nikki said.

"You don't have a big sister," Tammy challenged.

"So! I got a big brother."

While those two went at it, I twirled the Macy's box in my hand like it was a Rubik's Cube.

"Oooh. Look who's coming," Tammy whispered. I didn't even want to turn my head because I knew it was my daddy.

It wasn't until Nikki said, "I didn't know she lived around here," that I managed to crane my neck. When I did I almost wished it was Daddy instead of who was strutting down the street like she was in the Sweet Apple Elementary School Memorial Day Parade: Lucinda Hightower. Nikki ran to her bike and sat on it like she was showing off a new pair of Uggs. Tammy smoothed her hair that had been sticking up all around her head. Then they both started waving like they were in a fly-swatting contest. All Lucinda did was hunch her furry Juicy Couture purse on her shoulder. It was the same one that Nikki wanted for Christmas, but her mama said that Juicy Couture was for older girls.

"Hey, Lu Lu," Tammy said.

"My name is *Lucinda*, not Lu Lu," she snapped.

I just rolled my eyes. If my name was Lucinda, I'd pay kids my whole allowance to call me "Lu Lu," "Lucy," "Cindy," anything but "Lucinda." Plus, she knows that's what her friends call her at school. It's just that none of us were her friends. She stopped in front of Nikki's porch and sighed like she was doing us a favor. Lucinda's glitter eye shadow sparkled like crunched up bits of stars. Nikki's mama caught her wearing eye shadow like that and took her phone away for a week. I wasn't crazy enough to try it.

"You live over here now?" Nikki asked, still straddling her bike.

"Sorta, kinda. Staying with my auntie while my mama is out of town. Can't wait for her to come get me. This whole neighborhood is snoring boring."

"Yeah, it is," Nikki said, avoiding my eyes.

"I didn't know you lived over here, though." Turning her nose up, Lucinda scanned Nikki's street like even the air was one-star. Then her beady eyes lasered in on Nikki's bike. "Least there's somebody I can hang out with," Lucinda said, like Tammy and I were invisible.

"That'll be cool," Tammy said. Nikki and Lucinda ignored her.

"Wanna go bike riding later?" Nikki asked Lucinda. Nikki must have noticed Lucinda taking note, 'cause she rubbed her hands along the handlebars like it was a cat.

"Didn't bring mine," Lucinda said.

"Don't matter. I got an extra one."

"If it's as nice as that one, I'll think about it. Don't wanna sweat my hair out now anyways. Maybe tomorrow. Just us, right?"

"Yeah." Nikki nodded.

Tammy refastened a clip in her hair. "We were finna walk to my house and get some candy and stuff. You can come with us."

Reaching in her purse, Lucinda yanked out a phone with a pink rhinestone case. Nikki's eyes widened like a baby unicorn sat in Lucinda's hands.

"No, thank you. Anyway," she said as she poked her finger with light blue polish at Tammy's stomach. "You might want to miss candy for the rest of the summer. Unless you gonna audition for Santa Claus."

Tammy was the only one of us in *Ho, Ho, Ho: The Santa Claus Chronicles* last year. Kids made fun of her because she was the biggest elf. I found her crying in the coat room afterward, and it wasn't just because of that but because no one in her family made it to the play. Mama and Frank took her with us to Golden Corral.

Nikki laughed at what Lucinda said. I frowned and kicked her tire.

"When did you start making fun of your friends, Nikki?" I said. Tammy didn't say anything, but she held her stomach like she was scared it would jiggle when she breathed.

"Lucinda was just teasing, geesch," Nikki said. "Right, Lu Lu?"

Lucinda shrugged, then started scrolling through her phone.

"Ain't nothing wrong with a girl having some meat on her bones," I said. "Everybody don't wanna be skinny like you."

Lucinda looked up. "Skinny? Skinny or not, at least I'm not cut from *every* step team I try out for."

"I don't get cut from every one!" I shouted. I hoped Nikki didn't say anything. She was making me fire-hot mad the way she was cooing up to Lucinda, but I'd never forget how Nikki had quit a step team after I didn't make it. I was great at dancing with Peaches, and even in front of Nikki and Tammy. But when too many people are around my legs get all tangled.

Nikki didn't speak, but Lucinda wouldn't ease up.

"Yes, you do! And what boy even looks at you twice? Ahhhh, none of them. Oh, except that raggedy one. What's his name?"

I glared at Nikki and Tammy, daring either one of them to help her.

Lucinda put all her skinny weight to one side and rolled her eyes up like she was thinking hard.

"Kevin. That's it. Kept Back—" she said.

"You better shut up," I said. I balled my fist, and I was gonna sock her right in the middle of all that syrupy lip gloss until out the corner of my eye, I saw a car pull up.

"Georgie, get yourself in this car, now!"

7.

KEPT BACK KEVIN JENKINS

"Where's my daddy?" I asked as my eyes met Frank's inside his car. My voice started cracking at the thought of how much trouble I was in.

"Let's not start crying now, Georgie. There's something I have to talk to you about. I need you to listen to me real good."

"I know, sneaking out of the house. Daddy's so mad he probably don't even want to look at me, huh?"

"That's not what we need to concentrate on right now. Your father called us. They had to rush Peaches to Emergency."

"What?! What do you mean?"

"I don't have all the details, but she started vomiting. And she was running a high fever."

"Fever?" I repeated, like I'd never heard the word. My lips started trembling. Peaches told me herself that she wasn't feeling well, and I knew she was warmer than she should have been. She trusted me to take care of her. My heart beat faster. What did I do? I dangled the fact that I was such a good big sister over her head and pretty much told her to suck it up. I'd spent all that time calling out Lucinda for thinking the world revolved around her, and I was just as bad.

I stared out the window so Frank couldn't see the tears in my eyes.

"Can you take me to her now?" I raised up in my seat and put my hand on the dashboard like I could steer the car.

"We're on our way. Your mom, dad, and Millicent are there. Tangie sends her best. But hospitals . . . let's just say that we've been through a lot in them."

Then it hit me what he'd really meant: Morgan. Tangie didn't even have her baby sister on this earth and here I was mistreating mine. The tears flowed. I couldn't stop them. Peaches was in the hospital because of me. She needed me, and I let her down. I wanted to admit to Frank what I'd done, but it was too terrible to tell.

I didn't bother to wipe my tears. What was the use?

"Are we going to the hospital where they took your wife and little girl?"

"Yeah, we are. Emory." He said the word as softly as Tangie placed the picture of Morgan back on her dresser after I'd let it crash to the floor.

Frank turned on the radio and an invitation to shop at Big Lots rang out. I guess the whole thing was upsetting him, too, even though Peaches wasn't his "real" daughter— he'd forgotten about Mama's no-car-radio rule. "Families don't get enough time to talk as it is," she'd say.

I jabbed my elbows into my knees and something crunched. I eased my hand in my pocket and pulled out the Macy's box, then shoved it back. I was the worst big sister in the world. All I'd done to get Tangie to like me and I'd forgotten about the person who loved me more than anything. When tears trickled along my neck, I did my best to stop them and not make any crying noises except for an occasional sniffle.

Frank didn't say anything. But at a traffic light, he opened up the glove compartment and handed me a few tissues. We got out of the car, and he reached for my hand as we crossed the lot. I grabbed it like I would catch a grasshopper, knowing I'd let it go but wanting to see how it felt. Frank's hand was like a polished stone, hard but still smooth. Unlike Daddy's, who rubbed his hands with cocoa butter to keep them "soft as a baby's bottom." He used to say to Mama, "If I sold a car as often as I shook hands, we'd be millionaires."

Once we entered the hospital, Frank let go of my hand, and all I could think about was seeing Peaches.

"We need to go to the fourth floor," he said, and pushed the *up* button. Instead of the alcohol, Chlorox-y smell that I remembered from when Grandma Sugar had what she called "a scare," the hallway smelled of coffee.

Pediatrics, I read on the framed directions on the wall.

Frank held the elevator open for the lady and two girls

behind us. A skinny boy held a McDonald's bag, and the scent of french fries only made my stomach sink more. Peaches always ate up hers, then wanted some of mine.

As soon as the doors opened, the lady and kids got off, and Frank and I followed. I gritted my teeth to keep myself from crying. Frank put his hand on my shoulder, and I really wished that he would have held my hand again. But I didn't know how to reach for his yet, like I would Daddy's. Or maybe I didn't want Daddy to see me holding hands with Frank. All my thoughts were jumbled.

"You okay?" Frank asked.

"Yes, sir," I said, which was about the umpteenth fib I'd told that day.

Frank led me to a waiting room. It looked like a bigger version of Peaches's room at home, with Disney and Sesame Street characters and sunshine walls. Several shelves and tables overflowed with books, board games, and puzzles. Close to a picture of Big Bird, Millipede sat on an orange sofa. No Mama. No Daddy. Just The Pede.

"Is Peaches coming home?" I blurted out.

"No word yet, young lady," Millipede said.

"We should know something before long," Frank said, and sat down.

Millipede gripped my shoulders and held me at arm's length.

"You know you worried us like crazy, too!" she said to me. "Sick and all, Peaches wouldn't tell us where you were. Your daddy guessed you were at Nikki's."

I wiped my eyes with the edge of my sleeve.

She pulled me close and rubbed my hair. I just didn't have the strength to pull away.

"I didn't think she was really sick. Not this kinda sick." That might have been the most honest thing I'd said in a while. I really wouldn't have left her if I thought she was hospital sick. That didn't even matter now.

"I know that's not my G-baby crying, is it?" I heard Grandma Sugar's voice in back of me and turned toward it. She stood there with Eugene, one of the guys she took care of. She said that his body kept on growing, but his brain liked being a kid.

I ran over and hugged Sugar. It didn't matter what time of day, or where we were, Sugar always smelled of her dusting powder, Wind Song. One sniff was apples and the other roses. I saved up and bought it for her every Christmas. Her baseball cap had *Who Dat Nation* on the front, and her silver-and-black hair curled along her neck.

"Sugar missed her G-baby. Your daddy can think all he wants that it's George's baby, but we know what it means, don't we?"

"Grandma's baby," I said, hoping that hugging Sugar would make me not as scared, but it wasn't working. The volcano of tears that had been bubbling in me erupted. Sugar hugged me tighter and patted my flattened ponytail. My whole stomach just caved in. If it wasn't for Sugar, I couldn't stand.

For what felt like an hour, I held on to Sugar.

"Now, now, sweetie. Peaches will be home before you know it." She kissed my cheeks on both sides like rich people do on TV. She knows that always makes me smile even when I don't want to. Then she eased me down in a chair next to Eugene, and I wiped my eyes.

"It's small, small. It's small, small," Eugene said, and reached for my wrist.

I jumped. He sprung up.

"You know he won't hurt you, G-baby."

Sugar held up her wrist, and he poked it.

"Not small, small," Eugene said.

"Umph. You got good sense. Sit back down there and read. Later, we'll go for another ride. Would you like that?"

Eugene sat down. "Dark dessert on the highway. Cool Whip in my hair."

"Yeah, yeah. Those aren't the right words, but we'll sing 'Hotel California.' But you gotta behave yourself."

He bobbed and sang out, "What a nice surprise . . . bring your apple pies."

Sugar tapped his knee. "And hush up before you get us put out of here."

"Hush up before you get us put out of here. Hush up before you get us put out of here," he repeated.

"I was just bringing him over this way for an appointment when your mother called. I don't see how she was driving at all. Said Peaches had already been admitted before she heard a word."

Frank stood and she kissed his cheek, too. Then she said, "Milli," and just nodded to her. "Any word?" she said to Frank.

"Not yet," he said.

"Lord, I wish I could stay," Grandma Sugar said.

"Couldn't find a soul to take over my shift. Tell Kat I'll check back later. I'm sure this is just a stomach flu or something. Maybe, you know, ate something that didn't agree with her." Sugar glanced toward Millipede, who shifted in her chair. It wasn't a secret that Millipede wasn't on Sugar's, or Mama's, Christmas list. Mama don't know it, but I heard her tell Sugar that Millipede went after Daddy "long before the ink dried." And now it was all because of me that things weren't gonna get better anytime soon, if ever.

Sugar kissed my forehead. "You call Sugar if you need anything. Peaches will be out before you know it. I love you both to the moon and back."

Eugene was rocking. "Moon . . . Moon . . . The cow jumped over the moon. . . . The dish ran away with the spoon . . . spoon. . . . Hey, diddle, diddle. Hey, diddle, diddle."

"Come on here, boy," Sugar said. Before she took his hand, she dug in her purse. "Want to get yourself something out the vending machine while you're waiting?" she asked me.

"Yes, ma'am."

She handed me two dollars and kissed me again.

"Come right back, Georgie," Frank added and pointed up to the signs for the vending area.

"Yes, sir."

Grandma Sugar and Eugene headed toward the elevators, and I followed the arrows. The hospital floor was so slippery that I wished I'd worn my sneakers. Although I wasn't hungry or thirsty, I didn't want to see Mama right away. How could I ever explain to her that Peaches had been taken to the hospital and I wasn't anywhere to be found? My eyes felt like balloons about to pop with tears. Lights, people, just about everything looked blurry, like Peaches's finger paintings Mama always hung on the refrigerator.

About two minutes into my sad stroll down the hospital halls, someone sang out, "Look who's here, the smartest girl in Sweet Apple."

I recognized the voice, and my steps got tangled up.

"Don't act like you don't hear me, Georgie."

I dabbed at my eyes and wiped the corner of my mouth before I turned around.

"I won't be at Sweet Apple next year," I said.

"Well, you know what I mean."

I didn't have to walk back but a step or two before I was standing in front of Kept Back Kevin Jenkins. I'd never seen him outside of school or our old neighborhood.

"What are you doing here?" I said.

"Duh . . . Somebody's sick."

He was wearing a short-sleeve shirt with a picture of the Incredible Hulk on it. There was a tear at the knee of his jeans. His Afro was short and neat. At school, the teacher made him take out the tiny diamond in his ear. Nikki said it wasn't nothing but glass.

"Sorry . . . Is it somebody in your family?"

"Who are you? A caseworker?"

"Nah."

"You getting a drink?"

"Yeah, and some peanut M&M's."

"Well, you headed the wrong way. The best vending machine is at the other end. Follow me." We walked down the hall together. "So what about you?" Kept Back Kevin asked.

"What about me, what?"

"Who you know is sick?"

"Now who's a caseworker?"

Kevin smirked. "I can't be one. They're always women."

"No, they're not. Men and women can have the same jobs."

"Bet you don't even know what one is."

"Somebody who handles cases, like a lawyer," which is what Mama told me I'd have to be before I became a judge.

"Just like I thought. Are you gonna tell me who's sick?"

"My sister."

"Oh, that's why you've been crying."

I sighed. "Yeah."

"That would make anyone cry."

"Guess so."

"Is she older or younger?"

"Younger," I said, and wiped my hand across my eyes, glad tears didn't fall.

"She'll be okay," he said, then nodded toward the vending machines. "They're right here." Against the blandness of the hospital halls, they stood out like brightly colored robots.

We stopped in front of a row of them. Kept Back Kevin leaned so close to me that our arms touched. I almost expected Nikki to jump from behind the vending machine and yell, *Oooooh. You like him. You like him.*

But then I remembered why I was in the hospital in the first place. And what if Mama or Daddy turned that corner and caught me standing arm-to-arm with a *boy*? I moved over. What would Tangie do?

"Not gonna bite ya," Kevin said.

I straightened out my dollar. "Didn't say that you were."

Not wanting peanuts stuck between my teeth, I only got a Coke. "You never told me who was sick," I said as we walked back to the waiting area.

"My mama. I ride my bike up here every day to check on her." He shoved his hands in his pockets. "Don't bother saying sorry. She keeps doing it to herself. She got diabetes. The doctor told her to stop drinking and smoking, and she keeps doing both. She 'sposed to stay away from junk food and sodas." He pointed to my Coke. "That's her favorite. Drinks 'bout six a day."

"Gosh, that's a lot. Hope she can go home soon."

"What for? She never does what the doctors say do and ends up right back. That's why I can't wait to go live with my dad."

"Where is he?"

"Rochester, New York . . . It's nine hundred and sixty-two miles away."

"Wow. I heard of it," I said, and added it to my list of fibs, but I planned to look it up once Peaches was home and Mama let me get on the internet. "When you going?" I needed to keep talking about anything so I wouldn't explode again, though every word got harder to say without my voice cracking.

"Soon."

The word swirled around us and made the time seem magical and faraway.

When we got close to the waiting room, he kept walking with me while I let the unopened Coke sweat in my hand.

I glanced up and there was Mama rushing toward me.

Kevin whispered, "I better go."

"Okay . . . bye."

"See you around."

"See ya."

I didn't really hear the words I said. All I could think about was Peaches and how upset Mama would be. The closer she got, the more her eyes looked like Kevin's—way down deep sad.

8.

IT'S ALL MY FAULT

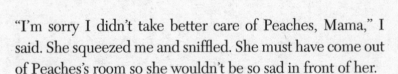

"I'm sorry I didn't take better care of Peaches, Mama," I said. She squeezed me and sniffled. She must have come out of Peaches's room so she wouldn't be so sad in front of her.

"Mama's not worried about that, G-baby," she said. "That's not your job. You weren't the grown-up. I called your daddy—I—" She stopped herself and glanced back at Daddy and Millicent, who were standing at the nurse's station down the hall. Daddy's hand rubbed the back of his neck again.

"Let's go have a seat, Georgie." Mama took my hand. It didn't feel like walking but standing still while everything changed, like when I stood on that moving sidewalk at the airport.

"Don't you want to wait for Daddy?"

"He'll come when he's done chatting with Millicent." Mama said her name hard like she used to do right after she and Daddy divorced. "Five seconds it would have taken either of them to call me about my baby girl, but she's here and admitted before her mama knows a dog-gone thing. This is all my fault. You didn't want to go with them. I should have listened to you."

"It's okay. I just wanna see Peaches." I couldn't bring myself to tell her what a rotten big sister I'd been. The anger she had toward Daddy and Millicent, I knew I deserved a heap of it. I no longer felt like just the worst sister in the world, but the worst daughter, too.

Once we got back to the waiting room, Mama sat down and pulled me between her knees. Frank came over and rested his hand on Mama's back.

"How are you feeling, Georgie?" Frank asked me.

"So-so," I said.

Before Mama spoke, she held her head down. Then she reached for my hands and squeezed them.

"Mama's gonna tell you this 'cause you're a big girl. You're Mama's big girl, right?"

"Yeah," I said, though I felt no bigger than an ant's eyeball.

"Baby, they're running tests on your sister," Mama said. "But they think she might have meningitis."

I let the word roll around in my head and didn't even attempt to say it. Not because I couldn't, but it felt like if I didn't say it, it would go away.

"Is it a bad cold, like the flu?" I asked.

"Well, it's—" Mama got that out, then her voice cracked again. "No, baby." Now Mama's voice was cracking, and my teeth were chattering like I was freezing.

Frank said, "It's a little more serious than that, Georgie. It has some of the same symptoms, so you're right, in a way."

"When can I go see her?"

"She's asking for you." Mama sniffled again and her tears streamed. "But Mama can't bring you in, baby. The doctor won't allow it." She dropped her head and cried, soft and sad.

Then I looked at Frank and remembered Tangie not wanting to come.

I stepped back, my fists balled tighter than when I wanted to sock Lucinda Hightower. But now, all I could do was punch my own legs, over and over.

"G-baby, stop that!" Mama said.

"It's all my fault, Mama," I cried. "You don't know, but it's all my fault!"

"What are you talking about? Stop punching your legs," Mama said.

"Is she going to die? Is Peaches going to die like Tangie's little sister?"

Mama reached out for me, but I didn't wait for an answer and took off down the hall, determined to find Peaches's room.

Before I could get very far, I ran into Daddy.

"Whoa, whoa!" he said.

I rammed my head into his chest. "You gotta do something. Peaches is going to die. And Mama says I can't see her. She wouldn't be here if it wasn't for me. Please make the doctor let me see her."

"What's this about dying? Peaches isn't going to die."

"Then why can't I see her? She's gonna die like Tangie's little sister. It's the same hospital, too. They might not be able to save her here."

Daddy drew me closer to him, which only made me cry harder, because it reminded me of how much I missed him.

Mama's voice surrounded me. "Georgie, I'm so sorry to scare you like that. I should have gotten myself together a bit before I talked to you." She rubbed the hair that had come loose from my ponytail. "Everything is going to be okay. Let's go back into the waiting room."

I didn't let go of Daddy. He walked with me, almost like when he was teaching me how to waltz before we went to the Sweet Apple Father and Daughter Valentine's Day Dance.

It was comforting walking in between Mama and Daddy again, even if I knew Millipede was lurking right in back of us.

As soon as I sat down, Daddy kissed my forehead, and Mama took my hand in hers like she does in church sometimes.

"Anybody need anything?" Frank said.

Everyone shook their heads.

"If I can't see Peaches now, Mama, then when?"

"Soon, Georgie. I promise." I remembered Kevin Jenkins's voice, and Mama's "soon" sounded even farther away.

I'd left my soda with Frank and started drinking it just to have something to do.

Daddy kneeled in front of me and patted my knee, like a puppy's head.

"Your mama and I will always do whatever we can, and then some, for you and Peaches. You believe that, right?"

"Yes," I said.

"I know you're upset about Peaches. We all are, but you gotta know that you can't go sneaking off."

"Yes, sir." My lips must have moved, but every other part of me was frozen solid. If I had a do-over, I wouldn't have never, ever asked to go over to Nikki's.

"Wait, what do you mean 'sneaking off'?" Mama glanced at Daddy like she'd do when he'd say he had to work late.

"Kit . . . I mean, Katrina, I told you when I called that I thought Georgie was over at Nikki's."

"But you didn't say anything about her going without your permission."

"Baby," Frank said to Mama. "I went to go get her. So he had to say it. Remember?"

Mama rubbed her forehead and shut her eyes. "If I remembered it, why would I be asking?" she shot back at him. Mama and Frank seldom argued, but when they did, it was never the type of argument that ended with Frank sleeping on the couch, or Mama hauling off Peaches and me to go stay with Sugar.

"Frank, I said that he might have said it, but this is the first I'm hearing that Georgie ran off without anyone knowing. What kind of supervision is that?" Mama said, scanning between Daddy and Millicent. Then her eyes zeroed in on Daddy. "So just how long was she missing?"

Daddy just shook his head but didn't speak.

"I don't think that's fair, Katrina," Millipede said, and that gave me chills because I'd never heard them say nothing but short, nice words to each other, face-to-face anyway. "It's not like we weren't there. Georgiana snuck out. I wouldn't stress about it right now." Millipede squeezed Daddy's shoulder. "I'm sure Georgiana knows it wasn't the right thing to do. Maybe we just all need to discuss this another time."

"No, first what I need for you to do is not add your two cents when I'm talking to my ex-husband about *our* child." Then Mama's finger swayed like a windshield wiper between Daddy and Millicent. "When you two have one, I'll show you the same respect. Second, what I need is to know that when my kids are out of my sight, one doesn't end up in the Emergency and the other doesn't go sneaking off, roaming the streets. You two barely make time for them, and when you do, all this happens. On your watch!" She slapped her hand on her shaking knees. "I told you before you left to take care of my girls, and you said, 'They're in good hands,' like you were the Allstate man. I even called to see how everything was going and you rushed me off the phone. Now look. *Look!*"

"Don't put this on me like that, Katrina." Daddy tilted his head back and blew a loud breath toward the yellow ceiling, then he stared straight at Mama. "We don't know what made Peaches sick. And I didn't move them out to Timbuktu. That's why G-baby wanted to see her friend in the first place."

If my lips weren't glued shut, I would have spoken. All I could feel was the Macy's box poking me in my side.

Mama's voice raised. "Are you serious right now? You left Georgia! Didn't see them for months at a time. Barely called."

"You know what we talked about."

"Please don't say because you two are living in our old house that makes everything okay. Why did we lose it in the first place? Answer that, George!"

"Don't do this. Not now." Daddy shoved his hands in his pockets and walked away.

"He loves his girls, Katrina," Millipede said.

"You are the *last* person I want to hear from. I don't even want to—"

"Enough of this, Katrina," Frank said. "They're right. This isn't the time or place." Frank put his arm around Mama's waist and hurried her to the opposite side of the waiting room. Millipede slunk over to the corner.

I sat there with a dunce cap higher than the ceiling. Crying again would only make matters worse. That's the last thing I wanted.

A nurse stepped in. "Mr. and Mrs. Matthews. Everything okay?"

"It's fine. A little emotional is all," Daddy said. Frank and Mama stepped out of the waiting room. Then Daddy walked over and sat beside me. I tilted my head to lean on his shoulder.

"Sorry for all that, Georgie. Shouldn't have brought up your leaving. Don't know what I was thinking."

"Not your fault. Mama just extra mad 'cause Peaches

is sick. When she comes home, maybe we can come back over. I won't leave her alone, I promise."

Frank returned to the waiting room without Mama and motioned for Daddy, who patted me two times on my knee and stood.

"Be right back, Georgie."

Millipede eased down and sat a seat away. "It's going to be okay," she said gently.

I nodded. Even though she wasn't my favorite person, I hoped Mama didn't hurt her feelings too much.

After about ten minutes, Frank marched into the waiting room. He clapped his hands once, then rubbed them together, smiling at me the whole time. Just like Mama, he didn't know that I could tell a fake smile from a real one. Mama and Daddy's separation made me an expert, especially when we'd have family dinner and they'd wear their mannequin smiles.

"Did you hear me, G-baby?" Frank's voice brought me out of my thoughts.

"No, sir."

"Your mom and dad are in with Peaches. But your mom says I should take you home. We can stop and get something to eat, then go for ice cream."

"You mean I can't see her before I leave? She's gotta stay here . . . by herself?" The hospital seemed to grow to a hundred times its size. "She don't even like to sleep in her own room by herself. I gotta tell 'em!"

"Your mom and dad are with her. They know exactly what to do."

Millipede put her hands on my shoulder again. I guess

that was her thing. "Your mom and dad will stay with her."

"They won't keep her in the hospital a second longer than they have to, Georgie. Your mama wants me to get you on home," Frank said.

"No. No, I gotta see Peaches. Please. She needs me."

"Stay with her, Millicent. I'll be right back."

Millipede rubbed my back and I flinched.

She was talking, but my brain turned her voice into something close to Charlie Brown's teacher—I could hear sound, but the words were jumbled.

Frank was back in a few minutes with Mama at his side. Mama's mask that was supposed to go around her mouth dangled from her ear. Millipede got up and walked away.

"Georgie, let Frank take you home now so you can get some rest."

"Can I see Peaches tomorrow?"

"We can't say for sure, baby," Mama said. "I need to get back now, okay?"

"Okay," I said, and stabbed my elbows into my legs. Something crunched.

That Macy's box. I wanted to snatch it out of my pocket and throw it against the wall. I could tell Mama and Frank the real reason I snuck off, but they might force Tangie to talk to me and she'd hate me more. I took it out and dropped it between the chairs. Somebody would find it and have better luck with those earrings than I did.

While the grown-ups talked about what to do with me like I wasn't even there, I lowered my head and squeezed my eyes tight. *God, I know I want a big sister, but Peaches is the best little sister in the world. Please, don't let her die like Tangie's little sister. I'll do anything to make Peaches better, anything.*

As I prayed, I held on to the edge of my chair as if that would stop the feeling that I would never see Peaches again and my world was about to spin out of control . . . forever.

9.

IF YOU'RE GOING, I'M GOING, TOO

After Peaches had been in the hospital three full days, Mama woke me up in the morning, smiling like those old-timey TV mamas. Her hair, up in a ponytail, sprouted gray strands like cat whiskers. The skin underneath her eyes was sagging more than the time she'd stayed up all night studying for her insurance exam.

"I talked to Nikki's mom, and I'm taking you over there for a while."

"The doctor still won't let me see Peaches?" I asked, though I knew the answer.

"Not yet, baby. But it's not good for you to be cooped up here by yourself."

"Isn't she getting better?"

Mama looked down and sighed. "She is. The final lab results confirmed it's a more serious type of meningitis than they first thought, though. Since she's so young, the doctors are being extra cautious. We need to continue to pray that she'll be home soon. Okay?"

"Yes, ma'am."

She clapped her hands like that gave her energy to talk.

"Now, about this running off the other day." I knew that was all Mama was going to say about Peaches then.

"Bad idea, huh?"

"You can say that again."

I deserved any punishment she dished out.

"Whether you're here or with your daddy, you know better than to disobey either one of us like that. And that includes Frank." She sighed. "Millicent, too."

"I shouldn't have snuck out," I said before sniffles took over.

"Your daddy and I think you've learned your lesson here. Right?"

I nodded into the pillow.

She rubbed my arm, and it soothed my chill bumps. "Get dressed and come downstairs." Mama stood and walked toward the door.

Before she opened it, Frank's and Tangie's voices exploded in the hall.

"If you want to participate in any protest, that's all fine and good, but just like before, I'm gonna be there with you," Frank said sternly.

"But I should be able to do stuff like this on my own. A lot of other high school kids are gonna be there!" she shouted.

"Oh. Good for them. They are, you're not. Not without me, anyway."

"I'm not a baby. I know this is about Marshall."

"The answer is no."

"It's only three years, Daddy. You were seven years older than Mom. And who knows how much older than your *new* wife."

"This isn't about me and your mother, or me and Katrina. This is about me letting you put yourself in harm's way, and about a boy who kept you out way past your curfew. Probably at some frat party."

"It wasn't a frat party. He's not even into that. I told you what happened."

"End of discussion."

"I hate you! You make me sick!"

I sucked in my breath, hoping Tangie didn't get smacked too hard. Mama put her hand to her mouth. But there was only silence as Tangie just stomped the rest of the way up the stairs and slammed her door.

After a few moments, Mama asked, "Think it's safe to go out now?" She tried to smile again, but she couldn't make her lips do it all the way. "That was a doozy," Mama said.

"A double-doozy." I wondered what Tangie was up to. It didn't seem like Marshall wanted her to tell Frank about the protest for Roderick Thomas. Was that even the one she was talking about? I couldn't think about that now. My thoughts immediately went back to Peaches. I had to figure out a way to see her so I could fix things like only her big sister could.

Less than an hour later, we were in front of Nikki's. Mama parked the car, and Nikki and Tammy came running up.

"Hello, Mrs. Matthews," they said.

Neither remembered that Matthews was her old name, not Frank's last name, which was Goodwin. I liked that Mama didn't correct them.

"Hello, girls. Nikki, where's your mom?"

Nikki pushed her bangs out of her eyes. The rest of her hair was in ponytails with the back loose. "She's in the kitchen."

I looked around to make sure I didn't see Lucinda Hightower walking around in perfectly ironed summer clothes and with her nose tooted up. I wasn't in the mood to hear her bad-mouthing Tammy, or watching Nikki acting like a minion.

As soon as Mama stepped on the porch, Nikki's mom (who I call Ms. Cora) opened the door. The sun made her reddish-brown hair shine like a fireball.

Tammy picked up the jump ropes. "We can double Dutch now."

"You can jump first, Georgie," Nikki said, which she'd never said before in her whole entire life.

Ms. Cora and Mama were still in the doorway hugging each other and rocking. Mama tried to keep her cries quiet, but her shoulders shook like they were pumping out the tears.

"Did you hear me?" Nikki said, her attitude popping with her gum.

"I'm not hard of hearing," I said. "One . . . two . . . three!"

I jumped into the middle of the ropes. As soon as they were under my feet, I felt better than I had since Peaches had gotten sick. The sidewalk was a trampoline that made me spring higher than I ever had before. But after the fifth routine, the sadness just dusted itself right off. I felt even worse for trying to have fun while Peaches was stuck in that hospital bed. And the way Mama cried to Ms. Cora, Peaches couldn't be getting better. As I thought about that, the rope tangled at my feet.

"Why you stopping?" Nikki asked, short of breath. She turned around and used her inhaler.

Tammy slapped her palms against her knees. "I don't care why, 'cause I'm ready for a break. I got freeze pops at my house. My mama's not home. We could get three apiece."

Nikki rolled her eyes. "You want our lips to freeze off?"

"Fine, two then," Tammy said.

Tammy re-braided the ends of her hair. Ever since I've known her, two cornrows on each side of her head was her only hairstyle, even on picture day. The thing with Mama was that she couldn't do hair either, but when she did, she tried different styles. I'd close my eyes and hope for the best. Nobody is good at everything.

"C'mon, Georgie," Nikki said. "My mom don't mind if I go to Tammy's without asking."

"Well, my mama is still in there, so I gotta ask."

"You spending the night with me. That means you get to do what I do."

Spending the night was news to me. But I didn't want to tell her about the mess I'd made when I snuck over.

"Wait right here," I said.

"The side door is open. Go in that way so you don't mess up the living room carpet. Jevon made me do all his vacuuming this morning."

"Got it!" I said as I cut across the lawn.

I opened the door and walked up a few stairs. But before I could announce myself, I heard Mama.

"The hardest part, Cora, was when I wasn't able to be in the room with her when they were doing all the testing. Before they put her under, I could hear her crying for me. They don't know when she can come home. My mother had to beg me to come home to change. I just don't want G-baby sitting in that room missing Peaches."

"That's understandable, Trina. She can stay here as long as you need."

"Thank you. That will help out. So much going on at once. Frank and Tangie at each other's throats. Can't talk to George a second without biting his head off."

"He understands, Trina. It's just stress."

"She'd been admitted before he thought to call me. What sense does that make?"

If Mama is mad at Daddy, I know she's just as mad at me.

"Cora?" Mama's voice sounded as tiny as Peaches's. "Cora . . . what if . . ."

"Don't you even finish that. Like we talked about

last night, if she needs the transfusion, we'll cross that bridge then."

"Her vitals," my mama said, and sniffled. "They're so weak. I've been reading up on it, Cora. It's possible . . ."

Transfusion? Mama didn't have to finish it. I could. What if Peaches can't get a transfusion and she dies? That's what Mama was gonna say. I knew it! *Nobody needs a transfusion when they are getting better.* I bit my lip to keep my teeth from chattering, slipped quietly out the door, then took off running.

I ran faster, trying to see how fast I could go. And the more my knees and arms pumped and the wind whipped across my face, the faster I ran. Mama was fibbing about everything. Peaches wasn't getting better at all. We could lose Peaches forever, and it was all my fault.

"Wait up!"

I couldn't tell if the voice was Nikki's or Tammy's. I didn't know where I was going, but it had to be a place where I could figure out what to do.

Then, a rock underneath my foot sent me flying like a kite. All I felt was wind and sunshine. I wished I could sail through the air forever. Even when I tumbled to the ground, the sharp pain and skinned knee didn't stop my mind from racing. *How to get to Peaches? How to save Peaches?*

"Oh no!" Nikki rode up. "You okay, Georgie?" she said, getting off her bike.

"I'll go get your mom," Tammy said.

"No, that's the last thing I want." I looked down at the bright red blood on my knee. Mama didn't let me watch those hospital TV shows on Netflix, but I saw one episode of *Grey's Anatomy* at Grandma Sugar's. I watched all the way to the end, and now I was glad I did. The patient was getting weaker no matter how much medicine they gave her. And, just like Peaches, she needed a blood transfusion, but the doctors couldn't find anyone with the right kind of cells or something in their blood. She almost died.

Maybe they couldn't find the right kind of blood for Peaches. We were sisters, so we had the same blood. I had to get down to the hospital to tell the doctors to use my blood. Mama was fibbing to me about Peaches. I had to get back to that hospital on my own.

Nikki searched a fuzzy Juicy Couture purse on her handlebars and pulled out her inhaler. "Can you make it to Tammy's?"

"Yeah," I said, and stood up, which took forever because I was trying not to bend my knee so it wouldn't bleed anymore. Needed to save every drop.

Tammy ran ahead of us. I held on to Nikki's handlebars like a crutch as we both walked beside her bike.

"Where did you get that purse? It looks familiar," I said, and tried not to roll my eyes.

"Jevon took me to the mall with his girlfriend, and I bought it. It's not exactly the same as Lu Lu's, if that's what you're thinking."

"Didn't she tell you not to call her that?"

"No, she told Tammy, then you. Not me, 'cause we're friends. She was over here earlier watching videos."

"Whatever." A few minutes later, Nikki leaned her bike against Tammy's steps, looped the purse across her chest, then helped me onto the porch. Tammy burst out the screen door holding a bottle of rubbing alcohol, cotton balls, Band-Aids, and a handful of freeze pops.

I reached for the alcohol.

Nikki took a cherry freeze pop and started reading the ingredients on the back. Then she tore it open.

"Lucinda said I should watch how much sugar I take in each day to help with my flexibility."

"Uggh. Stop acting like she's Simone Biles. You didn't hear how mean she was to Tammy?"

"She was just teasing."

"Give me the orange and grape, please," I said.

It took Tammy forever to decide what flavors she wanted.

As I dabbed alcohol on my knee, I tossed talk about Lucinda Hightower out of my head and focused on a way to get to Peaches. I didn't understand how the transfusion would work, but I was sure it involved a lot of tubes and needles. The hardest part would be getting there. Since Tammy's mama worked for MARTA, maybe Tammy knew what bus to catch. Even as I thought about that, Mama's words from this morning echoed in my thoughts. I was risking getting in trouble bigger than I'd ever known. She might let me skate once, but twice—no way.

"You gonna tell us what made you run like a lunatic?" Nikki asked.

"You don't even know what a lunatic is," I said as I secured the Band-Aid on my knee.

"Do so!" Nikki shot back.

"What is it, then?" I said.

She bugged her eyes at me. "Somebody who runs out

the house like you did. Are you gonna spill it or what?"

"Nah, not right now." I opened my freeze pop and sucked on it so hard my eyes shut for a second.

Nikki put her hands on her hips. "You better spill it tonight."

Tammy jumped in. "I want to know, too."

"She don't have to tell you," Nikki said. "She ain't your best friend."

"So what? That don't mean she's not my friend and I can't know."

Paying them no mind, I kept sucking on that pop until my lips were numb.

I was so busy tuning Nikki and Tammy out that I hadn't even noticed when they both stopped talking. At Sweet Apple Elementary School cafeteria, they never shut up. Well, unless something out of the ordinary was happening, like Lucinda Hightower and her crew sat at our table, which only happened twice: once when "Lucinda's table" was used to display science projects and the other when Lucinda was on the outs with her best friend, Sandy Franklin, the second most popular girl in school.

Nikki elbowed me. "Ooooh, somebody's got company."

When I glanced up, there was Kept Back Kevin Jenkins riding his bike straight toward us. I waved to him, not caring if my lips were purple.

"Ooooh, look at you waving! You like him, too," Nikki said.

"I don't!"

After skidding to a stop in front of Tammy's gate, Kevin said, "Thought you lived out in the country now?"

"I'm visiting," I said.

"All weekend?"

"Yessss!" Nikki said. Nikki pushed my shoulder and whispered, "Go up there, geesh."

"I was going," I said, and limped over to him. He smelled like peanut butter. There was a circle-shaped Band-Aid under his chin that looked like a tiny beard. Before I spoke, he said, "Messed up knee, huh?"

"It's not that bad."

"What happened to you?"

"Tripped."

"Sister still sick?"

"Meningitis," I said.

The word made us quiet, like a teacher was in front of us.

"Hey, can I go riding with you?" I said.

"Handlebars? Or you got a bike here?"

I shot a glance over my shoulder at Nikki and Tammy, who were on the steps, giggling. "Nikki, can I ride your bike?"

"This bike?"

"I don't see another one, do you?"

"Uh, no can do. But you can ride my old bike. It's back at the house."

Nikki acted like her bike was painted twenty-four-karat gold.

"Yeah, okay. Let's go get it."

My knee was stinging something crazy, but I wasn't going to let that stop me. Skipping past us, the gigglers headed to get the bike. Kevin and I trailed behind.

"How's your mom?" I asked.

"She's at home. Still smoking. Always sending me to the neighbors to borrow cigarettes. That's why I'm taking my time. Might even take me till the streetlights come on."

"She'll worry by then."

"About her cigarettes. Not about me." He spun the bike pedal. "It don't matter. Not now anyway. Have you gotten to see your sister?"

"No. They won't let me. And my mama said she was asking for me." I stopped walking for a minute. "Can you help me?"

"What you need me to do?"

"You know the way to the hospital on your bike?"

"Yeah?"

"Would you take me there?"

"It'll take about an hour, and we'll have to cross some busy streets. Don't know if you can do it with a hurt knee."

"That doesn't matter. I can do it."

"Okay, then." He stayed on his bike and let his feet paddle against the concrete. "You can get on the handlebars if you want."

Even if it stung, I bent my knee so I wouldn't walk like Frankenstein. "We're almost there. It's okay," I said. Nikki and Tammy were a few steps in front of us. I couldn't imagine what they'd say if I went speeding past on the handlebars of Kept Back Kevin Jenkins's bike.

When we were close to Nikki's house, she left Tammy and sashayed toward Kevin and me.

"What's the matter?" I said.

"*He* best stay back," Nikki said. "My dad's here, and he

don't allow strange boys inside our gate or in front of our house."

I faced Kevin. "After I get the bike, meet me at that big tree right next to Tammy's?"

"You can't go by yourself with him, Georgie," Nikki said after Kevin left. "You want to get us both grounded for the whole summer?"

"Where y'all riding to anyways?" Tammy joined in.

"He's taking me someplace is all," I said.

"It can't be to his house," Nikki said.

"You know I'm not going to a boy's house."

Nikki crossed her broomstick arms. "Tell me where you're going, or I'm not giving you the bike."

"He's taking me to the hospital." I told the truth like a dodo bird thinking she'd know how serious it was.

"What?"

"You heard me."

"That's far. Why don't you go on the MARTA?" Tammy said.

I thought for a second. "Your mom works for them. What if she sees us?"

"Oh, yeah. Forgot about that," Tammy said.

"If you're going, I'm going, too," Nikki said.

I shook my head. "You can't ride that far. . . ."

Nikki's hand raced to her hip. "Because I got asthma? Is that what you finna say?"

"Don't want you getting sick, too," I said, remembering the time she had an attack during gym once and had to leave in an ambulance.

"That's what inhalers are for, thank you very much."

"You two can go back and forth if you want to. I'm going home," Tammy said. "I don't wanna get in trouble."

"Well, you gotta stay inside," Nikki said to Tammy.

"What for?"

"Ugh. Do I have to spell out everything? If my mom or dad sees you without us, we're doomed."

Tammy squinted. She brought her hands up to her hair and started re-braiding. "Yeah, okay. Whatever."

Then Nikki looked at me the way Peaches would, her eyes wide, waiting for me to say something she wanted to hear.

"Let's go!" I said louder than I needed. I tried to drown out that little voice that comes sometimes when you might be making a big mistake.

10.

VENDETTA AGAINST VEGETABLES

Once we rounded the corner, I saw that Mama's car was gone. I was a little glad, so she wouldn't ask about my knee. Nikki and I hurried into the garage to get Nikki's old bike. It was neon green—her favorite color last year.

Before we could even get out of the garage, Nikki's mama hollered out the window.

"Where are you two going?"

"I'm letting Georgie ride one of my bikes back to Tammy's."

"Streetlights, Nikki. If they're on five minutes before you and Georgie are in the house, it's gonna be trouble. . . . Georgie?"

"Yes, ma'am," I said.

She poked her head out more. "Your mama waited, but I told her it was best for her to get on to the hospital. Sorry that Peaches isn't feeling well, but she'll be better soon."

"Thank you, Ms. Cora."

"You two want anything to eat?"

"Not right now, Ma," Nikki said.

"What about you, Georgie?"

"Ummm. Do you have any apples and beets?" I asked, thinking of my plan. If I was going to give Peaches a transfusion, my blood needed to be strong as can be.

"Beets?" Nikki said. "Are you feeling okay?"

"Not everyone has a vendetta against vegetables like you, missy," Ms. Cora said. "I'm afraid we're out of beets, but let me slice up some fresh apples for you."

"Thank you," I said, trying to avoid Nikki's eyes.

As soon as her mama left the window, Nikki scooted closer. "I would check you for a fever, but that don't tell if you're crazy. Why you holding us up for apples? And beets?"

"I need to eat better, and beets are good for my blood," I said. "You remember, that's what the health teacher said. Tangie eats them all the time."

"When did you start worrying about blood and stuff? Ohhhh, did you come on your—"

"Ugh, it doesn't have anything to do with *that*." I almost said it did. If I said that my Girl Time came before Nikki's, I bet she wouldn't speak to me for weeks.

Nikki's front door opened, and Ms. Cora stepped out. "Here you go, Georgie," she said, sealing the Ziploc bag. "I cut you up two whole apples and a half a carrot. Try to work some magic and make your BFF here eat some."

"I'll do my best, Ms. Cora."

"Have fun. And don't let them streetlights catch you."

"Yes, ma'am," we said together.

"Tell Tammy's mom I said hi," she added.

We bobbed our heads, and she waved to us as we ped-aled away.

Nikki sighed. "Whew, that lasted forever."

On the bikes, it took us less than two minutes to get to Tammy's. When we got close, Kevin didn't pay us attention but fiddled with the chain on his bike. Without looking up, he said, "I was 'bout to leave."

"Had to get something for energy," I said, and offered up my snacks. He downed an apple slice.

Nikki flipped her hand at him. "You wasn't going no-where, because you want Georgie to be your girlfriennnnd."

"Shut up, Nikki!" I cried.

"Y'all ready to go or what?" he said, and kicked dirt from his tire.

"You sure you know the way?" Nikki said.

"Yep. Go by myself all the time," Kevin said.

"We better get started. My mom don't play around about them streetlights," Nikki said.

I stuffed an apple slice in my mouth and put the bag in the pouch on Nikki's bike. Nikki turned to Tammy. "You remember what I told you."

"I got it. I got it. I'm not a nincompoop," Tammy said.

"You don't even know what a nincompoop is," Nikki shot back, copying me.

"I know I'm not one 'cause my mom said so," Tammy said.

Kevin took off. Nikki and I waved to Tammy and followed him.

"You three was gonna keep fussin' until it was too late to leave," he said, standing up and leaning his body from side to side as he pedaled.

I didn't answer, saving all my breath for the long ride and plus my knee was hurting like it was about to break in half.

When Frank took me to the hospital, we got on the I-85 North and were there in about fifteen minutes. Kevin's way took us through the side streets near the expressway. Horns blaring and engines rumbling made it difficult to hear. Kevin steered us away from any big potholes. I could tell that he could go faster than he was going. Anytime I heard loud voices, I thought for sure we'd been spotted.

After about twenty minutes, neither Nikki nor I did much talking. Instead of trying to keep up with Kevin, I glanced at Nikki and slowed down. Her bangs had looked like a big, fluffy caterpillar earlier, but now they had flattened and were nearly covering her eyes. Still, I'd bet she'd ride blind before she'd be the first to stop.

"Kept . . . I mean, Kevin . . . wait up!" I said.

He didn't stop but circled around and pulled up behind us.

Nikki moved her bangs out of her eyes, "Whatcha stopping for?"

I huffed. "'Cause I'm tired." I parked on the sidewalk under the shadiest tree I saw. After I caught my breath, I grabbed my apple slices and bit into one. Kevin didn't say anything as he took out a small towel and wiped his face.

"I could've gone another few blocks," Nikki said, sounding like the time she tried to blow up too many balloons.

"Plus my knee is hurting," I said. There was some truth in that, but if fibbing stopped Nikki from having an asthma attack, fine with me. Anyway, the apples needed time to get in my system.

Five minutes into our break, Kevin said, "If you two are finished resting, we got about another thirty minutes to go."

Nikki took a puff of her inhaler. "What you two waiting for?"

We headed off again. No one talked at all. Kevin kept us mostly on the sidewalk, but there were a few times we had to use bike lanes. As much as I could, I tried to keep Nikki in the middle whether she liked it or not.

"We're a couple minutes away," Kevin yelled.

When we entered the crowded parking lot, my arms and legs felt like worms. I barely had the energy to wipe my shirttail across my face. Nikki's chest was heaving so hard that she put her hand to her heart.

"You okay?" I asked.

"Yeah. I'm good," she said as her breathing slowed.

Before I knew it, Kevin had jumped off his bike. Lots of Lego block–looking buildings with sharp edges and rows of windows surrounded us. The main entrance to the hospital had huge revolving doors framed by trees sitting in gigantic pots, and the driveway circled to let patients off in the front where wheelchairs waited, like a hotel for sick people.

"It's best to walk the bikes from here, because of all the traffic from the parking garage," Kevin said. I caught up with him, Nikki at my side. "I got a place where our bikes will be safe."

He took us to the dental clinic entrance. A door led to an uncovered walkway between buildings. We followed as he opened the door and we bounced our bikes down a few stairs.

"I lean mine up against the side of the stairs. You can use the railing for your locks if you want."

"I'm always losing the key or forgetting the combination, so I left 'em home," Nikki said.

"Dang! I didn't think about 'em either," I said.

"Should be okay. I've been leaving my bike here without any problems."

"Look at your bike, then look at mine," Nikki said. "What if"—she wheezed a little—"what if there *is* a problem?" She finally broke down and took out her inhaler again.

I clapped my hands. "I got it. Nikki, you stay here with the bikes. We'll be back after I check on my sister and talk to the doctor."

Nikki stared at me like I had two heads. "What? You ain't a mama. You can't talk to the doctor." She sucked the inhaler again, this time longer than before.

"Well, I'm about to," I said.

Nikki twisted her mouth to one side. "Whatever-dot-com."

I sucked my teeth. "That's so played out."

"*Whatever* ain't played out."

"Nurses and doctors talk to me all the time about my mama," Kevin said.

He didn't have to help me convince Nikki that I wasn't crazy, but it made my case and shut up Nikki—two for one.

At that moment, I decided to stop calling him Kept Back and make Nikki stop, too.

"Are you gonna stay here or what?" I asked Nikki. I knew better than to mention it to her, but even the hallways in the hospital were a block long and her breath was still coming in wheezes.

She reached in her purse. "Yeah, I guess so. Bring me a soda."

I hit my pocket that was full of change. "I got it."

"Be back here in thirty minutes." Nikki sat on the stairs and folded her arms and pouted like a little kid in time-out, that copycat Lucinda purse flopped in her lap. "Not one minute longer."

"Okay! Okay!" I said.

If they needed to get me ready for the transfusion right away, Kevin could come back to get Nikki. I wasn't crazy. I knew they'd have to tell Mama, but she'd never suggest I do anything to help. She didn't even think I was strong enough to know Peaches's real condition. Maybe the doctors would convince her like they did on TV. Kevin opened the door for me.

"Not one minute longer, Georgie. I mean it!" she said right before the door closed. Kevin and I had started across the parking lot.

Nikki opened the door and shouted something else, but I couldn't make it out over the traffic noises.

Kevin stopped right before we entered the elevator. "Wanna go back and see what she said?"

"Probably just reminding me to get her soda," I said, hoping that was really what it was.

11.

'CAUSE I'M HER BIG SISTER

It took us about ten minutes to get to the pediatric floor. All the hallways were white and shiny, and everyone was at least a foot taller than us.

With all the confidence I had, I marched up to the nurse's station that was like a beehive on the quiet floor. "I need to see Patrice Ranee Matthews," I said.

"Good afternoon, young lady. Let me check that patient for you," the nurse said.

I folded my arms. "I'm her *big* sister."

The nurse stared at the computer screen for a few seconds. "I apologize, but she can't have any visitors."

"Why?"

"She's been moved to ICU. She's resting now." My stomach quivered, but I didn't speak.

"I'm on my way to check on her. Stay here and I'll tell you how she's doing when I return," the nurse said.

"Okay," I said.

ICU . . . ICU. Then I turned to Kevin. "That's the Intensive Care Unit."

He glanced down. "Yeah, I know. My mom's been there a few times."

"A few times? It's not the place people go before . . ." I thought I could get the words out.

"Before they die?"

"Yeah."

"I used to think that, too. But it isn't."

"I hope your mom stays out of there."

"When your sister comes out, she'll stay out for sure. My mom . . . ?" He shrugged.

His words encouraged me to do the transfusion even more. If the nurse got to my mother before I talked to the doctor, my chances of doing the transfusion were done.

I ran after the nurse. "I want to see the doctor who's looking after my sister. I need to talk to that doctor right now!"

I shouted it so loud, the nurse hustled back. She locked her arm with mine and ushered me back to her station. "I'm just coming on duty. Where are your parents?"

"No, please. They can't know I'm here, yet," I said. "They'll just take me home like I'm a baby."

"You have to calm down. Did you come with an adult?"

I pulled in my lips and held them tight.

"Georgie?" a voice called out.

Just then, Tangie grabbed my shoulders and turned me around to face her.

"What are you doing here?" she snapped.

"Did she come here with you?" the nurse asked.

"Yes . . . Yes, ma'am," Tangie said.

"I've been as understanding as I can be," the nurse said crossly. "We can't have outbursts like that. She doesn't want me to tell her parents she's here, so you're responsible for her."

Kevin stood nearby, not saying much, but not leaving me either.

"Sorry," Tangie said. "She's all right now."

"We have to be mindful of the other patients." The nurse scowled and hurried away.

Tangie rushed me to the nearest corner. "Now, answer me. What are you doing here? Your mom told me you were at Nikki's."

"I was. But Mama wasn't letting me see Peaches."

"Nikki's mama dropped you off?"

"No, we came on our bikes."

"All that way?" I nodded. "You can't be serious."

I nodded again.

"You came with him." She shot a look at Kevin.

"He comes here all the time," I said.

"You better be glad that my dad and your mom are in the cafeteria. Why didn't you wait for them to bring you?"

"'Cause they won't, and they keep treating me like a baby. I want to talk to her doctor myself. She's gonna die, and it's all my fault. I didn't mean to leave her alone." I sucked in my jaws, bit my lip, didn't blink. I tried every trick I knew to keep from crying, but I lost. I flicked tears with my knuckles. "Now she needs a blood transfusion. I gotta help her right now."

"Oh my goodness, Georgiana . . . You can't . . . I mean . . . You can't control . . ." She handed me some McDonald's napkins from her purse. "It's going to be okay."

How stupid did I feel? There I was talking about Mama treating me like a baby, and I stood there crying like one.

"What's your name?" she asked Kevin.

"Kevin . . . Kevin Jenkins," he replied.

"Do me a favor, Kevin. Take Georgie to that waiting room over there." She put her hand on my shoulder again, but this time it was much softer. "I'll go find the doctor for you, okay?"

"I'm not leaving," I reminded her.

"I know you're not, Georgie. I wouldn't have left, either," she said.

My knees were shaking. The sadness I felt about Frank and Tangie coming back to the same hospital where they lost Morgan piled on top of everything else. I couldn't speak.

Kevin motioned his head toward the hall. "Better get to the waiting room like she said."

I nodded and followed him. Kevin removed a few newspapers from a chair, and I sat down. I put my hand to my throat, hoping that would make the boulder stopping me from speaking go away.

"You want some water or something?" he asked.

"No, I just want to talk to the doctor."

"Was that your sister, too?"

"Stepsister."

"Oh. Least you have people at the hospital with you."

"I guess. It's not helping Peaches come home."

"It might." He bent down and retied his worn Chuck Taylors.

"Doesn't your dad ever come?"

"Not since he moved to Rochester."

"They got a divorce?"

"You only need one of those if you ever got married."

I twisted my lips to the side. "Not all parents gotta get married. My mom and dad did, but now they're divorced."

"Well, my dad wants me to move in with him. But my mom doesn't want me to go. She keeps going in and out of the hospital, and I was skipping school to see about her. Missed too much and had to repeat."

I wiped my eyes. Kevin walked over to a small table and yanked two tissues from the box.

"Thanks." I pressed the tissues against my face and tugged my nose, too embarrassed to blow. I was hoping that I felt stronger because of the apples. I only wished that I had known what to do the very first day Peaches was in the hospital. That way I could have eaten a bag of apples and two whole bowls of beets by now.

After a few minutes, Tangie returned with the nurse and a woman with tiny braids like Tangie's and a quarter-size birth mark on her temple.

"Are you Georgie?" she asked. She had a gap between her two front teeth.

"Yes, ma'am."

Kevin stood up so the doctor could have his seat, but she kneeled in front of me. I balled up the tissue and put it in my pocket.

"How are you, Georgie? I'm Dr. Harris, Patrice's doctor." She held out her hand for me to shake. It was warm, like I was putting my hand inside a mitten. If I decided to be a doctor instead of a judge when I grew up, I'd remember to shake hands with almost-teenagers like they were adults, not toddlers.

"I'm fine. . . . I want my sister to get better," I said.

"We all do. That's why she's here. I'm working on getting her better even as we speak."

"If that's true, why can't I see her?"

"Because the room she's in is for extra-delicate little girls, and we got to make sure that everyone who comes in contact with her has a strong immune system. You know what that is?"

"The science teacher said it's inside stuff that stops us from getting sick."

"Looka here! We got an up-and-coming doctor. And that system is stronger when you're older. That's why we can only let older people in right now."

I blinked to focus and cleared my throat. "I know a way I can help her."

"You're praying and thinking about her every day, right, Georgie?" Tangie said.

The nurse tapped on her clipboard. "That's the best medicine."

"But I want to do something else," I said. "Can I, Dr. Harris?"

"Why don't you tell me what it is and we'll see?"

A woman and a little girl walked into the room and sat on the other side. Someone was calling names on the loudspeaker. I tried to concentrate, but I couldn't stop rocking. I put my hands on my knees and squeezed real hard to stop them from shaking. I wouldn't mess up.

I stared into the doctor's eyes. "I've been eating apples. My blood is real, real red. I saw it myself today when I fell off my bike. It didn't look like sick blood. I want to give Peaches some of my blood. 'Cause I'm her big sister, you can take some of my good blood out and put it in with her blood."

"Hmm," Dr. Harris said, nodding. "A blood transfusion."

"Yes! Like on *Grey's Anatomy*. That way the men . . . men . . ."

"Meningitis," Dr. Harris said.

"Yes. That way it will leave her body. I haven't been sick in two years, not out of school once. Not even a cold. My grandma Sugar says I'm healthier than an ox."

Dr. Harris stood up and pulled me to my feet. "Well, you know your stuff. You're a smart girl."

"Was the smartest in our class," Kevin added.

"Is that possible, Doctor?" I asked. "Can we do it today?"

"What if I told you we can make her well without it, and because you love her so much that will make all the difference?"

"She's top in her field," the nurse added.

"Would you believe me?" Dr. Harris asked.

"I guess so . . . yeah," I said. "But Peaches can't stay here much longer. She likes to jump around and watch me dance."

"That transfusion is something I'll keep in mind. But filling her with a lot of vitamins and antibiotics will make her well, too."

I frowned. "If she's in ICU, whatever you're doing hasn't been working."

"You're right. Not as well as we hoped. That meningitis is a stubborn illness, but your little sister is strong and now we have a backup plan with the transfusion, right?"

"Right," I said.

"Now why don't you let me get back to your sister, and as soon as we can, we'll move her to her regular room. You'll be able to visit her then."

"Dr. Harris. Could she see her sister just for a second, please? It would mean so much to . . . her . . . us." Then Tangie just stopped talking. Her eyes were glassy like when I'd dropped the picture of Morgan. I really wanted to hug her, but we'd never done that before and I was scared she'd push me away.

"LaVerne," Dr. Harris called to the nurse. "Take her as close as you can." Then she turned to me. "Just so you'll know she's there and being cared for."

"Yes, ma'am."

Kevin and Tangie sat in the waiting room while the nurse walked me down the corridor.

When she got to room 403A, she stopped.

"She's in there?" I said. I'd never felt so far away from Peaches in my life.

"Yes. Step closer."

I peeped my head in, and there was Peaches. Mama and Daddy were back in her room, but on opposite ends, like those spikes Daddy used to hold down our tent in the backyard. Cotton-ball-white walls surrounded them.

"She's tough for such a little girl," the nurse said.

"Maybe she got energy stored up, too," I said.

"Most little girls do."

Though I focused, I couldn't see Peaches clearly, but it felt good to be closer to her than I'd been in days. Since I could only see the top of the bed, it looked like it was levitating. Peaches floated in the middle of the room. All the strange equipment with tadpole lines and zigzag graphs surrounded her. An IV going into her arm kept her from floating away.

There was some sort of cap on her head, maybe to keep her hair from getting in her eyes. I couldn't remember Peaches ever lying on her back. She always slept on her stomach or curled up like a caterpillar. I didn't think the nurse could do anything about that, so I bit my tongue. I hated that there were no windows in the room for her to look out when she woke up, and that her ceiling was plain white. If there was ever a room that needed stars twinkling above it, it was a room for a sick little girl, trying to come back home.

I felt the nurse's hand on my back and knew that was my signal to leave. I closed my eyes tight and concentrated really hard, hoping Peaches and I could be like those twins in my old class, Carol and Caroline, who said they could tell when the other was near and what the other twin felt.

"I'm so sorry I left you alone, Peaches. I'm not gonna leave you alone anymore. I won't ignore you when you say you're sick again, promise." I said it in a whisper, like I was talking more to myself than my little sister. "Just like sky, Peaches. Just like sky." I concentrated even harder, but I didn't feel a thing. Maybe those twins were fibbing after all.

"We need to get going now."

"Okay," I said. I made up my mind that I wouldn't ever tell Mama I didn't feel good just to get out of doing chores. Maybe that was bad luck and would make me sick for real. I'd just never want Peaches to have to miss me so much. I waved to her, and butterflies fluttered in my stomach. Maybe it didn't matter if those twins really felt something or not. As long as they believed they did.

The nurse walked me back to the waiting room and left.

"Feel a little better?" Tangie asked.

"A little. Think they would let me help Peaches if she needed it?"

"It won't come to that, Georgie."

"They got blood banks anyways," Kevin said. "She'll be good."

Tangie nodded. "You can wait here with me, Georgie, and we can take you home. Valerie should be here in a few." She raised her eyebrows. "You're cutting it close if you don't want your mom and dad to see you."

"I know. I don't want to give them anything else to argue about. Do you have to tell them I came to the hospital today?" I asked Tangie.

"If you promise to go straight to your friend's house, I'll ask the nurse and doctor not to say anything. It'll be another one of our secrets, okay?"

The feeling of wanting to hug her hit me again, but

I was scared I'd cry and get back on her annoying list.

Meanwhile, Kevin pointed to the elevator. "We should get going, Nikki is probably mad."

Tangie's eyes widened. "You didn't mention that Nikki was with you. Why didn't she come up with you two?"

"She didn't want to leave her precious bike," I said.

"Well, if I were her, I'd be bored out of my mind by now. Kevin's right. You two need to hurry back down there."

Tangie's phone buzzed, so I waved good-bye.

"We better go before Nikki tries to ride all three bikes home," Kevin said.

"Georgie," Tangie called to me, taking the phone away from her ear.

I stopped and took a few steps back to her.

"I'm proud of you for trying to help your sister."

"Thank you. It didn't work, though," I said. My head dropped, and I spoke to my sandals. "I thought the doctor would talk Mama into letting me give Peaches a transfusion and she'd come home soon."

"But you tried. I would've done anything to save Morgan. That's what big sisters do, Georgie. We don't always succeed in helping out little sisters, but we try."

Then her arms were around my shoulders, and she pulled me close to her. It was the type of hug that lasted for a while, where you could feel the other person's heart beating. And just when I thought she'd let me go, she embraced me a little tighter, like she was hugging someone she actually liked.

"Tangie . . . I . . ." But before I could finish she'd gotten back on the phone like it never happened.

❋ ❋ ❋

Kevin navigated the hospital halls like Sweet Apple. Without looking up, he remembered how we got to the nurse's station.

The change was rattling in my pocket. "Wait. Nikki's soda."

"Good catch," he said.

Once we got to the soda machine, I did a Tammy and couldn't decide what to get. I grabbed a Coke and a Sprite. "This should do it. Let's go."

Kevin's jeans had huge pockets on the legs, so he put a soda in each pocket for me. "We got about two hours before it gets dark. We should be good."

"Are you gonna get in trouble for not coming back home right away?" I asked him.

"Only 'cause I'm not getting her no cigarettes. I've stayed out overnight before, and she didn't say a thing."

"Whoa."

"It'll be different when I go live with my dad."

"When you going?"

"Not sure yet."

"Maybe I can come visit?"

"That'll be cool."

"I mean . . . if my mama brings me. If we both had cell phones, we could text and stuff."

"Might get one for my next birthday."

"Well, my mom would have to approve your number," I said, and dropped my head a bit.

"That just means she's looking out. No problem."

I was glad that Nikki wasn't with us at that moment.

If she heard us talking, she might not only think that Kevin Jenkins liked me, but that I might like him, too.

We stopped talking and raced across the parking garage. I saw the dental clinic. I hadn't realized how cold I'd been inside the hospital until I was back outside in the heat.

"I hope Tammy covered for us," I said.

"I'm sure she did."

"Oh, are you still going to get the cigarettes from the neighbors?"

"Nope. She was expecting me back from the store a long time ago. By now she's asleep, or . . ."

"Or what?"

"Just asleep is all."

When we reached the walkway door, minutes later, Kevin opened it. I was right on his heels.

"Nikki! Sorry it took so long but—" I wiped my arm across my face and blinked my eyes real hard hoping it would change what I saw.

Empty stairs.

I ran down them to check out the area.

One bike.

Two bikes.

No Nikki.

12.

THIS IS WHERE WE LEFT HER

I ran back up the stairs.

"Nikki! Nikki! Where are you?" I called.

"Let me check if she's out front," Kevin said. "Wait here." He jogged through the parking garage and disappeared around the corner, then reappeared a few minutes later.

"You didn't see her?" I asked. My voice was higher than I expected.

"Nah. Guess she got tired of waiting and rode home," he said.

"She wouldn't remember the way. Plus, we're supposed to be together. What if her mama sees her without me?"

"You're right. It was her idea for Tammy to stay and cover."

"That's what I was thinking. Anyway, she hates being grounded more than me. No mall. No phone."

"Guess she got bored like Tangie said. There's a park not too far from here. We should go there."

"Let's wait for a minute. It makes sense for her to come back here, right? This is where we left her."

"You're right. Let's give her a few more minutes," Kevin said.

We walked back to our bikes and sat on the steps. Kevin took the soda bottles out of his pockets. "Here you go," he said.

"Want one?" I asked.

He reached for the Sprite. "Thanks." It fizzed over a little before he took a big gulp. "Ahhh. Just like in the commercials. Thanks, Nikki. I needed that."

We laughed. After waiting another minute, I opened the second one, hoping Nikki would come along any second and fuss me out for drinking it.

Fifteen minutes later, we'd finished our sodas but still no Nikki.

"We better go look for her now," I said.

"I got an idea."

"What?"

"You stay here. I'll check the park. I'll go around once. I'm sure she'll be there."

"What if she isn't?"

"Deal with that if we have to."

We stood up at the same time. Kevin grabbed his bike, and I opened the door that led out to the parking garage. He rolled the bike onto the pavement.

"Be back in a sec." Kevin jumped on his bike and pedaled away.

After about ten minutes, I carried my bike up the stairs and straddled it in front of the entrance, ready to head home as soon as I saw Kevin's silver bike or a flash of Nikki's neon pink. Even if I wanted to, I couldn't sit there another second just waiting.

Another five. Nothing. There were cars honking and a few people walking around.

I bowed my head. "Dear God, I'm so sorry for not being a better big sister. Please keep making Peaches better and don't let her fall out of Your hands." I opened my eyes quickly and looked around, then continued. "And, if it's not too much trouble, can you help us find Nikki before them streetlights catch us? If not, we're going to be in a whole heap of trouble. But you already know that since you know everything. Amen."

No sooner had I said that than I spotted at least one of the two bikes—the silver one, not the pink.

"What are we gonna do?" I shouted, still searching behind Kevin.

"Gotta wait it out," Kevin said. "Only other thing is if she got mad and went home."

"Streetlights will be on soon," I pointed out.

"She could be sitting on Tammy's steps right now, waiting. We should circle around, check the park again, then get back."

"Got it," I said, and we sped off.

I thought about all the time I'd known Nikki. She once ripped my homework in two when I wouldn't let her copy it.

And she's the one who started "Kept Back" Kevin Jenkins. She won't fess up to it now, but she called him cute at first. When she thought he liked me, that's when she gave him that stupid name. But the longer we rode, those thoughts left my mind, and all I could think about was how Nikki kept my emergency sleepover drawer in her room neat and sometimes put new pajamas in there when she and her mom went shopping. And who else would practice with me so we both could make the step team, but give it up when I wasn't good enough? I needed to find her—ASAP. And, just my luck, my cell was useless, because Nikki's mama had taken hers away.

After about fifteen minutes of riding, Kevin and I were on a busy residential area that had sidewalks barely wide enough for both our bikes. I couldn't imagine that Nikki would have gone so far without a break. I was hoping to find her taking a rest, expecting us to catch up. I eyeballed everything I could to spot her. Another ten minutes of cars, bumpy sidewalks, but no Nikki. My legs felt like rubber bands, but stopping was out of the question.

One of our gym substitutes told us he was training for a big bike race called the Tour de France. That's what I felt like before Kevin said, "We're about five minutes from Tammy's."

"Yeah, I know where we are now," I said.

"Go straight to Tammy's?"

"Yup."

"Got it."

When we got to Tammy's street, I'd lost two barrettes and my shirt was clinging to my back. I pumped my knees higher, like a racer sprinting to the finish. We had about fifteen minutes before the streetlights came on. I felt like I was going a million miles an hour. My knee still hurt from the fall earlier, but I didn't care. Either I was riding much faster than Kevin, or he'd slowed down. In the distance, I could make out two people sitting on Tammy's porch.

"Thank goodness!" I shouted.

I left Kevin in the dust and pulled up to Tammy's gate just as the lights flicked on. When I stopped, a cramp crippled my leg. I bit my lip to keep from hollering. My legs went wobbly and my arms felt as weak as noodles.

"Where have y'all been, Georgie?" Tammy said. All I could do was stare at Crystal, Jevon's—Nikki's brother's—girlfriend.

"Jevon is out looking for you now," Crystal said. I nearly turned to stone. I was hoping that Nikki was in the house.

A few inches taller than me, Crystal was probably about the same age as Nikki's brother, seventeen. She wore her hair in diagonal cuts, flips, and bright colors, like tie-dye.

"Hellooo?" Crystal said.

Tammy jumped in. "Georgie, I told Jevon since you missed your old street you went riding." Standing next to Crystal, Tammy said those words so convincingly that, for a second, I even believed her.

My heart was a conga drum. I was sure each beat could be heard for blocks. "Like Tammy said. Just riding."

"Fine. Then where's Nikki? Jevon came down here to get you two. We were going to the movies, but your mom said she needed him to watch you and Nikki this evening. So where is she? Well?" Crystal studied Kevin's old Converses but didn't say anything to him.

I kept peering around, expecting Nikki to yell "Gotcha!" But when I met Crystal's eyes, her lips twisted to the side, and she folded her arms across her chest, as she tapped her foot.

"Uhhh," I got out.

"Psst. Kids. You two have messed up our plans. Hellooo? Where is she?"

"Is Nikki's brother driving?" Kevin asked.

"No, he was going to take me to the movies in his go-kart. What do you think?" Crystal said. "Why do you need to know that? And who are you anyways?"

"I'm Kevin . . . Kevin Jenkins."

Nikki and I agreed on one thing at least: I didn't like Crystal like that either.

Crystal rolled her eyes at him, but they landed on me.

"We don't know where she is," I said.

"What?" Crystal said. Before she could say anything else, a van with a *Your Mary Kay Representative* sign on it rolled up in front of Tammy's house, and Jevon jumped out. He was a tall kid and wore an Atlanta Braves baseball cap and OutKast *ATLiens* T-shirt.

"We got a problem!" Crystal said.

"Other than I gotta babysit?" Jevon scanned the porch. "I know Nikki is going to have big-time problems unless she pops up from behind that bush or something right now."

"They don't know where she is, Jay," Crystal said.

Jevon reared back a bit, then turned to me. "Georgie, what's up? Where's my sister?"

I made some odd popping sounds before I spoke. "I don't know."

He chuckled. "Okay, cool. I get that you two are best friends, right?" I nodded. "You keep each other secrets and all that girly stuff. But unless you want Nikki to get in more trouble than she's ever even imagined, you best tell me where she's at."

I shot a hopeless look to Tammy, then put my hand on my stomach to speak. "We went to the hospital."

"What do you mean 'the hospital'?" Jevon said. "Nikki ain't supposed to leave this block. Did she take her inhaler?"

"Yes, she has it."

Then he took in the entire street in one glance and held up his palms. "Wait, wait, wait. You're back. He's back. Tammy's here. You mean she's *still* at the hospital?"

"I'm sorry! It's all my fault. She tagged along with me to check on my sister."

"I'm sorry about your li'l sis, Georgie. But what happened to Nikki?"

I took a deep breath. "I don't know. When we came back to the spot where she said she'd wait, she was gone." I shoved my hand into my pocket, yanked out a tissue, and dabbed my eyes.

"What do you mean . . . *gone*?"

"Oh my God!" Crystal said.

"We left her at a spot outside the hospital. She wasn't there when we got back, so Kevin rode around to a park looking for her. I stayed put in case she showed up. We came back here thinking she was sore at us and found her way home."

"What hospital?" Jevon asked.

"Grady."

"Are you joking? On a bike?" Jevon punched the inside of his palm. "How long was she by herself?"

I couldn't even get out those words, so I stared at Kevin.

"Close to an hour," he said.

Jevon swallowed hard. "That long? Georgie, you should have come back sooner when you realized that she wasn't there." He clasped his hands in back of his head for a second. "You two, leave the bikes with Tammy. We'll take the van back up to the hospital."

"I want to go, too," Tammy said.

"This is serious," Jevon said. "Somebody's gotta stay here in case she comes back. You have a phone?"

"In the living room," Tammy said.

"Well, if she shows before we get back, have her use that and call my cell. She knows the number."

Tammy nodded. "I'll make her do it ASAP."

Then Jevon shook his head. "'Preciate that, li'l bit, but that won't cut it. I know Nik. She barely listens to me." He turned to his girlfriend. "Crystal?" he said, and rubbed his chin.

When she tapped her foot, her baby-pink Skechers mushed the grass. "I hear you. I'll stay. Matter of fact, I'll make sure she calls you from my phone," Crystal said. She yanked the phone from her back pocket.

"That's what I'm talking about," Jevon said. He hugged Crystal, then waved his left hand several times. "Hurry up, you two."

Kevin and I dropped our bikes in Tammy's yard and hopped into the van. The streetlight was shining above us like the sun.

13.

FOREVER 21

On our way to the hospital, Jevon called home.

"Hey, Ma . . . Yeah . . . Nik and Georgie are with me. We're going to take them with us to grab a bite and hit up Redbox. . . . We'll be home in a few. . . . All right. Have a good time." He hung up and said, "Now that's my neck for sure if we don't find Nik."

He was the only one who was allowed to call her that. I tried hard not to think what I knew Jevon was thinking, what Kevin was thinking. Something bad could have happened—Felecia Williams bad. She was only nine years old when she went missing. Frank and Mama were upset because they'd only showed her face once on the news, and she had on a Hello Kitty shirt like mine. Mama said if she was a little girl called JonBenét Ramsey they'd show her face every five minutes. When the police found Felecia Williams, she wasn't alive anymore. I grabbed my stomach but still couldn't stop the queasy feeling like I was upside down.

"Hey, you okay, Georgie?" Jevon asked.

My lips felt like they were glued with Elmer's. "I'm fine. Stomach just hurts a little."

Jevon's left hand tapped on the steering wheel like it was his keyboard. "No time to get sick now. Need you alert to help me find Nik."

"I'm fine," I said, but I couldn't even hear the words.

"Come on, sis. Come on, sis. Don't do this to me," Jevon sang, tapping harder. When he gets on Nikki's nerves, she calls him a wannabe John Legend.

When we got to that parking garage, I grabbed the door handle. As soon as Jevon parked, Kevin and I dashed out of the van, and Jevon followed us. I was so scared that Nikki wasn't gonna be there that I didn't want to open the door to the walkway where she was supposed to wait. I crossed my fingers *and* said a quick prayer. I called that "a double."

Kevin pushed the door. "She's not here," he yelled as we all looked at the empty steps.

My hand flew to my mouth. "Oh my Josh! It's really getting late now."

"Let's check out the park," Jevon said. "And here's the thing: if she ain't there, gotta go ahead and call the police."

When he said the word "police," I got that stinging feeling in my head I had when I sucked the freeze pop too fast.

Oh, God. Please, please . . . don't let my best friend be an Amber Alert. I couldn't make myself believe that Nikki would go alone to a place neither one of us was familiar with. I took a deep breath before I spoke. "Kevin already checked the park, Jevon. You know how Nikki loves the mall."

"That's my roadie. Makes sense," Jevon said. "Her allergies keep her out of parks anyway."

We hopped in the van.

"We better get there soon. It's almost nine," I said, this time louder than I thought. I straightened up in the front seat and held on to my knees.

Jevon turned his baseball cap backward. "Gotcha. Lenox isn't that far away." Then he muttered to himself, "C'mon, sis, be there."

Once we were out of the hospital parking garage, Jevon picked up speed. No one spoke. I strained my eyes peering out the window, hoping to see Nikki pushing her bike along the sidewalk.

Minutes later, we were pulling up in the mall parking lot. I thought about all the stores, halls, and corners of the mall. I used to love them, now they were just places Nikki could be and no one would find her. Instead of the castle Lenox used to look like to me, it seemed like nothing but a massive cave. The size of it scared me. Its glass *Lenox Square* sign seemed as big as that Hollywood sign you see on TV. The lower roof in the front spread out like humongous eagle wings, with crisscrossed beams swooping down. But it wouldn't even matter if Drake himself swooped down from the ceiling, all I would want to see was my best friend. How could I be so stupid to leave Peaches alone, then Nikki?

Jevon zoomed up to the front of the mall doors where people have to pay to leave their cars. He parked along the curb. "You guys jump out here. Wait for me right inside the doors." A guy wearing a red polo shirt and black pants rushed up to Jevon. From the inside of the mall it looked as though I was watching Jevon on TV.

"Think she's here?" Kevin asked.

"Yeah," I said, but I wasn't telling the truth. It's just all that I could say.

"Probably is," Kevin said.

Inside the mall, the cool air made me shiver.

Seconds later, Jevon was standing next to us. "Hopefully it'll be four of us on the ride back. So where to?" Jevon asked, looking around.

"We should go to Forever Twenty-one, that's her favorite store," I said.

"You know better than I do," Jevon said. "Let's give it a shot."

I led the way. The boys followed. I felt like I was doing that funny-looking speed walking that we'd do around the track. But the next thing I knew, the speed walking wasn't fast enough. I was running to the far end of the mall.

As soon as I saw the empty bench out front of the store, my heart sank again. "Dang," I said.

"She could be inside," Jevon replied. He and I rushed in. Kevin didn't come in the store with us, but I could see him peeking into Express.

"Hi, I'm Sherry," said the girl at the front of the store straightening T-shirts. She smiled at Jevon, then spoke to me. "There's two-for-one boyfriend tees today and two-for-one graphic tees there on the middle table. Let me know if I can help." She wasn't much older than Jevon, and her red blush and blue eye shadow looked like watercolors.

"We're looking for my li'l sis. 'Bout eleven," Jevon said. "This tall." He held his hand up to my nose.

"She has a whole bunch of hair. Probably has it in a ponytail like mine." I pointed to my hair like she couldn't see it.

Sherry stopped refolding T-shirts and let her head rest in her hand for a second. "Gosh. I've seen so many girls today, I couldn't remember."

"This one would have a pink-and-turquoise bike," I added.

"Well, I'd doubt she be riding it in here," Sherry said.

My shoulders drooped.

"Never hurts to ask. You don't know my sister." Jevon scanned the store. "What about those fitting rooms?"

"Just cleaned them out. Empty."

"Gotcha. Thanks," Jevon said, and turned to me. "What's next?"

I took a few quick breaths. "Let's check the food court."

"Since the mall is closing in a few minutes, stopping by security first is your best bet," Sherry offered. "It's on this level, next to Things Remembered. Hope you find her soon."

"Thank you," we said as we exited and linked up with Kevin.

"The food court. That's where we should go. Auntie Anne's Pretzels," I said. Whenever we go to the mall, we meet in front of Auntie Anne's if we get separated.

I started walking faster, then running again. Jevon knew where he was going this time. Kevin and I were right behind him. Jevon slowed a little when his phone rang.

"Anything?" he said. "No, nothing there. . . . Not yet. . . . Yeah. . . . We were gonna try to make it there next."

A voice came over the loudspeaker. "On behalf of all the employees of Lenox Square, we appreciate your patronage today and want to help you in making your final selections. The mall will be closing in fifteen minutes."

Jevon jumped on the escalator, taking two stairs at a time. Kevin and I did the same.

"Security after this," Jevon said. "Police are next."

That word turned my stomach to sludge, though my legs kept moving. Kevin wasn't familiar with the mall, but Jevon and I weaved through it like Kevin did the hospital. My shoes were slippery, but I still didn't let that stop me from getting to Auntie Anne's Pretzels. An employee was cleaning the tables and pushing chairs underneath them. Most of the tables directly in front of us were empty.

Then I glanced to the right at a row of tables next to the down escalator. A girl with her arms folded and her head resting like she was taking a nap on a school desk was sitting there alone. Running up the escalator made me so dizzy I couldn't remember exactly what Nikki had on, but there was no mistaking those huge ponytails that flopped down like bunny ears.

"Nikki!" I shouted loud as a fire drill. Several people turned my way. "Nikki!"

Her head shot up.

"'Bout time! Thank God!" Jevon huffed.

Nikki ran up and hugged me, tears streamed down her face, and she breathed like a tiny engine starting and stopping. I pulled her closer to me, my tears streaming, too. If I wasn't holding on to Nikki, I would crash to the floor. Her favorite sweet-pea body spray floated around us.

"You're the best friend I've ever had, Nikki. I don't want anything bad to ever happen to you." I took a shaky breath. "I love you," I said, and couldn't remember if I'd ever told her before.

"I love you, too, Georgie," she whispered, and tilted her head back. "You're making me cry more."

Kevin grabbed a few napkins off one of the tables and handed them to Nikki. "We've been looking for you all day," he said. "I thought you'd been kidnapped or something."

It took me a second before I remembered Jevon was even there. When I looked at him, he had his head hung low and he was scraping his sneaker on the floor like he was kicking dirt. Nikki walked toward him.

"I'm sorry, Keys." She always called him his nickname when she was in trouble.

"Don't give me that 'Keys' business. Y'all excuse us for a moment." He wrapped his arms around Nikki's shoulder and scurried her off a few tables away. Then he kneeled down to her height, said a few words to her as she wiped her eyes with a napkin and nodded.

"She's in major league trouble," Kevin said.

"I know it," I said. I could still smell her sweet-pea body spray on my shirt. Next thing we knew, Jevon reached over and hugged Nikki, then lifted her off her feet and spun around with her. He held her so tight, it was like he was scared to let her go.

As we walked out of the mall, Jevon held Nikki's hand. When he answered his phone, Nikki lagged back with us.

"What in the world happened to you?" I said. "Jevon was playing it cool, but he was about to lose it. You had us worried sick."

Nikki sniffled. "Did he tell my mama and daddy?" she asked me.

"He was getting ready to. After the police."

"The police?" If Nikki thought she whispered, she didn't.

"Yes, the police," Jevon said. He held the door as we walked out into the muggy air. "Do you know how many girls get snatched up around here? What did you expect me to do, Nik?" He had his regular big-brother tone back. "After Mom and Dad, I'm the most responsible for you in this world. Don't worry me like that." His voice raised that time. But I couldn't blame him. Nikki deserved it.

Jevon got back on his phone, and Nikki, Kevin, and I walked to the van. Kevin said, "Where's your bike?"

His question hit me like ice water splashed on my face. Nikki didn't say a word. She reached in her bag and gave herself another squirt of sweet pea. If I wasn't still glad to see her, I would have knocked it right out of her hand.

"Well, where is it?" I said.

"Ugh. The guard wouldn't let me bring it in. I mixed it in with bikes that were locked, thinking no one would bother it. When I got back to where I left it, it wasn't there."

"Stolen?" Kevin asked.

"Yeah." That made more tears fall. I waved another napkin at her and she grabbed it.

"Well, we can't worry about that now. We're just glad you're safe. It's just a bike." But my eyes watered again when I remembered how happy she was when she first showed it to me. She smiled as big as Peaches did when Daddy gave her Girl. I'd made an absolute mess of things. All because I wanted nothing more than to get Tangie to like me. Now, Peaches was in the hospital and Nikki's prized bike was gone.

"Let's just get out of here," Jevon said as he opened the van's door.

Kevin turned to me and whispered, "Want me to stay behind and start looking for Nikki's bike?"

"Right now?" I asked back.

"Yeah. Whoever has it might be still around."

"Thanks, but we should all go. Your ma— I mean, it'll probably be better to find it during the day."

"Yeah, you're right."

Nikki got in the front. Kevin and I hopped in the back. Soon as we buckled up, Jevon drove off. "I'm missing something here, Nik. Your friends said you went bike riding. Where's your bike?"

Nikki squirmed a bit before answering.

"I got bored waiting and caught the bus to the mall.

132

I put my bike on that rack thing. It was too late when I remembered I didn't have my lock. It got stolen."

"First things, first. You shouldn't have taken off," Jevon said.

"I told you I was bored."

"Are you catching an attitude, sis? You're getting off easy. What if I go home and tell the folks? I'm going to get blamed either way, so I got nothing to lose. And who you think they can ground, huh?"

"Sorry . . . I shouldn't have left. I didn't mean to be snappy."

"Where's that game I got you?"

"Right here," she said, and pointed to that fuzz ball of a purse.

"If you were so bored, you should have whipped that out. And, Georgie . . ."

"Yeah," I answered.

"Going up there in the first place was the wrong move. If your folks thought you should be there, they would have taken you, right?"

"Yes," I acknowledged, lowering my head.

"You've been by yourself this whole time, Nik?"

"Not really. As soon as I got to the mall, I saw some kids from Sweet Apple." Nikki planted her entire face in the napkin for a second, wiped, and continued talking. "They told me that they'd show me the quicker way to get back to the hospital. So I hung out with them. I was gonna stay with them, but when we started walking around the mall I found out they planned on stealing." On "stealing" she let out a cry that made me reach out and pat her back.

Lucinda Hightower. Nikki didn't say her name but it's all I heard. *Lucinda. Lucinda. Lucinda.*

"I'm glad you got good sense. You know I've been down that road once. Ain't worth it," Jevon said.

"They tried to talk me into it. But I left."

"Good job. Still not happy about all this, but you haven't completely lost your mind," Jevon added.

"When I left the kids, I browsed around in a few stores and when I tried to get back to the hospital, I went to get my bike and it wasn't there. First, I thought someone moved it. I searched for the kids and didn't see any of them. I was scared to start walking by myself because I couldn't remember the way."

"If it wasn't locked up, one of hundreds of people could have thrown that bike in their trunk. Maybe surveillance cameras or something could help us."

"But I can't even remember where I left it. The mall is so big."

That was odd to me because Nikki could find Bath and Body Works in Lenox blindfolded.

"We'll get back to that later, but you've known the house phone number since you were five, and you know my cell. You could have found a phone to use."

"I didn't want to get us in more trouble."

"Sis, I don't think you realize how close you were to being an Amber Alert. Please never scare us like that again. None of y'all. You hear me?"

Jevon turned on the radio. "Two minutes from being an Amber Alert. And that's the truth. That's Mom calling again now." Jevon answered his phone. I closed my eyes and thanked God for bringing Nikki home. Something worse than a missing bike could have happened. I just hoped that this was a sign that Peaches would come home next.

14.

LU LU TO ME

When Jevon pulled up in front of Tammy's house, Tammy came running to the gate. She opened it for us, and we got our bikes. "Oooooh, where were you?"

"Tell you about it tomorrow," Nikki said.

"Nik, you don't think you're leaving the house tomorrow, do you? If you even think about it, you better think again. And you too, Georgie," Jevon said. "Let's get home."

"Just glad you didn't get snatched," Crystal said. She hugged Nikki, then Jevon.

"Psst. You ain't the only one," Jevon said.

He opened the back of the van and put the bike I was riding inside. "Put yours in here, Kevin, and we'll drop you off," he said.

"Nah. I got it."

Jevon held out his hand to Kevin. "Good looking out, man."

"No problem," Kevin said as he shook Jevon's hand.

While Jevon chatted with Kevin, I eased over to Nikki. "Think he's gonna tell my mama about this?" I asked.

"Uggh, if he's not telling our mama and daddy, why would he tell yours? Think it through!"

"Don't tell me to think it through. Not like you think things through all the time either."

"See you guys later," Kevin said.

"Bye," Nikki spat.

"See you later," I said. "Thanks for helping me," I shouted, right before he rode off.

"No problem." He waved and pedaled faster.

As soon as he was far enough away, Jevon said, "Ain't that the boy with the drunk mom?"

I shook my head. "I don't think so."

"He lives across the way on Culberson, right?" Jevon asked.

"I don't know."

Nikki stepped up, bumping shoulders with me, but I hoped she didn't say anything mean about Kevin or his mama. I watched Kevin's reflectors glow in the night and wanted to believe that his mama missed him when he went away.

Once we loaded up back in the van, it took a minute for Jevon to drop us off in front of Nikki's.

"Mom said that she and Dad were heading out for a while," Jevon told us as he parked in front.

"Can we hang out on the porch?" Nikki asked.

"You got jokes, Nik!" Jevon said. "It's a bite to eat and bed. Period. Peanut butter and jelly or turkey sandwiches, knock yourself out. And, Georgie, you might wanna check in with your folks."

"Okay," I said, and followed Nikki inside. Jevon and Crystal stayed on the porch.

Nikki smacked her lips. "I know why he wants to be alone with her." She tossed her fur ball purse on the stairs, and I waited to let her lead the way to the kitchen. "You think Tangie kisses boys?" she asked.

"Who knows?" I tried to sound casual. The timing couldn't have been more perfect for me to tell her about Tangie and Marshall, but I just couldn't risk it. Plus, I'd made a promise to Tangie and didn't want to be a snoop tattler for real. Nikki turned on the faucet, and we both barely let the water wet our fingers.

"When do you think your parents will come home?" I said.

"Who knows?"

I sat at the kitchen table and put my head in my hands.

"What's wrong with you?" As soon as I sat down everything that was going on with Peaches dunked me into a deep pool. If I uttered a word, I'd drown. "Peaches?"

I nodded. Now that Nikki was safe all I could think about was Peaches asking for me. "She must think I'm the worst big sister ever."

"Oh please. Peaches loves you more than ice-cream cake and pizza."

"Think so?"

"Know so! She'll be home soon, I bet."

Nikki stood on a stool and scoured inside a cabinet for a few seconds, grabbed the peanut butter, then hopped down and stood in front of the fridge. A pineapple magnet held a picture of her posing on her bike. We'd snapped a bunch on Memorial Day, and her mom had them printed at Walmart. Nikki stared at it so long I thought she'd start bawling, or snatch it down and stomp on it.

"We . . . we can post pictures of your bike around the mall. Even around here. Who knows. Anyone could have seen it. I can help with money for the reward. I got almost twenty dollars in my piggy bank."

She yanked the refrigerator door open. "No thanks," she said in a short, sharp tone and took out two jars of jelly.

"Well, we have to do something. You can't keep it from your folks forever. Jevon already knows."

"Just forget about it." I stared at her to see if she was tearing up—nothing. Just them sneaky, catlike eyes of hers.

Something didn't seem right.

"Grape or strawberry?" she asked.

"Don't matter," I said, waiting for her to say anything about her bike.

"I'm gonna mix 'em." She dropped the bread on the white countertop, then jabbed the knife into the peanut butter. "I bet Tangie kisses boys. Just like you and your boyfriend."

"What does that have to do with your bike?"

"Nothing. How many times I gotta tell you to forget about that."

"Whatever. But don't say stuff about Kevin and me. We never kissed. And he's not my boyfriend," I said, then remembered Jevon's telling me to call home. I'm glad I thought to call at that moment. Anything would be better than arguing with Nikki.

My phone was really dead, so I used the house phone to call. Nikki just went about clanging plates on the counter. Sometimes it was like she had a Nice-or-Mean switch, and I never knew how I triggered either.

After two rings, Tangie answered.

"Hey, may I speak to my mom?" I was nervous because I didn't know if the niceness Tangie had shown me at the hospital had ended.

"Hey there. How are you?" Her voice was soft like I was the one sick.

"I'm okay."

"Good. Your mom said you'd probably call soon. She's back at the hospital."

"How's Peaches doing?"

"She was sleeping during most of my visit. Are you coming home tomorrow?"

"I don't think so. My mama wants me to stay here longer."

"That's cool if you want. But if you're ready to come home, I could use some help taking out my braids. Finally ready to do it. After that we can do our nails."

"Together?"

"Of course together. Only if you wanna come home tomorrow. If not, we'll do it another time."

"You've never wanted to do anything like that before."

"Well, just need some help and you offered, remember? If you've changed your mind, that's okay, too."

"Oh, I wanna do it." We said good-bye and hung up. It was almost as good of a feeling as when she hugged me at the hospital. "Tangie wants me to help with her hair," I told Nikki, twirling my own at the thought of it.

"So?" Nikki said. She loaded her bread with peanut butter and clumps of strawberry and grape jelly, then cut it straight down the middle. "Big whoop."

Jevon stepped in the kitchen. "Did you check in?"

"Yeah," I said, knowing that was all he wanted to hear.

"Good. I'll be out on the porch. After you two eat, it's upstairs and get ready for bed, nothing else."

"Okay," we said.

The front door opened and closed.

"See how he just wants to get rid of me? That's how Tangie's gonna be, too," Nikki said.

While I was making my sandwich, Nikki grabbed a bag of potato chips and plopped a handful on top of her sandwich, then poured us glasses of milk and started upstairs to her room. Eating in her room was one thing I liked about Nikki's. It was against the law at our house.

"Are you coming or what?" she asked.

I took my sandwich and milk and followed her upstairs.

Nikki was being extra snappy. Something wasn't adding up. But with her, sometimes the best way to find out stuff is to act like you don't want to know.

In her room, Nikki had half a wall dedicated to Chance the Rapper and Drake and the other to Future and Kendrick Lamar. She had one poster of Beyoncé and Jay-Z performing together. There was a picture of Nicki Minaj wearing a pink gown with two pink toy poodles on either side of her, and another picture of Rihanna wearing purple, orange, and green feathers that fanned out like a peacock's tail. Nikki had a canopy bed and pink everything. Though we didn't play it as often as we used to, there was an Xbox in the corner. On her dresser were several miniature elephants. Ever since we've been friends, she and her mama liked collecting them.

She closed her door, tossed that Lucinda Hightower–imitation purse on her dresser, and sat on her bed. I grabbed a seat at her desk.

After her first bite of her sandwich she asked, "So you don't think it's strange that Tangie wants you around now?"

"Guess she's trying to be nice since Peaches has been sick."

"Her wanting to do girly stuff with you sounds fishy. Big sisters are just like big brothers: hug your neck one second and send you to bed without TV the next."

"Yeah, or she could really like me."

"Georgie, you've been my friend for, like, forever, forever, and I know you're worried about Peaches, but sometimes you can be such a big baby."

"A baby? You're the one who got lost and your bike stolen," I blurted out.

"Least Kept Back Kevin Jenkins with the drunk mama ain't my booooyfriend."

"Stop calling him that! Especially after all he did to help us. And you don't know if his mama is a drunk."

"I do."

"How?"

"Security had to throw her out of the Walmart on Old National. My brother and I were there."

"Could have been a mistake. Anyway, he's not my boyfriend."

"Is so!"

"Is not!"

"I don't care either way. What'd you think 'bout these?"

She flipped back one ponytail that covered her ear to show me her earring. It was a sparkling silver hoop with a heart dangling from it.

"Those aren't the same earrings you had on today," I said.

"Duh and double duh. And these, too?" She got that fuzzy thing off the dresser, opened it, and pulled out three other pairs.

"Where did you get them?"

She fluttered her eyelids and put her hand on her hip. "That's for me to know and you to find out."

"You stole 'em!"

"No shirt, Sherlock," she said, and handed one pair to me.

She started saying that—"no shirt"—after she got a note home for cursing at recess.

I backed away. "I'm telling your brother right now!"

"*Please*. Do that, and I'll spill how you and Kevin left me alone so you two could kiss."

"That's not what we were doing!"

"Don't matter. Bet that will stop you from blabbing."

I hated it, but she was right. When Peaches was better,

Mama was bound to ask me about the boy she saw me with at the hospital. My science teacher says elephants have the best memory. Elephants and Mamas.

"You better not say a word," I finally said.

"I shouted that I would leave if you took too long. You ignored me."

I immediately knew what she meant and wished I'd gone back to check like Kevin said. "I didn't hear you."

"Well, too bad. If all three of us would have gone in, I wouldn't have gotten so bored and—"

"And what?"

"And none of your business. F.Y.I., I know where my bike is."

"Oooh. You made that whole thing up?"

She took a big bite from her sandwich.

"Where is it?" I demanded.

Just then, I heard Jevon coming up the stairs. He stopped halfway. "Is everything cool up there?" he called to us.

"Yes!" we both yelled. Nikki stuffed her mouth with potato chips and sat there munching like a big squirrel.

"I want both of you in bed ASAP," Jevon said.

"Okay," I called, just to get back to Nikki's story.

As soon as Jevon jogged back downstairs, I lowered my voice but made it deeper. "Where is your bike?"

"My friend borrowed it."

"What friend?"

"Lucinda to you. Lu Lu to me."

"Are you serious?" I yanked my pajamas out of the emergency sleepover drawer and tossed them on Nikki's other bed. "How did she get her wormy fingers on it?"

"And what do you care? You're so ready to go back home to *Tangie*."

"That doesn't have nothing to do with nothing. Lucinda's not your friend. She's a bully."

"You are so third grade. I ain't never heard of Lucinda taking anybody's lunch money, or beating up nobody."

"So what? Those aren't the only kind of bullies. What about that time when Sherry didn't want to write her essay for her and Lucinda started telling everybody that Sherry peed on herself?"

"Big whoop. She probably did. You're just jealous that Lucinda likes me now and not you."

"She stole your bike!"

"I told you, she borrowed it." Her voice was insistent, but her eyes landed on every single thing except me. "She was supposed to drop it off at Tammy's, but maybe it got too late." Nikki bit her sandwich again, but not before I saw her flick away a tear. "I'm sure she'll probably do it tomorrow." She looked up at me the way Peaches would sometimes when she wanted me to tell her that Daddy would keep his word.

I sat down next to her. "Nikki, she *steals* stuff, she doesn't *borrow* it. She's not dropping it off nowhere. She's going about her business on it like it was hers. Your daddy had that painted for you. We gotta figure out a way to get it back."

"I shouldn't have told you a thing. I can get it back whenever I want. How many times I gotta tell you that she's my friend now."

"And how many times I gotta tell you—no, she's not!"

"Jealous Georgie. That should be your new name."

I stood up and stomped back to my bed. "I'm not jealous. I'm your best friend. Who else would have known where to find you in the mall. . . ? Oooh, you knew that, didn't you?"

"Figured you'd find me to save your own behind. You're the one who talked me into going with you, then you left me. Hope I worried you a ton. Serves you right for thinking I wasn't as good as you 'cause I got asthma. Lucinda didn't care about that. Said we could be best friends, too."

"First, I didn't want you even coming along. And second, I don't care about your asthma, either."

"'You should stay here with the bikes.' Who said that, huh? You were treating me like a sickie, and I'm not. Point-blank. Period." She bit into her sandwich.

I'd lost my appetite, so I sat down and picked at my sandwich before I spoke. "I didn't want you to be in the hospital, too. You needed to catch your breath."

"If you don't want me treating you like a baby, then don't treat me like a sickie. A sickie couldn't do what I did. Lucinda said so, too." She stood up and slid the earrings into the back of her drawer.

"You better not steal anything again, or I'm telling. I really will. Threatening me about Kevin won't work. I'm your best friend. Lucinda is only friends with people who do what she says. That's it. I'm not gonna let her get away with stealing your bike."

"Stop acting like you care so much. Matter of fact, stop saying you're my best friend. You don't even want to stay the night. You hardly ever want to talk on the phone anymore. The only best friend you want is *Tangie*. Remember, I was trying to help get her to like you when she was treating you like a mosquito."

"Well, maybe she's sorry for that now."

"She's not sorry. I bet she's only pretending she can stomach you while Peaches is sick."

"You don't know that! Maybe she just wants to be a good stepsister."

Nikki laughed. "You are so lame. All you want to do is talk about Lucinda and how she uses people. But what about Tangie? I bet she's getting something out of the deal. Probably more allowance. Who knows. She wouldn't give you the time of day last week, now all of a sudden she wants to do a mani-pedi like y'all the Kardashians."

"You think you know everything all the time, and you don't."

"More than you. Don't let Tangie fool you like you're five. You're eleven. Almost twelve, next is thirteen."

"I know how to count."

"Don't seem like it. Lucinda says I can't act like a baby and hang with her and her crew. Neither should you." She took another bite of her peanut butter and jelly sandwich and put two chips in her mouth.

"That's gross!" I said.

"What's it to you?" She slapped on her Beats and put her head under the cover.

I yanked at it a few times. "Now who's acting like a baby?" I said.

I stood over her, bending down until my lips were as close to her ear as possible. I whispered, "Don't come crying to me when you need help getting your bike. Girls like Lucinda Hightower don't change overnight."

Then, in grand Nikki fashion, she flipped the cover back, yanked off her Beats, and said, "You should be thanking Lucinda and me instead of talking junk."

"Seriously? Why?" I snapped. She just got quiet and rolled her eyes. I folded my arms and leaned forward. "Really, Nicole Denise Shepard, you tell me why right this minute, or I swear you'll regret it."

Nikki gave a deep sigh like a teacher had just asked her to read aloud.

"There's a step team at the Boys and Girls Club that's starting in September. And Lucinda's the captain." As soon as Nikki said "step team," Lucinda's words about how I got cut from everything punched me in the stomach.

"Big whoop. You can make that with your eyes closed," I said.

"Not if Lucinda doesn't want me on it. She says that for letting her ride my bike for a while, she'll make sure that I'm on the team."

"So, you're giving up your favorite bike, and fibbing about it, to do something you can do anyways. Lucinda wants to win, she wouldn't keep you off the team. . . ." She folded her lips in. "What else, Nikki?"

"Uggh, do you ever stop?"

"What else?"

Nikki's sigh sounded like a tire going flat. "Oh my Josh! If you must know, she says she'll let Tammy on the team and make sure no one teases her."

"So basically, they're just going to not bully her. We

both know she's made a team on her own, remember?" One of Sweet Apple's first step teams was the Apple Dumpling Dancers. When she made it, the girls bullied her about her size until she quit.

"And . . ."

"And who?" My stomach tightened up a little.

"You. She said that she'd make sure *you* are on the team."

My stomach fluttered. I could see Peaches, maybe even Tangie, watching me dance in front of strangers. I didn't know whether to hug Nikki or holler at her. But she was Best Friend Nikki now. And regardless of the other fibs she may have told, I knew this one was true. Lucinda would want Nikki on her team because Nikki can dance circles around anybody. Tammy can dance, especially Dab, almost as good as Nikki. But me in a crowd, not so much.

I sat on the bed alongside of her. It felt like we were back in the gymnasium on the bleachers after I found I didn't make the team.

She'd put her head on my shoulder. "We can practice more, next time," she'd said. We both knew that wouldn't make a difference if I forgot the moves soon as I stepped in front of a crowd. We'd sat there until the noise in the hallway quieted down, then we walked to her house. I put that out of my head and tried to focus on this New Nikki.

"This isn't how it should be. We gotta stop Lucinda from thinking she can use people. If she wants to help us all be on the team, that's cool, but she can't take over your bike as a reward. That's not fair to you. It'll only get worse when school starts." After I'd stopped talking, I wished that I'd made each word as strong as Marshall's when he was talking about his friend.

"You never get it, do you," she snapped. "I'm letting her ride it, not giving it up. Just worry about *your* new BFF."

I folded my arms, trying to think of a quick comeback. I had nothing but a quivering bottom lip.

"Whatever!" I shouted.

Nikki rolled her eyes and plopped those Beats back on her head.

I could feel with everything I had that Lucinda was just using Nikki. Then I thought about Tangie wanting me to help with her hair and do our nails. I just got madder. Nikki didn't need to say a thing because the more I thought about it, the worse I felt: If Lucinda couldn't change so quickly, could Tangie?

15.

QUEEN OF PAC-MAN

The next morning, Nikki and I barely spoke as we made our own breakfast of Frosted Flakes and peanut butter toast, then headed back to her room. I didn't sleep all the way through the night but woke up and counted the neon stars that Nikki's daddy had painted on her ceiling. I'd wished that instead of her lying in her hospital bed, Peaches and I were playing hopscotch up there lost in a circle of light. As soon as I came back to reality, I got a sick feeling in my stomach that wouldn't go away.

"Wanna play Pac-Man?" Nikki asked, instead of apologizing.

"I guess," I said.

Nikki had lots of games, but we always ended up

playing Pac-Man because she was always trying to prove she could beat me. It's my dad's favorite, and I'd play it with him for hours. Mama didn't allow me to download games that made you kill people to win, and I was never that good at Angry Birds or Candy Crush. But I was queen of Pac-Man.

"You still mad?" she asked.

"Yep. Who wants a fibber as a best friend?"

"You act like you never told a story. You don't want your mom to know we were at the hospital."

"That's different."

I usually felt sorry for her during Pac-Man and let the Ghosts touch me on purpose, but not this time. I didn't care if she never got a turn.

"What about the other stuff?" Nikki said.

"What other stuff?"

"You know, about Lucinda and Tangie."

"Well, Lucinda has your best bike. Tangie doesn't have mine."

"That's all you could come up with?" Nikki laughed.

"Whatever," I said, knowing that it sounded better in my head.

"Georgie!" Mama's voice rang from downstairs.

I tossed the controller on the bed. "Gotta go."

"Geessh, you didn't have to throw it down like that," Nikki said, as the controller bounced. As I started heading out the door, she said, "If you leave, that means I won."

"That's not what that means," I shouted, and dashed down the stairs. Seconds later, I flung my arms around Mama.

"Georgie, lower your voice," Mama said, and smoothed my hair.

"Hey, Mama," I whispered, lower than I needed to.

"Hello, silly," she said, and hugged me tighter. When she called me "silly," I knew she didn't know about my hospital visit. That would have gotten me a "young lady," or worse, "Georgiana Elizabeth Matthews."

Mama smelled like Ivory soap. She hadn't worn any perfume since Peaches had gotten sick. Instead of curls, Mama had combed her hair back and used my big butterfly clip to keep it in place. She didn't even have on earrings, which Grandma Sugar says a lady should wear from the time she learns to talk until she says her last words.

"Are we going to see Peaches today?" I asked.

"Cream and sugar for your tea, Katrina?" Ms. Cora said over the whistling teapot.

"Just sugar," Mama said, then she took my hands and kissed them. "Sweetie, your sister was in a special section called ICU."

"Is she out now?" I asked.

"Thank the Lord. They moved her this morning. . . . But . . ."

"She still needs a transfusion?"

"No, thank God. . . . Wait, where did you hear that?"

I shrugged. Mama was too tired to challenge me.

Ms. Cora walked into the living room and set saucers and teacups on the coffee table.

"But what, Mama? When is she coming back home?"

Mama shook her head before her words followed. "They still can't say exactly, sweetie. She has bacterial meningitis. And . . ." She glanced around for Ms. Cora before she spoke. "They caught it early, so that's a blessing. But baby, Peaches may not be well for some time, even after she comes home."

"What does that mean?" Pictures of every sick person I'd seen in my life flashed in my head. "Will she be able to talk or walk? She'll have to take medicine every day?"

She shot another look at Ms. Cora, who seemed just as sad as when Mama brought me over yesterday.

"We'll just have to take care of her, Mama," I said hesitantly. "Right?"

"Baby, Mama doesn't know what condition she'll be in yet. The doctors are doing all that they can." Every time I watch a TV show where somebody is about to die, someone says, "The doctors are doing all that they can." I put my hand to my stomach as if that could stop it from somersaulting.

"You and Nikki didn't give Jevon a hard time, did you?" Ms. Cora said, changing the subject.

If I thought I could get away with it, I'd have stomped so hard that the elephants on Ms. Cora's coffee table would've tipped over. I wasn't ready to change the subject, but it didn't matter. "No, ma'am."

Mama wrung her hands together like she used to do when Daddy upset her. She didn't meet my eyes anymore, and I thought she'd start bawling any minute. She cleared her throat, her eyes glassy. The sadder Mama got, the less I held out hope that Peaches would ever come home. "I need to ask you a question, sweetie."

"What is it?"

"Since we're going to be at the hospital so much, would

you like to stay here with Nikki for a few days?" Whatever they knew was locked in the Mama Vault. Mama wasn't even gonna let me know what was going on with my own sister. All of that "big girl" stuff was for the birds.

I folded my arms. "No. I don't want to be here. I wanna come home." I didn't know Nikki was behind me until I heard her stomp back up the stairs and slam her door. A part of me wanted to go to her, but right now, all I could think about was Peaches.

"What was that all about?" Ms. Cora asked. "Georgie, are you and Nikki getting along?"

"Probably mad 'cause I won't stay and let her try to beat me in Pac-Man."

"That's all there is to it?" Ms. Cora asked.

"Yes, ma'am. I just wanna be home and in my room. All Peaches's stuff is there." Ms. Cora nodded, though I don't think she bought it. "Did you feed Girl, Mama?"

"Tangie did." Mama tugged at my ears. "I understand, honey. Give me a moment with Ms. Cora while you go get your things." Mama picked up her tea.

I hurried back upstairs. Nikki had already cleared out my emergency drawer and put all my stuff in a bag. "If you don't wanna stay over, I don't want you to either, ever again," she fumed.

Sometimes when she's mad, she tells me that twenty times an hour. But she'd never cleared out my drawer before.

"Just want to be in my own room," I mumbled.

"That's not it! You wanna suck up to your new best friend."

"Tangie's not my new best friend. She's my big sister.

155

She's a stepsister, but that's good, too. You got a big brother. Jevon looked out for you yesterday. Ain't nothing wrong with me wanting someone like that. Anyway, I think there is something no one is telling me."

"About Tangie?"

"No, Peaches. My mom is hiding something. Your mom knows what it is I betcha."

"Oh, they put it in the Mama Vault?"

"Pretty sure. And the only way to know for certain is if I go home and wait for someone to slip up. Frank's not as good at keeping stuff like Mama."

That was kinda true, since he asked Peaches and me wouldn't it be cool to go to Disney World so many times, I swear even Girl figured it out.

"But what do you *think* it is?"

I could feel the chill bumps all over my arms. Within seconds I was back in Tangie's room staring into the sadness in her eyes. It was possible that little sisters go away and never come back. It happened to Tangie's li'l sister.

My lips parted, but no words came out.

"Well?"

"It can only be one thing—that Peaches is sicker than they want to say. Maybe"—I swallowed, my throat tight— "maybe she's not ever coming home." Even saying the words left me feeling like I wasn't able to stand. I wrapped my arms around myself.

"No, Georgie. Don't say that. Peaches is coming home. I promise."

Hearing Nikki's words made my eyes well. She only "promised" when I was really hurt and she didn't know what else to do. Like the first night I told her I thought my parents were getting a divorce, and she said, "No, they'll just argue sometimes like my parents. But they won't get a divorce. I promise."

I didn't want to remind her of that. She was doing the best she could.

"If she's coming home, then why does it feel like they're not telling me everything? Mama keeps saying, 'You're a big girl.'"

"Parents just say stuff like that. Then treat us like we can't handle grown-up stuff. We're eleven. Not two."

"I know," I said. My shoulder slumped so far down, I felt like I was going to crumple to my knees.

Nikki pulled me by the elbow until I sat down next to her on her bed.

"If your mama's not telling you, then my mama's not telling me. That leaves us with one thing to do?"

"What's that?"

"Secret mission."

Nikki loved the word "secret." Anything she thought anyone else didn't know, she wanted to know. I was so desperate to find out about Peaches, it sounded like the best idea ever, whatever it was.

"Something's better than nothing!"

"Trust me. This will work. I'll make sure I listen to my mom talking to my dad or Jevon after you leave. I won't let them find out I'm listening, though."

"Eavesdropping?

"No, that's sorta by accident. I'll make sure I'm hidden away close by."

"Spying?"

"Yeah. You got a better plan?" Her folded arms looked like skinny rails.

"Nothing," I admitted. "Thank you, Nikki."

"What are you thanking me for? I'm your best friend, and I'm good at spying. Big whoop. Just need to find out how Peaches is really doing."

"Tell your mom that I need to talk to you to cheer me up, and she might give you your phone back."

"Already thought about that."

"Good. What about your bike?" I asked.

"What about it? I can get it anytime I want." But then she glanced away and her lip drooped.

"What's wrong?"

"Nothing!"

"Tell me what really happened."

"If I do, will you forget about it?"

"Yes."

"And don't cross your fingers!"

"Okay," I said. "I'll let it go." I mentally asked God for forgiveness at that second because I was fibbing—big-time.

"Georgie!" Mama called. "Unless you're staying, you need to get yourself down here."

"On my way, Mama!" I said, rushing Nikki with a flap of my hands.

"I didn't tell her to drop it at Tammy's. I said that she could keep it until the step-team tryouts."

"That's the rest of the summer!"

"I know. She said it was that or nothing. She'll probably give it back if I told her I changed my mind."

"Yeah, she might," I said. She'd tacked that last sentence on with a feather. I didn't have the heart to blow it away. But I was already thinking of a way to get her bike back and teach Lucinda Hightower a thing or two.

"Georgie!"

I hugged Nikki. "I'll talk to you soon."

"Duh. I gotta come downstairs with you. If I don't, they'll think I'm still mad."

"Oh, you're right."

When we got downstairs the curtains were wide open and the living room furniture's emerald-green color glowed.

"Call me if you need anything, Trina," Ms. Cora said, and kissed Mama's cheek. They held hands for a few seconds and rocked their arms like little girls do. "Peaches will be home in no time."

"Thank you for everything, Cora," Mama said as they walked to the door together.

"Peace out, rainbow trout," Nikki said, and hugged me for show. "I'm on it," she whispered.

"Bye, bye, butterfly," I said as Mama and Ms. Cora hugged. I gave Nikki a thumbs-up. She winked at me like the time I ran for class president against Theophilus Jackson. He was sure he'd win, 'cause he told the boys that his big brother would give them discounts at Foot Locker if they voted for him. Don't know what Nikki did, but I won by three votes.

At the door, Mama and Ms. Cora were still whispering, and between Nikki and me, we had to find out what that was all about.

I had to admit that being Nikki's best friend was hard.

But one time when we had a fight and weren't speaking to each other, Mama told me that a best friend was a relative that you make for yourself. I thought about that every time Nikki made me mad. I figured since I made her, I just might as well keep her.

16.

YOU'RE A FAKER

When we got outside, I saw that someone had written "Wash Me" in the dust on Frank's van. I'd never even seen the windshield on his van or car dirty before.

As we buckled up, I glanced at Peaches's booster seat. I closed my eyes and imagined that she was in it, her head bobbing to music that only she could hear.

Since Mama didn't talk, I didn't either. I'm sure she was working on "getting her thoughts together." I bet they were scattered all over the place.

A couple minutes later, at a red light, Mama said, "Thank you for being such a big girl through all of this, G-baby."

"You're welcome, Mama," I told her, and gave her my best smile. But a part of me was hurt inside, because if

Mama thought I was a real big girl, she would tell me the truth.

A horn blew when the light flashed green. Mama waved her hand in the rearview and hit the gas.

"Your daddy sends his love. Says he tried to call but your phone was dead."

"Left the charger home. You still mad at him?"

"We'll get through this," she said.

"You forgive me for leaving Peaches?"

"Baby, I was mad at the entire world that day. You shouldn't have left without your daddy's permission. But neither you or your daddy are to blame."

"What about Millicent?"

She shook her head a few times before finally speaking. "No, G-baby. No one. We might not ever know exactly when she contracted it. Nurses did their due diligence, but no outbreaks or anything reported."

"Who's there with her now?"

"Sugar and your daddy. He wants to know if you want to stay with him and Millicent. He's at the hospital most of the time and his dealership the other, so you'd be with Millicent a lot. What about that? You'll be closer to Nikki."

Not that I didn't think Daddy wanted me there, but it seemed like something Mama was just thinking up so I wouldn't be home.

"Do I have to?"

"No, baby. Just know it's an option. Everybody's trying to make this as easy on you as possible."

Thirty minutes later, Mama parked in our driveway instead of the garage.

"Heading right back out," she said.

"Is Tangie here?"

"Probably in her room." She tugged at her clothes, then stared at her hands and dingy sneakers. "I look a mess. I'm going to jump in the shower and try to make myself resemble a human being." She laughed. "I don't want to scare Peaches."

Once we were inside, Tangie pranced around in the kitchen rummaging through the fridge and talking. Took me a second to realize she had on her Bluetooth.

"Just a sec, Val," she said when she saw us. I wondered if it was Marshall on the line.

"Hey, Georgie! I got the manicure and pedicure sets. Let me know when you're ready."

"Okay, I will," I said. I wished Nikki was here so she could see Tangie just being regular.

But right before I went upstairs, Mama mouthed "thank you" to Tangie the way she did after Tangie babysat us or made us lunch. All I could think about was Tangie's meanness to us then. I wanted to believe Tangie liked me for real. That she was really proud of me like she'd said. I just didn't know if that was true.

As soon as I started upstairs, I missed Peaches yelling, "What you bring me?" Even if I didn't have anything, she'd just say, "Get me something next time, G-baby." Anytime I left the house without her, it seemed like she'd imagine I was on some magical adventure, complete with fairies, chocolate fountains, and gifts that I could pick from trees. I'd give anything for the two of us to be somewhere like that. This whole world was impossible to imagine without Peaches in it. The knot in my stomach tightened at just the thought of her in a hospital bed with tubes sticking in her arms and no windows that let her see the sky.

I couldn't even manage to go up to my room right now and see my empty twin bed, so I turned around. Mama darted upstairs, and I went back to the kitchen with Tangie and got a glass of water. I kept wiping my sweaty palms on my shorts. Tangie sat at the breakfast nook and peeled the lid off a cup of yogurt.

"We can get started whenever you want," Tangie said, digging the spoon in her yogurt and swirling it.

"I'll be ready in a minute. Going to go put my stuff in my room." I'd said it, but as soon as I turned around, it was like I hit a cloud of thick smoke. My eyes burned and I just couldn't breathe. It took me seconds to even feel Tangie's hand on my shoulder.

"It's okay if you're a little sad to go upstairs, you know."

"Why would I be sad? It's not like Peaches isn't coming home," I snapped.

"Didn't mean it that way," Tangie said. "Ready when you are."

I couldn't even stop my tone. All I could think about was Mama mouthing "thank you," to her. All my feelings were a big, jumbled mess.

I went upstairs like it was no big deal. Mama was taking a shower to quickly freshen up. If she were "luxuriating," the upstairs would smell like pearberry—her favorite Bath & Body Works scent—and Nair.

All the time I was wishing and praying for Tangie to like me, I guess I forgot to add that I wanted her to like me for real—for real. And never would I ever have even thought to ask for her to only like me because my sister was sick.

Now I knew why maybe Tangie didn't want to cheer anymore. Maybe she couldn't jump so high because there was the same sinking feeling in her stomach that I had that kept her feet on the ground. Ever since Peaches got sick, there'd never been a moment that I felt like dancing, not even for a second.

After about thirty minutes, Mama was dressed and off to the hospital, leaving me alone with Tangie.

"Georgie," Tangie called from downstairs while I was checking on Girl. I sprinkled dots of fish food onto the surface of the water.

When I got to the living room, she held up a tiny makeup bag. "Is it okay if we get started?"

"Yeah, I guess," I muttered.

"You don't sound excited. What's up?" She twirled a fingernail file between her fingers.

"I'm hungry."

"What do you want?"

"Pizza."

"Did your mama leave pizza money?"

"No," I said as we walked into the kitchen.

"What about Steak-umm and fries? You can whip up that special sauce you like."

"It's mustard and sugar, nothing special. I don't want that, anyway. I want pizza." I pouted.

"Okay, okay, pizza it is. I got some money saved . . . Garden Crust, okay?"

She only ordered from places that made pizza that looked like a salad on a thin slice of bread.

"No, I want Pizza Hut."

"It's too greasy, but if that's what you want, that's cool. What you want on it?"

"Sausage, pepperoni, and ham."

"All that meat?"

"On the *whole thing*. You can pick it off." I folded my arms and let my weight fall to the side. I probably looked like one of those bendable pencils, but I didn't care.

She raised her eyebrows and stepped back a little from me. "Are you okay?"

"I'm fine."

"Well, I'm not that hungry, anyway." She glanced at the time on her phone, then placed the order. When she hung up, she said, "It'll be here in about forty-five minutes. While we're waiting on it, we could handwash the dishes and use paper plates and cups. What you say I wash and you dry?"

"I don't feel like washing dishes." I sat down at the kitchen table.

Tangie sat next to me. "Well, we got to do them before the manicures, that way we won't mess up our nails."

I tried to force words out of my lips, but I just shrugged and clasped my hands. Tangie stared at me for a long moment. Then she said, "I get you're upset about Peaches. Did anything else happen at your friend's house once you three got back?"

"No . . . nothing."

"Are you sure?"

"Very."

"I didn't mention a thing," she said.

"Big whoop."

We locked eyes.

"Okay. Look, Georgie. I know this is hard on you."

"And why now are you calling me 'Georgie'? It's been Georgiana. All this time, remember?"

"That was me being mean. Seems childish now. I know how hard this is."

She reached over and touched my shoulder, and I flinched like she was Millipede. I bit the inside of my jaw to keep my lips from quivering. It burned me up that Nikki was right about Tangie not liking me for real.

"I'm tired of everyone saying they know how hard it is and treating me like a baby."

"Nobody means any harm. Peaches would want you—"

"Don't tell me nothing about what my sister would want!" I shouted, and banged my fist on the table. "You don't know her or me. You don't even like us. Peaches knows you don't. Since we've been here, you've done nothing but treat us like bugs. Bedbugs. Now you're trying to be nice. You're a big faker! A big, phony faker."

"A big faker?"

"You're in high school. You know what 'faker' means."

"What are you talking about?"

"You'll never like us because your real sister is in heaven."

As soon as I said it, I wished I could snatch it back. Tangie's head lowered like she was saying a prayer. When she looked up at me, water pooled in her eyes.

"That's not true, Georgie."

"No one wants to tell me what *is* true," I said, trying to forget how much I wanted to trust her.

Just that second, Frank walked into the kitchen carrying a bag of groceries with a loaf of bread sticking out of the top. Without a doubt he was in on it, too, so I jetted past him and stomped upstairs, shaking the African mask Mama had on the wall.

I slammed my door and plopped on my bed. As soon as I stared up at my starless ceiling, I missed the fluorescent twinkles in Nikki's room. While her daddy was busy painting stars on her ceiling, mine was off somewhere with the Millipede. Yeah, sure, he bought our old house back, but that was just like Tangie's fake niceness now—guilt. Didn't matter. As soon as enough time had passed, both of them would be back to their regular old selves. At any moment, I expected Frank and Tangie to come knocking, but I didn't hear a sound.

So what if Tangie doesn't like me for real? From now on, I'd focus on being a better big sister to my *real* sister.

I got off my bed and wandered over to Peaches's, wishing I could erase all the times I didn't want her in my room. And even though I didn't say it to her all the time, I'd be telling a big, fat story if I said I wasn't thinking it a lot.

I plopped my head on Peaches's pillow, and it sunk right in. My hand touched something underneath her pillow. It was *The Princess and the Frog.* I opened the book and read,

"Tiana works hard. She has no time for fun." I couldn't help thinking of all the times Peaches wanted me to read to her, but all I wanted to do was get to Tangie. I slammed the book shut and slid it back underneath Peaches's pillow.

Then—knock, knock.

"Georgie, can I come in?" Tangie asked.

"No!" I shouted. "You're a faker. Go away!"

My lips trembled, but I was ready to call her a faker again.

I stomped as hard as I could back to my bed. So I wouldn't have to hear her knock again, I put on my headphones and turned my iPod up as loud as it would go. Then I yanked the cover up over my head.

That still wasn't enough to block out the sound of the knocking. And when I didn't answer, the door opened and Frank's deep voice bounced off the walls.

I'd done it now.

17.
NOBODY'S 100%

"Georgie. What's the matter?" Frank said as he sat down on the bed and nudged my shoulder.

I didn't say a word, even as my bed rocked when Tangie sat on the other corner of it. "I'll do the dishes. No problem," she said.

"That's thoughtful of you, but I don't think this is about doing the dishes. Take the cover off your head, please, Georgie," Frank said.

I sat up and dropped my headphones around my neck.

"I should have understood she didn't feel well, Dad. I told you she was okay," Tangie said.

"Georgie, I'm waiting," Frank said.

"I didn't feel like her telling me what to do. That's all."

He darted his eyes between us. "Well, nobody is themselves lately, so I understand. We all have to work on holding it together and not losing our tempers with each other," he said to me, and glanced at Tangie.

"'Kay," I said.

When the doorbell rang, Frank asked, "You girls expecting somebody?"

"Too soon for the pizza guy," Tangie said.

Frank peered out of my curtains. "One of my bowling buddies," Frank said. "Coming!" He jogged downstairs.

Tangie's eyelids closed and opened slowly like she was trying to bring me into focus. As soon as she glanced at me, I looked away. I wasn't a "big baby" like Nikki thought, so I had to keep Tangie from fooling me. It was possible for her to be sad about Peaches but still not really like me–like me.

"Dad's worried about you," Tangie said.

"He's not my dad," I said. "He's *your* dad. Just like this is *your* house."

"But this house is your house, too. And I'm sure my dad wants to be a good stepdad."

"Maybe he does. He tries hard just like my mom tries hard to be nice to you. But you . . . you've treated Peaches and me lower than dirt."

She fluttered her eyelids like I'd blown sand in her face.

"I didn't mean to." She reached out to touch my arm. I backed away.

"Don't lie!" I heard the word that I'm always telling Peaches not to use fly from my tongue, and I didn't care. "You knew what you were doing when you slammed the door in our face. I could take it, but you really hurt Peaches.

She didn't understand why a person older than us would be so mean. We didn't ask to be here."

Tangie clasped her hands together and brought them to her forehead. She shook her head and sighed before letting her hands drop to her side. "You're right. You, me, or Peaches really didn't have a choice in any of this. But I'm the oldest. I should have handled myself better. When Peaches comes home—"

"No. Don't use my sister! Don't say how you're going to be nicer or whatever. You don't mean it. You're only being nice to me 'cause she's sick. And you're only pretending like you want to be nice to her, too, just in case she goes to heaven like your sister."

I didn't know tears were streaming until I tasted the saltiness of them on my tongue. I wiped my eyes with the edge of my blanket.

Tangie's face scrunched up like I'd slapped her. "Don't say that, Georgie. Please."

She wasn't fooling me with that surprised look. I hated that she thought I was some silly little girl who couldn't put two and two together.

"I'm not stupid. You've never wanted anything to do with us. You're only doing the nails and stuff because you're getting something out of it. My mama is paying you because you're helping them keep secrets."

Tangie shook her head. "Your mama isn't paying me a dime. And what secrets do you think we're keeping?"

"That Peaches might never come home. Nobody is telling me the truth." Just saying the words aloud made it feel like the floor gave way and we were falling. It was like being on one of those scary amusement rides except it was going to go on for the rest of your life.

"Oh my goodness," Tangie said.

I scooted closer to the wall. "And keep your pizza. I'm not hungry."

"Look at me, G-baby."

I didn't move.

She rocked my side, but not with enough force to turn me toward her. "Please, look at me," she said.

Don't really be a baby, I told myself, and turned around.

"Peaches is gonna get better. She's coming home. Dr. Harris said that taking Peaches to the hospital right away helped save her life. But I know what it's like when grownups keep you out of the loop. My dad and aunts didn't tell me about my sister for days. They even kept my mom's condition from me."

"Then you do think they're hiding something."

"I don't know, Georgie. Your mom did talk to me."

"Then she is going to die." My head hit the wall. I wanted it to come tumbling down. Tangie grabbed my shoulders before I could do it again.

"No, no. Stop that," Tangie said. "She's not. You gotta believe that I'd be honest about that. But your mom said that she won't be a hundred percent."

"She said that to me, too. But I don't know what that means."

"That's because she doesn't know. Not even the doctors know sometimes."

"It must be serious for them to say it. I'm not stupid. Nobody's a hundred percent after they've been so sick.

But then you get better and it's like you were never sick at all."

I thought about after Nikki had her tonsils out Mama let me go over and visit her. She didn't talk above a whisper. Sometimes I had to lean in real close to hear what she had to say. But, next thing I knew, she was back to screaming at the top of her lungs.

"Well, that's just it, Georgie. Sometimes the person never gets to be a hundred percent, physically anyway. Your mother told me that there may be some 'lasting effects.' She may never be like the Peaches we were used to."

"I asked my mama if she meant that Peaches wouldn't be able to walk or something?" I felt my stomach somersault and my eyes well again.

"Don't think they know exactly what will happen right now."

"I mean . . . but even . . . even if she couldn't walk or something wouldn't she be the same Peaches on the inside? She'll still love me, right?"

"Of course!"

"Why you think my mama is protecting me from that? Aren't you supposed to love someone even when they're not at a hundred percent?"

"Yeah," Tangie said. "Maybe even more," she added, but turned her head away from me a little. "I would have loved Morgan no matter how she came back to us."

I didn't say anything else but just sat with Tangie for a while and listened to the birds chirping. They were happy now, but would be just as sad as those lonely crickets when the day went away.

As Tangie got up to go back in her room, she said, "Do you need anything?"

I shook my head. "I'm sorry for what I said, Tangie. I know you miss your sister a lot."

"Thanks," she said.

"Can I . . . ?"

"What?"

"Can I see more pictures of her?"

She wiped her eyes with the heel of her hand. "Maybe another time," she said. I didn't speak, just nodded like she could hear it. Before she opened the door she said, "Do you really want to?"

"If it's okay," I said. I sat up hoping she'd tell me she'd be back with the pictures.

"Well, you coming?"

"In *your* room?" I asked, putting my feet on the floor.

"That's where they are," she said, and opened the door.

As soon as I stepped in her room, I caught a whiff of strawberries. Maybe it was the same as before, but I was so scared when she caught me, I couldn't remember nothing but the sound of Morgan's picture hitting the floor.

She pointed to her bed. "Have a seat. I keep one of my mama's old photo albums up here."

She reached for the top shelf in her closet. I quickly eyed the rest of it and decided to make sure all my clothes were neatly folded and hung up on hangers, too. Once she got it down, she sat next to me. Resting the album on our legs, she opened it and started from the first page. "Morgan wasn't even born yet. It was just Dad, Mom, and me," she said.

When she got to pictures of her sister and mama, she ran her fingertips over them like it helped her see them better.

"I even got a few of her the night before it happened, but it's still too hard to look at them."

"How'd it happen, Tangie?"

Soon as I said it, I bit my tongue. I was sure Tangie was going to toss me out. I'd heard the words "car accident," but that's as much as anyone ever said.

It took her a little while to answer. I kept my lips glued shut.

"Morgan was seven and made the junior gymnastics team. Mom was taking her to an early morning practice. Morgan woke me up and asked me to go with them. I told her I was tired and she could do the routine for me when she came home." Tangie's voice cracked. I reached out and rubbed her back in small circles like Mama would do with Peaches and me.

"On the way there, or coming home, Mom's tire blew out, and they were hit by another car. Their car flipped a few times. Mom and Morgan were in intensive care. Mom, for nearly a month. Morgan, just for a few days, then she died. Mom and Dad seemed to fall apart after that."

"I'm sorry. I shouldn't have asked." My hands collapsed into my lap. When Tangie didn't say anything, I figured I'd messed things up again. But when I had the nerve to look at her, her tears were falling and she didn't bother wiping them. I didn't know what to do. What if I touched her and she flinched away from me?

I eased closer to her. I was too scared to hug her, so I just sat there. When I got up enough courage, I patted her back.

"It's gonna be okay, Tangie," I said. I just kept sitting there without trying to think of anything new to talk about, but she didn't ask me to leave and that was just as good as her asking me to stay.

18.

NOT SCARED OF NOTHING

"Special delivery," Frank said, and knocked on the door.

I realized then that the doorbell had rung a couple times since I'd been in her room. "Come in, Dad," Tangie said.

Frank entered with the pizza. "The captain of my bowling league stopped by with all kinds of goodies for you girls. And this came a few minutes ago."

"I forgot we ordered it," I said. On top of the pizza box were cups and plates. In his other hand was a jug of sweet tea. He sat them on Tangie's desk.

"Upstairs?" I said, and knew Peaches wouldn't believe it. But it still didn't feel as good as when I got to eat in Nikki's room. It was just because Peaches was sick. That sucked the happiness right out.

"Didn't want the pizza to get cold," he said.

"Thanks, Dad," Tangie said.

Frank's eyes darted to the pictures of Morgan on Tangie's lap. He sat the pizza down on the table and reached for the album.

"Daddy's beautiful little girl," he said quietly. Then he glanced at Tangie. "You need to talk, Tee?"

"I'm good, Dad," she said. Frank handed her the album and she stood to put it back in her closet.

"We have to remember what the counselor said."

"I know. I know. Don't be afraid to schedule more appointments if I need to."

"We agreed?"

"Yes, Dad," Tangie answered, and stared out her window.

"Are you holding up okay, Georgie?"

Talking to Tangie had made me feel a little better. A thousand words were on my tongue, but all I managed to say was "Okay, I guess."

"That's the best any of us could do right now."

I nearly held my breath thinking he'd say something new about Peaches.

"I'm gonna go back up to the hospital, but first I'll stop and pick your mama up a fancy salad. That was her on the phone. Told me something to tell you."

"To behave myself?" I asked.

"Nope. Peaches has been cleared for visitors."

I perked up instantly. "Really? When can I see her?"

"First thing tomorrow," Frank said. He did the head-rubbing thing again and walked toward the door.

"Are you sure?"

"As sure as we can get. Your mama wouldn't let me say a word until she cleared it with Dr. Harris herself. Didn't want to get your hopes up."

"That's good to hear!"

I was nervous to look at Tangie because of the mean things I'd said, but when our eyes met, she had a little smile that even showed in her eyes.

"Frank!" I called out. I wanted to run up to him and wrap my arms around him like I would my very own daddy, but I lost my nerve.

"Present!" he said.

"Can you eat with us?" I asked, opening the box.

"You know what? Roger that. I could use a little something to hold me over." He slid a chair from under Tangie's desk and took a slice. Tangie and I grabbed slices, too. "Pepperoni, sausage, and ham . . . Love it."

Tangie nodded. "Not too bad," she said, and poured our tea.

"You're eating the meat?" I said, noticing that she wasn't picking off the toppings.

"Can't eat like a bird all the time, especially after good news," she said.

"If you want to taste the pizza in a boot camp chow hall, just take a heap of tomato sauce and pour it over one of those right there," Frank said, pointing to one of the sneaker boxes stacked in the corner of Tangie's room.

I laughed and took a bite so big it filled both my cheeks. I couldn't wait to call Nikki and tell her that she was wrong about Tangie, but most importantly, I'd see Peaches tomorrow!

We'd been eating and talking for about ten minutes when the doorbell rang again.

Frank wiped his mouth and stood up. "You didn't order from two pizza places, did you?"

We shook our heads, although it wouldn't have been the first time. Frank headed downstairs to answer the door.

Tangie sipped some tea. "Peaches having visitors is a good sign. I'm so glad your dad got her to the hospital when he did."

"Yeah, but they could have gotten her there quicker."

"What do you mean?"

"I'd snuck over to Nikki's. My daddy and Millicent didn't know where I was. Millicent said that Peaches wouldn't tattle even when she was sick." Since Millicent tried so hard to be nice to me at the hospital, I was going to forget about "Millipede."

"Georgie," Frank said as he trotted upstairs a couple of minutes later. "You have a visitor, young lady."

I bugged my eyes. "Really? Who is it?" I was hoping it was Nikki so she could see Tangie and me in action.

Frank tapped his foot but still had a smile on his face.

"Who?" I asked again, and took a bite of pizza.

"A very polite fella," he said. "Told me his name was Kevin. Kevin Jenkins, to be exact. Says it's important."

I swallowed before I could stop myself and almost choked.

"He's having a glass of apple juice and some crackers

at the kitchen table." Frank smiled. "Quite the industrious guy. He brought it himself."

Frank walked down the stairs with me, and Tangie followed us carrying the pizza box and tea. I tried to act like it wasn't a big deal, but there was a jackhammer where my heart usually was.

In the kitchen, Frank stood with his arms folded, eyeing Kevin like he was a mini soldier. "So where do you live, young man?" he asked.

Kevin's shoulders straightened. "Culberson Street. It's not 'round here, sir, but in Georgie's old neighborhood."

"He's our friend from Sweet Apple," I said. I wasn't sure if Frank knew the "our" was for "Nikki and me," but my mouth was too dry to add anything else.

"That is a long trek on a bike," Frank said. "Where are your folks? They okay with that?"

Kevin bobbed his head as Frank asked the questions. "My mom is home, and my dad is in Rochester."

Frank tipped back on his heels. "Rochester, New York? That's quite a ways away."

"It's nine hundred and sixty-two miles from here. Not far from Buffalo," Kevin added.

"Upstate. I've been through there a few times. Far cry from Georgia."

"I'm going to live with my dad soon."

Frank nodded. "Ready for that knee-deep snow, young man?"

"Count me out of any place dealing with snow," Tangie said, and set the pizza and tea on the counter.

"Gonna make money shoveling," Kevin said.

"That's the way to think. . . . Well, I'm off to the hospital. You two can visit in the kitchen, living room, or front porch." Then Frank turned back to Kevin. "Don't stay more than an hour, young man."

"Yes, sir," Kevin said.

"Did you hear me, Georgie?" Frank added.

"No more than an hour," I repeated when I got my tongue to work again.

Frank saluted us. Kevin saluted back, and I waved.

Once Frank left, Tangie playfully tapped her foot like Frank. "Guess I'm the official chaperone," she said. "You were at the hospital, right?" Tangie asked.

"Yes, ma'am," he answered and reached out to shake her hand like Daddy would a customer at the car lot.

"Just call me, Tangie. That's fine."

"Yes, ma'am," he said again, and she giggled.

"Hope my dad didn't scare you," she said.

"No. He's kinda like my dad."

"Do you want something else to drink? What about a slice of pizza?"

"Thata be cool."

"Georgie, pop Kevin here a slice in the microwave and pour him some tea. I'll get started on my nails."

"Okay," I said.

As soon as she left the kitchen, I grabbed the pizza, put it on a plate, and slid it in the microwave. "How did you know where I live?"

"I stopped at your old house first, but nobody was home. Then I saw Nikki. She told me."

When I tell Mama something and she doesn't feel like writing it down, she says, "I'll make a mental note of that." I made a mental note to wring Nikki's neck. She could've at least called and told me she'd talked to him. She didn't have a problem calling me any other time.

"You rode your bike all the way here?"

"Halfway until I caught a bus that let me bring my bike along. Like Nikki *said* she did." He raised his eyebrows a bit. I almost forgot about that part of her fib. I was bursting to tell him the whole story, but Nikki would bite my head off if I spread the news she was bullied. I did a mama move and changed the subject.

"So what did you want?" I asked. "You told my stepdad it was important."

"Guess who I saw at the Boys and Girls Club?"

"Probably Lucinda Hightower," I said, thinking of her being captain of the new step team.

Kevin nodded. "Guess what else."

"What?"

"Lucinda is the one who stole Nikki's bike."

My eyes widened. "How did you find out?"

"I saw her with it. But the crazy part is that I was ready to go take it from her and she told me that Nikki knew all about it."

At that moment I hurt even more for Nikki. Lucinda was flaunting Nikki's bike right in her own neighborhood. Didn't even have the decency to ride it on some other block. Just rubbing her face in it.

"I hate to say that's true, but it ain't that simple."

When the microwave dinged, I opened the door.

"Hope this is hot enough." I set the slice in front of Kevin.

"Thanks." He bit into it right away. After he swallowed he said, "So what's the deal with it?"

"Nikki keeps telling me that Lucinda 'borrowed' it."

"Looking like it's hers now."

"Nikki says she and Lucinda are friends."

"You don't buy that, do you?"

"Not one bit. But I got other stuff to think about right now."

"Well, that's why I'm here, too." He lowered his voice. "Wanna go see your sister again? I could help sneak you in her room. I've snuck into my mom's room before."

"Oh, they moved her out of ICU. My mom said I'll be able to see her tomorrow."

"If they moved her, she's getting better?" He twirled a piece of cheese on his finger and popped it in his mouth. Then he wiped tomato sauce off his face with a napkin.

I put another slice in the microwave for him. "Yeah. I hope so. Everyone keeps saying that she might not be a hundred percent, though. But they won't say how or anything."

"My mom doesn't see too well out of one eye 'cause of the diabetes, but she can still see okay."

I shrugged. "Maybe it's something like that?" I really did want to know, but another part of me just wanted to be happy about visiting Peaches, not wondering about what Mama wasn't telling me. "Thanks for checking on me."

"My dad called my mom last night," Kevin said in between bites.

"Oh, to make plans to come see you?" I asked.

"More like plans for me to come live with him before school starts. My mom argued him down, but since I had to repeat, she says that he's threatening to take her to court."

"I thought you were going to stay here for the rest of the summer."

"Nah, my dad said the way it's situated now ain't working. Says somebody's gotta keep an eye on me. He wants me there to stay as soon as possible."

"When's he coming?"

"Next week."

"Wow, that's soon." I put my hand to my stomach while the butterflies went haywire.

"You okay?"

"Yep. Too much pizza, I guess."

"It makes my stomach hurt when I eat too much, too. But I eat it anyway," he said.

"Yeah, me too," I said, and smiled.

"Guess I coulda waited, but I didn't know when you'd be back over Nikki's. Plus, I wanted to tell you about Lucinda." He took a big gulp of his tea, holding the glass up until the bottom pointed to the ceiling.

I put the other slice in front of him and refilled his tea. As he ate, we chatted about Sweet Apple, our old teachers, but the conversation circled back to Lucinda Hightower. One good thing about talking about Lucinda was that I could be angry. I'd take angry over sad any day.

"That Lucinda thinks she can get away with anything," I said.

"'Cause she usually does," Kevin said.

"Well, not this time. I don't care what Nikki says, soon as Peaches is home, if I find out that Lucinda still has Nikki's bike, she's gonna be in a whole heap of trouble."

"What you got in mind?" His eyes lit up like when I asked him to help me get to the hospital.

"I don't know yet, but it's gotta be something good to teach her not to mess with my friends anymore."

"Whatever it is, count me in." He held up his hand, and I high-fived him. There was always the chance that Lucinda would give Nikki's bike back on her own. But that had about as much chance as Nikki admitting she liked Kevin before she started saying he liked me: Zip. Zero. Zilch.

About thirty minutes later, Kevin said, "Guess I better be going."

"How do you know when the bus comes?"

"It's every forty-five minutes. I ride until I see one. Do you have a pencil and paper? I can write my e-mail address for you. We don't have a house phone, and my mom only has the kind of cell that uses minutes."

I ripped off a grocery-checklist memo slip from the refrigerator door and found a pencil in a cabinet drawer. Before I gave them to him, I said, "My mom opens my e-mail all the time. If there is anything in it she doesn't like, she deletes it and blocks the sender."

After he wrote his address down and I gave him mine, we walked through the living room to the front door. "I won't send nothing bad," he said. "Just tell you how school is going and stuff."

"Leaving?" Tangie called, and waved from Mama's favorite couch with big roses printed on it. Mama found curtains that matched a pink color she called "mauve" and ordered them from Sears. The room looked like spring-time. "Be safe getting home."

Kevin waved back. "Thanks."

Outside, a warm breeze hit me, and I could practically taste Mama's sweet gardenias on my tongue. Kevin's bike leaned on the edge of the steps, right next to them.

"Is your dad driving here?" I asked.

"No, he's flying. Then we're flying back within the next couple of days, I guess. If he can't get off work, he says he might send me a ticket and I'll fly by myself."

"We flew when we visited my aunt Elvie in Louisiana. It was kinda scary."

He jumped on his bike. "Well, I wouldn't be scared. *I'm not scared of nothing*." His voice was louder than before.

"I didn't mean you'd be scared," I said.

He inched his bike along. "No biggie."

I walked next to him. "Hope you get a pilot that lets you see the cockpit and learn how everything works."

"That'd be cool. I hope your sister comes home soon. We don't have a computer, but I'll ride to the library and e-mail you."

"Okay!" I said.

I waved as he sped off. But then he stopped and came back.

"Oh, I meant to give this to you." He jammed his hands in his pocket and kept whatever he pulled out balled in his fist. He drew his arms closer to his chest, and I leaned in. "Do you want it?"

"I guess. Is it another address for you or something?"

When he opened his hands there wasn't anything there.

"Did it fall out?" I asked, looking at the ground.

"Nope, it didn't."

Just then, I felt his lips on my cheek like a buzzing bee had landed on it.

"Hey!" I said as he zipped off.

"I'll e-mail you," he said again, and I watched him pedal down the street.

I stood there with my hand on my cheek, like the kiss was gonna fly away.

19.

KISSING BANDIT

When I got my feet unstuck from the ground, I walked back inside the house. Tangie was standing at the kitchen sink with her hands plunged in the dishwater. "Kevin leave okay?" she asked.

"Yeah, he's gonna ride until a bus comes."

"That's smart. I've pretty much finished the dishes. I just filed my nails while I waited. Didn't feel like tackling my braids today, but let's get to your nails."

"That'd be cool."

Once we were back in her room, I sat on her bed. "What color do you want?" she asked.

My cheek was still tingling. "Probably bubble-gum pink?"

"Sit on the chair at my desk. I'll go get one from your room."

A minute or two later she returned dragging a chair with one hand and balancing a bowl of soapy water in the other. I jumped up to help.

"Grab that towel and put it on my desk for me. You're getting ready to see a real manicurist at work."

As soon as I did, she placed the bowl on the towel. "Go ahead and put one of your hands in here," she instructed me. "You know, just your fingertips."

The water was the warmest it could get before it would've been hot. "There's baby oil in there to give your nails some moisture," she explained.

She sat in the chair across from me. After she took my hand out of the water, she put the other one in.

"Just pretend you're at the beach," she said, as she dried my free hand and started to massage my palm. I giggled. I blocked the kiss out of my mind, so I could pay attention to my manicure. I decided that when Mama came home, I'd give her a manicure, too, so she could luxuriate.

Once Tangie finished the massage and dried my other hand, she started clipping my nails.

"Think we'll be able to visit with Peaches long?" I asked.

"Hmm, thirty, forty minutes," she said.

"Better than nothing. Wonder if I could sneak her a peanut butter and banana sandwich?"

"We better let the nurses keep her on the diet she's on so she can keep getting well. When she's home, she can eat that for lunch and dinner if she wants. Hold your hand still."

Tangie told me to think about the beach, but when I tried, I just thought of my kiss.

Oh, I meant to give this to you. I could hear Kevin's voice. "Tangie . . ."

She glanced at me. "What's up?"

"Is telling a big sister something—I mean telling a stepsister—the same as telling a mama?"

"You're Peaches's big sister, right?"

"Yeah."

"So what do you think?"

"She could tell me anything. I wouldn't tell Mama. Well, I guess if someone was trying to hurt her and I couldn't stop it, then I would."

"That's the way I feel, too. Unless it's something that could hurt the other sister, sisters are the best secret keepers. Even stepsisters."

"And the best manicurists, too."

"You got that right. Other hand, please."

I took a deep breath. "Kevin kissed me."

She stopped clipping, her eyes bright. "He did?"

I pointed to the exact spot like a bull's-eye. "Yep."

"How did you feel?"

"Surprised."

She laughed.

"He kissed my cheek, then sped off."

"Like a kissing bandit."

"Yeah, just like that."

"It was probably his first kiss, too, and was scared you'd be angry."

"I didn't know if I was supposed to be angry. It wasn't like it was on the lips."

"He knew you two would need to be older for that."

"Fifteen?"

"Sometimes it happens earlier. I was thirteen. His name was Elston Grimes. He lived around the corner. Used to walk me home from school when Dad wasn't waiting for me. One day he walked me all the way to the porch. And I kinda knew it was coming, because I closed my eyes."

"Like in the movies?" I asked.

"Kinda. It lasted about five seconds. When it was over, he ran down the stairs."

"Did you like it?"

"Neither one of us knew what we were doing. It was okay."

"Was he your boyfriend after that?"

"Nah, his family moved to Tennessee a couple weeks later. Plus, boys weren't much on my mind then . . ."

"Kevin's leaving, too. Going to live with his dad in Rochester, New York."

"I remember. Up near Canada."

"Not sure, but it's nine hundred and sixty-two miles away," I said, remembering Kevin's words.

"There's no worries about distance these days. There are lots of ways to keep in touch." She dried my hands and glanced back and forth between them both. "I think they're all even. Time for the first clear coat, then bubble-gum pink."

"I have Kevin's e-mail address."

"That's the best. They don't change like cell numbers."

"Tangie?" I bit my lip. "Is Marshall your boyfriend?"

"Sorta, kinda."

"Frank don't like him 'cause he's in college?"

"Yeah."

"That's all?"

"Well, I stayed out with him past my curfew. That made it worse. But then my dad found out that I went to a Stop the Violence rally downtown without his permission. If I would have told him, he'd okay me to go, but he'd be there right by my side. Who needs a babysitter at a protest rally? Can't imagine what he thought we were doing. Thing is, it wasn't *all* Marshall's fault we were late."

"Your daddy doesn't like anybody late for anything."

"Don't I know it. College lets you get involved more with helping the community than high school."

"Like march—"

"Yes, like marching," she said, and didn't seem irritated that I'd overheard that, too. "College is all about speaking up when you don't agree with something, right?"

"Right," I said quickly, though I didn't know.

"Before the accident, my mom was always on the lookout for ways she could help. I was young, but I remember her and my dad protesting when a man named Oscar Grant was murdered. Dad is all for me doing whatever I can, but he doesn't trust Marshall. And it sounds like a lie, but people really do have flat tires." She chuckled. "Not in my dad's world. You'll find out soon enough. It's gonna be a trip when you start dating."

"Why you say that?"

"You got two dads. I'm catchin' it with only one."

"Yeah, that's gonna be a trip." I didn't think I was supposed to like the thought of two dads, but I did. "How often you get to talk to Marshall?"

"Almost every day. Dad doesn't know I do."

"I won't tell."

"Thanks."

"Can I ask you something else?"

"'Course."

"You kiss Marshall on the lips, huh?"

"Yeah. Don't be in a hurry to do that, though. You'll be old enough before you know it. That's what one of my older cousins used to say. I didn't believe it, but it's true."

"You'll be around to talk about it?"

"'Cross the hall. Until I go to college."

"Far away, huh?"

"Not if Dad can help it. He's thinking Clark, Spelman, but I'm thinking Howard, FAMU. Out of state. It'll be cool, though. We can Skype, FaceTime, or whatever."

I didn't want to spoil our time together, so I didn't mention more of the conversation I'd overheard between her and Marshall and left well enough alone.

Tangie put the quick-dry on my nails and used a little mini fan to make them dry even faster.

"Wow! They look like a picture in *Seventeen*," I said.

"Glad you like," Tangie said.

"G-baby," Mama called from downstairs.

"Didn't even hear them come in," Tangie said. "Did you?"

"Nope," I said.

"Girls," Frank's voice followed.

"Just a sec!" Tangie shouted, and tightened the cap on the polish.

I ran down the stairs to the kitchen first. No one there. All I wanted was to go to the hospital to see Peaches, no matter what her percentage.

"We're in here," Mama called from the living room. She was sitting on the couch. When I entered the room, she held out her hand and pulled me on her knee. My heart sank—she does that to give me bad news, like when she and Daddy got their divorce.

"What is it, Mama?" I asked. "I can't go tomorrow either, huh?"

"No, you can't go tomorrow," she said.

My bottom lip felt like a brick pulling down my entire face. I just tumbled onto Mama, who rubbed my back. I wished Frank hadn't told me I could go, so my hopes wouldn't have been up so high. I heard his footsteps in the hallway but couldn't look his way.

"Remember what we talked about?" Tangie said. "Peaches is going to be okay."

"But it's taking too long," I mumbled without lifting my head from Mama's shoulder. It felt like the safest place in the world.

20.

FOR REAL?

Mama kissed my forehead before she spoke. "There's something else Mama needs to tell you . . ." But then she stopped talking.

Another reason I can't visit Peaches, I thought.

"G-baby! G-baby!" a voice called.

I whipped my head off Mama's shoulder and turned toward the doorway. There, with arms wrapped around Frank's neck as he carried her, was Peaches!

I tried to jump up immediately, but I couldn't because my legs were trembling. Everything about me was full of jitters. I grabbed on to Mama, and she rubbed my back. I blinked my eyes really hard. Somehow, I couldn't make myself look at my sister. I was so scared that she'd look like the real Peaches, but when I'd reach out to touch her, there'd just be air. Our house would go back to a house with no Peaches who we needed like sun. And I'd go back to just being a bad big sister who could never make things right. Mama gave me a little push. I finally got up and walked closer to Frank and Peaches, but I kept my eyes on the ground. "You're home for real, Peaches?"

"We're surprising you," she said. Her voice sounded like it does right before she nods off to sleep. I still couldn't meet her eyes.

"This is the best surprise I've ever had." I didn't care how fast my tears were coming.

"I'm so sorry, Peaches. I've been the worst big sister and I'm so sorry."

"Georgie, baby. What are you talking about?" Mama said.

"It's all my fault. If I had called you earlier, or if I hadn't snuck over to Nikki's, maybe she wouldn't have to be in the hospital."

Mama pushed my head into her chest and there was the faint scent of Red Door that relaxed me more than her touch.

"G-baby." Tangie's voice was soft like when she spoke to me at the hospital. "Your sister is home. Look at her. Peaches is here." I was so scared to look at Peaches. To get used to seeing her, for fear she'd disappear.

"Mama's baby is home," Mama said.

I lifted my head from Mama's chest and stared at Peaches. She wasn't pudgy like she was before and her hair was braided into two small plaits along the side of her head, but she was still looking like the prettiest girl I'd ever seen in my life.

Peaches wiggled out of Frank's arms, and I scurried across the living room so fast, I almost knocked him down.

"Take it easy," Frank said as he let Peaches stand on her own. But when he did, her legs weren't sturdy like before, and she wobbled.

"Oooh! Careful, careful," Mama called, nervousness wrapped tight in her voice.

After Tangie hugged Peaches, Mama opened her arms wide, and Frank took Peaches over to Mama with me right on his heels. I sat close enough so that Peaches's feet stretched across my lap. I cuffed her jeans and tugged at the top she wore that had a picture of a surfing dolphin on it.

"Remember what we talked about?" Mama said, and kissed her forehead.

"Not to . . . to . . . overdo it," she said. Peaches blinked. But her eyes didn't open right away. They twitched underneath her lids, then opened. She reached out for Mama, but it took two tries before her hands touched Mama's face. Mama kissed Peaches's fingertips, but it was strange not hearing Peaches's giggle.

"That's right. Just take it easy. Your body just got to get used to you being at home."

"I'm not gonna be able to dance with G-baby anymore, Mama?"

I held my breath, waiting for Mama's answer.

"Of course, you will. Just gonna take some time." Mama looked over at me. There were tears in her eyes that were in that place in between happy and sad. Mama kissed the top of Peaches's head. "Just some time. That's all."

My mind was already ticking. Whatever I needed to do to help Peaches, I'd do. She's the only one who I feel comfortable dancing around. It doesn't matter what dances I do, new or old, or if I don't even get them right. She thinks I'm the very best.

I put my hands on my hips and eyed her straight on. "You'll be back jumping on my bed in no time," I said. "Right, Mama?" Mama didn't speak but just nodded. I glanced at Tangie, hoping she'd give me any sign that maybe this was what the not 100 percent would be.

"Like your mama said, it's just gonna take some time," Tangie said.

"G-baby . . . did you . . . ?" Her voice was low, and she was struggling to keep her eyes open.

"Did I what?"

"Feed . . ." she managed to say.

"She's asleep already, Mama?"

"That's that medication kicking in," Frank said. "It's going to make her sleep quite a bit."

"That's fine with me," I said. "As long as she gets to be here and not that enormous hospital." Those words eased out of my lips, but the ones that scared me were the ones I couldn't say: What if she has to go back? What if the medicine they've given her doesn't work all the way?

"I was in the IOU," Peaches mumbled.

"It's ICU, girl," I said, and just the thought of it made my stomach cave in. I leaned over and kissed Peaches on her cheek. "I'm glad you're home."

"Me too, G-baby," she said, and then she really fell asleep.

Mama shook her head when Frank tried to take Peaches upstairs. "No, sir. Not now. I want to sit and hold my baby girl."

"Understood, honey," Frank said.

"She not gonna be able to walk anymore, Mama?"

"Sure she will. Just not right away. Sometimes doctors don't have all the answers."

Tangie had her arms crossed in front of her, giving herself a hug. "Mama used to rock Morgan like that."

Frank drew Tangie close to him and planted a kiss on her temple. "Sure did."

Tangie leaned against Frank. "I'm glad she's home," she said.

"Thanks for all your help lately, Tangie," Mama said. And once again, I felt like an idiot for ever saying Tangie was a faker.

"Daddy know she's home, Mama?" I asked. She didn't answer right away. Then she sighed like she used to do back before they were "happily divorced."

"Yeah, he knows."

"Is he coming to see her?"

"When she's up to it, *we'll* take her by to visit. Your daddy had the wild idea that Peaches would recover better back in her old room. Obviously that isn't happening."

Mama was still mad at Daddy for not calling her as soon as he knew she was sick and letting me sneak off to Nikki's.

"You two aren't gonna start arguing again like at the hospital, are you?"

"No, sorry, baby. Nothing like that."

I wanted to forget that Mama and Daddy weren't on the friendliest of terms again until I could think of how to fix it. But first I needed to tell somebody Peaches was home besides Nikki. *Kevin. I could tell Kevin.*

Mama tried to stand up with Peaches still on her lap. I grabbed Peaches's legs to help, but Frank rushed over.

Peaches slept so hard that I stared at her chest, making sure I saw it rising and falling.

"She needs some good rest," Mama said. "Let's get her upstairs, Frank."

"In her own room or Georgie's?" Frank said to Mama, but he smiled at me.

"Mine, please, Mama?" I pleaded.

"That's where she's gonna end up anyway," Tangie added. I grinned at her and wiggled my fingers, letting light shine on my pretty pink nails.

"Adorable," Mama said. "Your handiwork, Ms. Tangie?"

"Yep," she said proudly.

"You're looking at your next customer, soon," Mama said, then faced me. "Your room it is, G-baby. But we got to watch her. Her coordination may take a while to balance out."

"I can help her. I'm never gonna want her to sleep in her own room again," I said.

Mama's smile danced in her eyes. "Never is a long time," Mama said. Mama and Frank strolled upstairs to tuck Peaches in.

As soon as Tangie and I were alone, I said, "Think she'll be okay soon?"

"She will."

I nodded. When I thought about telling Kevin she was home, I thought about the kiss again. "Oh, you won't forget and tease me about the kiss in front of Mama or Frank, right?"

"Will you tell about Marshall?"

"No way!"

"Then you don't have to worry about me either."

"To be sure, can we make a pact?" I asked.

"Okay," Tangie said. "Hmmm, what about the Sister Secret Pinky Pact?"

"Did you do that with your little sister?"

She nodded and curved her pinky, waiting for me to loop mine around it. "Now here is what's special: we pump three times, tug at our ear once, and then snap."

As I did it, I smiled.

"Teach Peaches, too, okay?" Tangie said. "Remember not to do it around your mom or my dad, not even Nikki. It's only for us sisters."

"That's cool," I said. "Oh, I better call Nikki before someone else tells her about Peaches." I took off.

When I got upstairs, Mama and Frank were walking out of my room. "Try not to wake her, G-baby," Mama said.

"I won't," I promised. "Just want to call Nikki."

Frank headed downstairs, but Mama stayed around for a moment. "Talk in Peaches's room, and keep your voice low," she suggested. "Then come downstairs after you're done and tell me about this young boy."

My knees shook. Frank must have told her when he got to the hospital. "It's nothing to tell, Mama," I muttered.

"I'll be the judge of that. Call Nikki and come downstairs. There's something else we need to talk about."

"Okay," I said.

She can tell. The kiss. She can tell. That spot on my cheek tingled.

I forgot about calling Nikki and ran in the bathroom and locked the door. Tangie didn't say a word about it, but Mama could probably sense that I was more grown-up now. In the mirror, I stared at my face from all angles. My eyes were still a little puffy. But no other difference. Guess you had to be a mama to see it.

Wait a minute. Peaches. This isn't about the kiss, but Peaches.

Everything I'd been thinking about all day swirled in my head so fast that the room spun like a pinwheel. Now with Peaches home, Tangie liking me, not to mention I just might have a boyfriend like Tangie's. I twirled myself into Peaches's room, where everything became a humongous, colorful blur. I took a few minutes to catch my breath before I called Nikki.

"What are you doing?" I asked as soon as she answered.

"Watching *Everybody Hates Chris.*" She snapped her gum in my ear.

"Stop that," I told her. She popped a bubble and snapped again. "Fine, I'm hanging up."

"Okay, okay," she said. "I know your good news. I'm happy, too."

"How did you find out?"

"Spying . . . hellooo. Your *real* daddy told my daddy. My daddy told my mama. My mama told my brother. My brother told me. I wanted to call you so you wouldn't be so sad anymore, but Mama said not to spoil the surprise."

"Thank you for not spoiling it, but you could have told me Kevin had asked about me and was coming over here."

"Oooh, he really came over there?"

"Yeah. And Frank was home."

"Gimme all the details."

"Maybe later."

I hadn't decided if I was gonna tell her about my kiss or not.

"You'll spill it sooner or later. You can't hold water."

"That's what you think."

"And that's supposed to mean what?"

"Never mind. I just called to tell you about Peaches. I'm glad she's home."

"I know. I missed her. She's like my little sister, too," Nikki said in an honest way that reminded me why she was my best friend. Now I felt a little guilty for getting mad.

"How is she?"

"Mama said that she'd need a little more time before she's like before."

"It'll happen. Jevon said that when I was little I stayed in the hospital two weeks with the flu. I was even sicker than Peaches." She popped her gum again.

"The flu wouldn't make you sicker than Peaches. Anyway, why don't I remember that if it *really* happened?"

"'Cause, duh, it was when I was a little, little girl, before you even knew me."

"Still, I don't ever remember you saying anything about it."

"Whatever, anyway, when I came home, my family was so happy they threw me a surprise party."

"What a coincidence. Me and *my* big sister are planning a party for Peaches," I fibbed.

"Geez, Louise! You're only saying that 'cause I said I had one."

"You'll see. And guess what?"

"What?"

"Peaches is home, and Tangie is still being nice."

"We'll see how long that lasts."

"I gotta go. She's calling me to come help with the guest list."

"I better be invited," she added.

"Maybe, maybe not. We'll see. I'll talk to you later."

I hung up the phone and sat on the bed wondering what I'd gotten myself into.

If I didn't have a party, Nikki wouldn't ever let me forget it. If I had a party and it was lame like Tammy's tenth birthday party, with only four girls, six cupcakes, and milk instead of ice cream, everybody would talk about how horrible it was. My only option was to have the biggest, best welcome-home party for Peaches that the world has ever seen. Well, maybe not the world, but all the kids we knew.

I went to my room, sat on my bed, and watched Peaches sleep. She wasn't snoring, but sometimes she'd make a sound like baby bird wings flapping. I kissed Peaches as softly as I could, then left the bedroom. Maybe the party would make her so excited that it would help her get well even quicker. My mind was running like a racehorse. For the first time, I wasn't even scared to knock on Tangie's door.

Two knocks and she opened it wide. She yanked out her earbuds. "Peaches still sleeping?"

I nodded, then blurted out, "I want to give Peaches a welcome-home party."

"Shh. Let me close this door. We don't want to wake her."

"Oh, yeah. Sorry."

"Okay. Good idea," Tangie said. "Soon as she's up to it, we'll get a cake, ice cream, and balloons. I'm sure your mom wouldn't mind if you called her friends."

I shook my head. "That's not the kind of party I'm thinking about."

"More kids?"

I spread my arms out real wide. "More of everything! On *That's So Raven*, they had this party with a big glass ball on the ceiling and a quick flashing light that made everyone look like they were starting and stopping. Afros, too. A lot of people had Afros. Like Mama's pictures of the Jackson Five."

"You are cracking me up, G-baby."

"All the pants were wide, and the shirts had strings hanging from them."

"Bell-bottoms and fringe. And that light you're talking about is a strobe light. Girl, you want to have a throwback party. A seventies party."

"That's it!" I cried.

"Those always look like fun," she said.

"Think my mom and your dad will think so?"

"Probably. Have you seen all the old records in my dad's den? It's like he's George Clinton."

"Who?"

"Leader of Parliament-Funkadelic. They play him all the time on V-103. Trust me, you'll know who they are before the party's over. Dad has a record player down there, too. He could use his dad cave for us older kids, and we could set up the den for the younger ones and the living room for the adults.

"So you think we could do it?"

"Oh, it's doable!"

"Do you think my dad and Millicent would come, too? I mean, they've never been over here together before."

"Maybe, because it's for Peaches."

I kept thinking of how Mama was mad because I snuck out and they didn't notice. I had to do something to help things get back to the way they were.

And as if Mama heard us talking, there was a knock on the door. Tangie opened it, and sure enough, there stood Mama. "G-baby, I thought I asked you to come downstairs when you were off the phone," she said.

"Sorry, Mama. I forgot."

"Don't worry about it. Just come down now. You too, Tangie."

"Okay," we said at the same time as Mama went back downstairs.

Since Tangie left the door cracked, I lowered my voice. "I bet since it's mostly a kids' party, your dad will let Marshall come."

"If only. Trust me, my dad won't let Marshall take me

to a church carnival. Marshall says he'll talk to him. By the end of the summer, who knows? I might not have to sneak around. But you're right about one thing: there's something going on."

We peeked in on Peaches, then hurried downstairs.

21.

BOGA-WHAT?

Frank and Mama sat so close on the couch, they looked joined together. One of the throw pillows was on Mama's lap, and her elbows rested on it. She didn't look happy the way people on TV look when they about to share good news. So that was out.

Since Tangie didn't sit down, neither did I. We both stood right behind the coffee table that separated the four of us like a small fence.

"You've got our undivided. What's up?" Tangie asked.

"What's up?" I echoed.

"At ease," Frank said. "What's the rush?"

"Best to get it out," Mama said, and looked at Tangie and me. "Remember I told you that Sugar got a call from one of her sisters today?"

"Is she okay?" Tangie asked, which was what I was thinking, but she was quicker.

Mama nodded. "She's fine. But she received some news about one of her sisters, my aunt Elvie. She's the oldest."

"Something bad happen to Aunt Elvie?" I asked.

I only met my great-aunt Elvie once at the family reunion. She had her own restaurant that made the best sweet potato pie I'd ever tasted, and she looked so much like Grandma Sugar that a few times I'd accidentally called her "Sugar."

"Well, baby, she has a condition called Alzheimer's that causes her not to remember things like she used to. It's been happening for a while, but it's to the point now where Sugar needs to go help her."

"Will she know us?" I asked.

"I'm praying she will," Mama said. "You remember her diner and hotel, G-baby?"

"Uh-huh," I said. "In Louisiana? It was a long time ago. Peaches wasn't even walking."

"That's about right. When we visited, it was popular, but not like it used to be. You wouldn't believe the stars who've come through that place," Mama said.

"Aunt Elvie said Tracee Ellis Ross had eaten there," I said.

"From *Black-ish*?" Tangie's voice shot up a notch.

Mama chuckled. "Think you might be confusing her with Diana Ross, sweetie. That's Tracee's mama. I used to work there when I was a little girl. The diner hosted everyone—James Brown, the Supremes, and even the Jacksons."

"The Jackson Five?" Tangie asked.

Mama lifted her chin a bit. "She's served Michael him-self. But now she needs help remembering day-to-day things."

Frank put his hand on Mama's knee. "That's what we wanted to talk to you two about."

Mama took over again. "Sugar wanted me to go with her to Louisiana a few months ago, but with moving and you girls adjusting, it wasn't the right time. That was even before we realized Aunt Elvie's condition was worsening. There's so many decisions we need to make about the hotel and diner. Since they're connected, it's not feasible to keep one without the other. Gotta get down there and sort things out."

"You're leaving Peaches and me, Mama?"

"No, baby. I'm taking you and Peaches with me as soon as we get the doctor's okay." Mama paused for a few sec-onds. "And Tangie, too, if she wants to come."

I held my breath.

Tangie frowned. "To Louisiana?"

Frank made a drumroll with his fingers. "I'll be there to visit a week or two after you leave."

"One of the girls on my old gymnastics team is from New Orleans. That's in Louisiana. She says it's the best city in the country," Tangie said, and put her iPod on the coffee table.

"Some of the most delicious food in the world," Frank added.

"And Peaches will love it. That's where Tiana from the *Princess Frog* lives." I couldn't remember much, but I wanted Tangie to like it.

Mama raised and lowered her hands the way she does when she wants us to slow down. "Just a second. Our hometown isn't exactly New Orleans. About sixty miles north. It's a small town called Bogalusa."

Tangie reared her head back like she caught a whiff of the paper mill.

"Boga—what?" she said.

"Bogalusa," Mama said.

I jumped in. "Not forever, huh, Mama?"

"No, just the rest of the summer," Mama reassured us.

"But it's only June, Dad," Tangie said. "That's like forever. I don't want to be stuck in some small town all summer. Snellville is bad enough, but Atlanta isn't *sixty* miles away."

"Think about this, Tee," Frank said. "You'll be paid for helping out at the diner, so it'll be a chance to earn money and save for a car."

"Wow, your own car," I said.

"I'd make you a deal. Whatever you earn working at the restaurant, I'll match it," Frank said.

"Tips are good," Mama added.

"Hmm," said Tangie. "Nice try, but no thanks. I'm good. I'm staying here with you, Dad."

Frank sighed. "Tangie, you know the hours I work."

"Well, Mama . . . I can stay with her," Tangie offered.

"Already discussed that," Frank said. "She agrees that you should go to Louisiana."

"Wait! You two aren't *asking* me if I want to go. Are you?"

"Just for the summer, Tangie. To help our family," Mama said. "I'm sorry, baby."

Mama never called Tangie "baby." *This is bad*.

"*Your* family, not *mine*," Tangie shouted. Then she snatched her iPod off the coffee table. Two magazines hit the floor as she stormed out of the living room.

The room turned upside down. Everything, all the work for us to be sisters, was going down the drain.

"Get yourself back here!" Frank shot up from the couch and stomped his foot.

"Frank, let's not wake Peaches," Mama said.

I bent down and picked up Mama's *O* and *Essence* magazines.

Every stomp Tangie made up the stairs beat hard in my chest. I looked at my fingernails and wondered if I'd ever get that close to her again. After all, it was *my* mama's fault that *her* daddy was trying to get her to go someplace whose name sounded like something in your nose.

"Give her some time, Frank," Mama said, then turned to me.

"This diner and hotel is going to require that we all work hard and be on our feet a lot. Think you can handle that?"

"I guess." Tangie's reaction poked a huge pin in my balloon. I really wanted to help Aunt Elvie, but I wanted Tangie there, too. Then I thought about Peaches. She wasn't even all the way well and Tangie was gonna be back to growling at us. But what if we could all have so much fun together at our party that Tangie wouldn't mind going away with us? What if Peaches had such a good time with her friends that it made her stronger sooner than anyone could have ever imagined? And what if Mama and Frank would be there and Daddy and Millicent? Maybe Mama and Daddy wouldn't have to go back to pretending they liked each other again, and Mama wouldn't be upset with Millicent anymore. Maybe it wouldn't work, but I had to try. The more I thought about Peaches playing with her friends, who knew that she'd been sick, the more I thought about kids who wouldn't know.

"Mama, will there be lots of other kids where we're going?"

"More than you can fit in one room, I bet," she said. "Why? What's on your mind?"

I flicked my tongue like I was moving words around.

"Even though the doctor says that Peaches can travel and stuff what if the kids there aren't nice, or play too rough with her?"

"Baby, most of them will be your cousins. We'll keep an eye out to make sure there's no roughhousing."

Mama tried, but nothing she said made me think Peaches would be okay. Mama hadn't been a kid in a long time. If we protected Peaches too much, kids could make fun of her. But if we didn't she could get hurt.

"Mama?"

"Yes, Georgie."

"Before we go anywhere, do you think we can do something special for Peaches to welcome her home?"

Mama smiled. "It's wonderful that you're thinking of your sister like that."

"It wasn't just my idea. It was Tangie's, too. We talked about it before we found out about Boga—Boga—"

"Bo-ga-lu-sa," Mama said.

215

"Bogalusa," I repeated, and it didn't sound so bad.

"You and Tangie talked about it?" Frank asked. He seemed more interested than Mama.

"Uh-huh. We want to have a big party for Peaches." I spread my arms as wide as I could, the way the kids did in the Sunshine Children's Choir when they sang "He's Got the Whole World in His Hands." "Not just *any* party. A special one. A throwback party. That's what Tangie called it. A throwback seventies party. It'll be for the adults and kids. Everyone who loves Peaches. Daddy and Millicent could come. Grandma Sugar. And we all get to dress up."

"Don't one of your uncles still think it's the seventies, Frank?" Mama laughed.

"You got that right. More than one of 'em." Frank flopped back on the couch. "What do you say, honey?" Frank asked.

When Mama grabbed the back of her neck like Daddy, I knew I was in trouble.

"We've never had a party since we've been living here, Mama," I said. "Not ever. We used to have them at our old house. Remember?" I dug my fingernails into the seat cushions.

"What you think, baby?" Mama said to Frank.

"A chance for me to strut around in some bell-bottoms and slap on an Afro wig. You think I can resist that?" He winked at me like Daddy would do. "Why don't you two ladies talk it out? I'll check on Tee. This can be a welcome-home *and* going-away party."

Mama removed the pillow from her lap and put it back

on the couch and fluffed it. "You still want her to go with us?" she asked Frank.

"As opposed to her being home alone with even more opportunity to plot like a mini Angela Davis with that college boy behind our backs, which I'm sure she's doing anyway?" Frank replied.

I tried not to move a muscle, so they couldn't tell I knew a thing.

"Is forcing her the best way?" Mama asked. "Teens can be awful stubborn."

"What choice do we have? She says she's not ready to rejoin any of her old gymnastics, dance, or cheering teams. She's already out on a limb about her curfew. And her mother's not in a position for Tangie to visit for the rest of the summer. We both know what happened when she didn't want to live here, remember?"

"Yeah, I do," Mama said.

Frank headed upstairs. "Her at home by herself won't work. That's a fact."

As soon as he turned the corner, Mama said, "So where did this idea come from, G-baby?" I bit my lip. I had that feeling I get when Mama is asking me a question, but she already knows the answer. "I'm waiting."

"I want to make Peaches happy since she had to stay in the hospital?"

Mama put her hand under my chin and lifted my head up. Her eyes weren't glassy with tears like they'd been for so long. There were a few gray hairs sprouting from her eyebrows that she hadn't plucked away.

"That's sweet of you. Is there any other reason?"

If I told her that I didn't want her and Daddy to be mad at each other anymore, she might think I was "in grown folks' business."

"No, ma'am."

She rubbed the side of my face and kissed my cheek.

"Not sure if I'm buying this hook, line, and sinker. But okay. A throwback party it is."

"Thank you, Mama! Thank you!" I squeezed her until my arms were weak.

"You might not be so happy when you learn how much work goes into a big party," Mama said.

"It doesn't matter. I'm ready," I said, and clapped like a circus clown.

"Look who's up." Frank reentered the living room carrying Peaches. She leaned her head against his shoulder but waved to us in that way she does that looks like she's grabbing chunks of air.

"Hey, Mama's baby." Mama reached for her, but not before Frank planted a big kiss on her cheek. I think that was the first time he kissed one of us. When Peaches got out of his arms, her steps toward Mama were wobbly, like Frank had swung her around and she was still dizzy.

"Take your time, baby," Mama said. I saw Mama and Frank exchange glances, neither one surprised at her unsteady steps. Mama clasped her hands like she was keeping herself from reaching for her.

I didn't quite know how to feel. One part of me was just happy to have Peaches home, the other part was sad that she wasn't running and jumping. It was like the meningitis just wouldn't let her go.

When Peaches made it to Mama, Frank said, "Let me see if I can pry that other member of the family out of her room and we'll go pick up something for dinner."

"Get whatever you three want," Mama told him. "I'm going to cook Peaches and me a little something."

"Popeyes?" Frank gave me a thumbs-up like a human emoji.

"That sounds good," I said. Frank headed upstairs to talk to Tangie. Then I turned to Mama. "Can I tell Peaches?"

At first I thought it would be a surprise party like Nikki said hers was, but then Peaches would have missed the fun of planning it and getting dressed up.

"Sure," Mama said, and smoothed Peaches's hair.

"Guess what, Peaches?"

"What?"

"Mama and Frank said it's okay if we have a party for you!" I spread my arms wide. "I mean a big, *big* party with all the friends we have."

"It's not my birthday, G-baby," Peaches said. "Tell her, Mama. It's not my birthday, is it?"

"No, baby," Mama assured her. "But we are so happy you're home, and we want to celebrate."

"And it's a seventies party like we saw on *That's So Raven*, remember?" I said.

"We get to wear the funny clothes and make pets out of rocks?" she asked.

"That's right!" I said.

"I can invite my friends, Mama?"

"Anybody you want," Mama said. Then Peaches got quiet and buried her head in Mama's chest.

"What's wrong?" I asked.

"What if I fall down instead of dancing?"

"Know how you've seen me dance in front of people and fall down?"

"Yeah," Peaches said.

"What do I do?" I asked.

"Get up," she said.

I would do anything just to keep her from falling, but it was out of my hands.

"You'll do fine. Nobody cares about that anyway. Your legs just not used to walking around. It'll be okay," I said. I glanced at Mama.

"Your sister's right, baby. You'll be stronger in no time."

And just when I was about to get sad, I saw Frank coming down the stairs with Tangie behind him.

"We can have the party, Tangie!" I said. "Mama and Frank said we could. You can invite *all* your friends! There'll be food, music. You like music, right? We can go buy some old clothes."

Tangie stared at me. She took her earbuds out but still said nothing.

I needed words that would make Tangie want to be a part of it all. But the fear of saying something goofy fastened my lips airtight. Then, just like in a football game where a player throws the ball down the field and his teammate catches it and makes a touchdown right before the end of the game, Peaches's words were sailing in the air.

"It's because I don't have to be in the hospital no more!" Her voice was louder and stronger than I'd heard it since before she'd gotten sick.

LESLIE C. YOUNGBLOOD

Tangie put her arms around my shoulder. "Well, I can't think of a better reason to have a party."

"Thank you, Tangie!" I wanted to give her a big hug but figured that would be too sappy. "We're going to have so much fun." I threw my arms up like runners do when they've crossed the finish line, which made me look pretty stupid. But I didn't care. All I could do was run and call Nikki to tell her what was going on. I hoped I'd hear Tangie talking to Frank and Mama about the party as I jetted up the stairs. But I didn't hear any words at all.

22.
WOULDN'T IT BE PERFECT?

A couple days later, after Mama's Sunday dinner of meat loaf, mashed potatoes, and lima beans, she said it was time to start planning the party. I guess Mama had been too busy taking care of Peaches and "getting the house in order" before that. I didn't mind, though. Getting Peaches well was the most important. Anytime Daddy called, Mama didn't say much but just called Peaches and me to the phone. Sometimes I'd think about that day he came to pick us up and he and Mama laughed like they could never be a pain in each other's necks. I'd even heard Frank telling Mama that she needed to "get herself together before the party."

"We don't have long to prepare," Mama said. "We

should be ready to leave for Bogalusa a few days after."

"We can have it Saturday," Tangie said. I stared at her, waiting for something to tell me she was just teasing. But she gave me a smile that told me a whole bunch of nothing.

Peaches leaned against Mama's leg. I couldn't help holding my hands out just in case she fell. "No school on Saturday," she said like we weren't on break.

"Sounds good, Tangie. Decorations, next."

"You ladies worry about everything but the music and the meats," Frank said. "I'm taking care of that. Getting one of those barrel grills." He closed his eyes for a second and breathed in like he could smell sizzling steaks.

"Are you gonna cook a whole pig?" Peaches asked.

"Not a *whole* one, but it'll be plenty."

We talked about who we wanted to invite to the seventies party, and I thought about Kevin. *Wouldn't it be perfect if he were there?* And just as if my mama was skating around inside my brain, she said, "So tell us about this visitor you had the other day, G-baby."

I shot a hopeless look at Tangie. After everything had gone haywire about going to Bogalusa, I thought Mama had forgotten.

"Well?" Frank said.

"Just one of my friends from Sweet Apple," I whispered.

"He's a perfect gentleman," Tangie jumped in.

"Seemed very mannerable. Nothing wrong with having friends your age," Frank said.

Mama sipped her water and pointed to Peaches's juice for her to drink the rest of it. "Well, as long as it was just friendly. Start your guest list for the party, G-baby. Put him and his parents on there."

"His mama doesn't leave the house much, and his dad's in Rochester," I told her. "He's moving there to live with him."

"Well, invite her, anyway. She might make it," Mama said.

"Okay," I said, and sped off to e-mail Kevin. I'd memorized his e-mail. The family computer was in a corner in the living room. Tangie had hers in her room, but Mama said that was a no-no for me, because of the creepy strangers who try to talk to young girls when their mamas and daddies don't know.

While I waited for our computer to boot up, I checked out all of Mama's Dummy books. She likes to try new hobbies, but she loses interest in them like Peaches loses interest in every toy except anything Barbie. There was *Acrylic Painting for Dummies*, *Embroidery for Dummies*, *Making Candles and Soap for Dummies*. I wondered if there was *Kissing for Dummies*. What if one day Kevin tried to kiss me on the lips, and I just stood there like a real-life dummy? I was so deep into that thought that I jumped when the computer finally booted up. I went straight to my e-mail and started typing.

Hi! We are having a welcome home party for my sister. You and your mom are invited. It will be out at our house this Saturday at 6 p.m. Lucinda still has Nikki's bike. We gotta think of a way to get it back. Bye!

As soon as I wrote "bye," I felt stupid. I should have said, "Talk to you soon," "Take care," or something like that. Even though the chances of Kevin sitting in front of a computer right at that moment weren't the greatest, I waited for a while, refreshing my e-mail every few seconds, and each time my stomach flipped. I'd be happy to get any response. I wondered if that was the way Tangie felt about Marshall.

23.

A SPECIAL RSVP

The week cruised by, and Saturday came before anyone was ready.

A little after eleven o'clock, Peaches was munching on a peanut butter and banana sandwich that Mama let her have as a treat for taking her medicine like a "big girl," and I was wolfing down a peanut butter and grape jelly one. Frank and Mama walked up from the basement.

Without even fussing, Mama put the milk back in the fridge that I'd left out. "Did you fold all those clothes I washed last night?"

"Yup," I answered.

"Did you and Peaches clean your rooms?" she asked.

"We did, Mama," Peaches said, though I did all the work and let her play vacuum.

"Checked the weather and it's going to be eighty-five for the high, seventy-one for the low, and only a five percent chance of rain," Mama said.

Frank rubbed his hands together. "Gotcha! That's my confirmation to crank this shindig up a notch. Grill master mode in full effect."

"And what does that mean?" Mama said.

"That's for me to know and you ladies to find out." He raised one eyebrow higher than the other like an evil genius.

"Mama, we got to get together what we're going to wear, and remember about our Afros," I said.

"We'll get to it, G-baby, but first, if you two are finished eating, Frank and I have a surprise."

Peaches gulped the last of her milk. "What is it, Mama?"

"Go check out the front closet."

I took off but stopped and waited for Peaches. I tried not to feel sad when she tried to run, but it was like she was sloshing around in mud. If I could take back every time I stopped her from jumping on my bed and crashing to the floor, I would. I thought I was helping her not get hurt, but when she really needed me to protect her, I was running off to Nikki's.

"You open the closet door, Peaches." As soon as she did, a huge Walmart bag tumbled out.

"It's like Christmas!" said Peaches. I helped her lug the bag to the couch as Mama and Frank strolled into the living room.

"Trouble, Sorry, Pik-Up Stiks? I've never heard of some of these games," I said.

"Oooh, a Pet Rock kit!" Peaches said.

"Can't have a seventies party without the right games," Frank said. "Just make sure you feed and walk it yourself."

Mama elbowed him.

"Thank you!" we said. Mom and Frank walked back to the kitchen, and Peaches studied the instructions on the back of Sorry.

While she did that, I went to the computer. As fast as I could, I checked my e-mail and saw Kevin's "Hi." If Mama had a chance to open that, she would have. I quickly clicked on it.

> Dad driving in to get me this morning. He wants to go back the same day because of his work. If it changes, I'll e-mail you. I should have just taken that bike from Lucinda. Sorry.

I remembered his dad was flying in, but I guessed he changed his mind. I typed back.

> Not your fault. Glad your dad is coming. We're gonna have a lot of fun. I'll tell you all about it. Hope you like Rochester. Talk to you later.

The only good thing about Kevin not coming would be that I'd have more to write him later. At least that's what I told myself.

After I e-mailed him, I joined Mama and Tangie in the

kitchen. Tangie had taken her braids out at Valerie's and had them redone. They were as skinny as before and dangled against her shoulders. She told me that I could help her undo them next time. Now, I was a little nervous about that, since I really had never taken any braids out before, except for Peaches's.

"G-baby, we need to make it to the store before it's too late, but we got to get you and Peaches's hair started first," Mama said. "Tangie, can you wash G-baby's hair for me and I'll take care of Peaches?"

"Sure," Tangie answered.

"Then we'll blow-dry it and put it in rollers," Mama said.

"With all the hair these two have, they gonna have Afros bigger than those old pictures of Michael Jackson," Tangie said.

"I don't have as much hair as before," Peaches said.

"Still looks like a lot to me," Tangie said.

"Me too," I added. "Plus, you know you're tender-headed anyways."

I didn't know if Tangie really had stopped being mad about going to Bogalusa. Or if she was just pretending. I hoped that she liked me more now and would tell me the truth.

"C'mon, let's put a move on it. Need to stop at a couple stores. Can't be late to our own party," Mama said.

"My dad will be on time," Tangie said.

Mama laughed. "Yes, he will."

An hour later, Peaches and I were walking around with a head full of foam rollers. It looked like we already had pink and squishy Afros. We took turns holding the blow dryer to our heads to speed things up. Mama knew it was useless to do it the night before, because Peaches and I couldn't sleep with rollers in our hair, like Mama could.

When Daddy called to check on Peaches, Peaches got on the living room phone, and I grabbed the one in the kitchen.

"Millicent and I will be there this evening," Daddy said.

Tangie had sent him an e-mail invitation like he was a regular person.

"You coming to Bogaloosie?" Peaches asked.

"It's Bogalusa," I said.

Daddy laughed. "You know it. Be there before July is out."

Mama called to Peaches.

"Gotta go, Daddy. See you later."

"See you in a bit, baby," Daddy said and sighed. Peaches hung up.

"Daddy," I said. "You and Mama still mad?"

He cleared his throat the way he used to do at dinner before he prayed.

"Just say we were on a good track but hit a bump in the road. Both of us said things we probably shouldn't. Got worse when we were alone."

Daddy was always more honest with me than Mama. Mama used to say because he was trying to get me on his side, but she doesn't say that anymore.

"Mama didn't want to have the party at first. I think she didn't want you and Millicent to come. But she changed her mind."

"We always try to put you and Peaches first, G-baby. We'll both be on our best behavior."

"You coming to Bogalusa by yourself?" I asked.

"Not sure yet. Millie will probably come, too."

"Oh," I said.

"G-baby, I thought you were giving Millicent a chance. You know she was the first one to suggest taking Peaches to the hospital. We all need to be thankful for that. Okay?"

"Okay," I said.

"Plus, just between us, it wouldn't hurt if she picked up a little bit of Aunt Elvie's cooking skills, huh?"

"A li'l bit," I said, not knowing if Daddy was joking or not. "Mama said Aunt Elvie might not be remembering everything like before."

"That's why it's good for her to do stuff she loves," Daddy said. "And you know one thing she loves most?"

I thought for a second. "Making sweet potato pie."

"Not just that, but she loves cooking for folks she loves. That's why she has the diner. She also makes the best black-eyed peas and collard greens you've ever tasted."

"Better than Mama and Sugar?" I asked.

"Plead the fifth," he said, and laughed.

After I talked to him a little longer, I went back upstairs to get ready. But now and then, I'd sneak back down to the living room and check my e-mail just in case Kevin's plans changed. That happened sometimes to Peaches and me when Daddy lived in North Carolina. He'd want to see us, but something would always come up. It didn't matter how many times it happened, Peaches and I cried every time.

Mama caught me about to check my e-mail before I could act like I wasn't on the computer.

"I want to run to the store around two," Mama said, as she turned it off. "Enough of this for today."

If I told her I was double-checking for an e-mail from Kevin, she might think I liked him too much, so I said, "Okay," and rushed upstairs to Tangie's room. "Mama turned off the computer. Can you check my e-mail for me?" I asked her.

"Expecting a special RSVP?" she asked.

"He already said he couldn't make it but that he'd e-mail me if that changed."

Tangie opened up Gmail, and I entered my information. *Nothing.* I closed it out and started back to my room.

"I'm sure he'll update you when he can," she called after me. "Everybody doesn't have a couple computers in their home like we do."

"Yeah, he said they don't even have a phone."

"I'd check back in a little while. It's still early. Wanna help me with my hair?"

I turned around and came back to her door. "What are you doing to it?"

She showed me an old picture she'd found online of a singer called Patrice Rushen who had a head full of braids with beads all over them. Then she flipped to a picture of Stevie Wonder, and after that, old pictures of my favorite athletes, Venus and Serena. They were still kids then and wore their hair plaited with white beads on each one.

"I gotta tell you something."

"What?"

"I don't really know how to take out braids like I said. I've been practicing, though."

"It's okay, Georgie. Trust me, it's not hard. I'll show you when I'm ready to do it again, okay?" I nodded. "What I need help with now is really simple."

Tangie opened her closet and pulled out a plastic tub of multicolored beads.

"Wow, where did you get those from?" I shoved my hand in the tub and lifted the beads up, then let them fall like sand. She took a dish of black rubber bands off her nightstand and she taught slide the end of the braid through the beads and then twirl the rubber band at the end to hold them in place.

"My mom would put these in Morgan's and my hair sometimes," Tangie said.

"These are even better than Afros!" I exclaimed.

For a while, I worked on Tangie's hair, taking a water break when my arms got tired.

"Did you ask your dad if Marshall could come?" I asked her.

"I tried, but he won't budge. Says college boys are different from high school boys. He says he's the only one of us who's been both."

"Do you like any other boys?"

"No, just him. He understands things other boys don't. Daddy thinks all Marshall thinks about is girls, but that's not close to being true. He volunteers. Tutors. He's even organizing—" Then she stopped.

"Organizing what?" I asked, like I didn't know.

"Nothing you need to be concerned about."

"About the police?"

"Figured you heard that, too."

Embarrassed, I said, "Not the whole thing," which was true.

She glanced back at her door. It was closed, but she still lowered her voice. "A boy at Marshall's school got beat up pretty bad. Roderick Thomas. Busted lip. Black eye. Police stopped Roderick on his way home from a friend's house over in Buckhead. Said he 'fit a profile.' But Rod did exactly what he was supposed to do, gave the police his name and driver's license. That wasn't good enough. Officers said when they told him that he needed to come with them to the station, Roderick resisted and was belligerent."

I felt a little guilty because I hadn't thought about Roderick much since Marshall mentioned him.

"Won't his mama and daddy help?"

"Thing is he's on scholarship, and his parents think if he makes a big to-do out of it, he'll lose it. But now, it's not even just about Roderick." Tangie's eyes were fiery and her voice was so full of energy that my skin tingled. "It's happened a couple times since then. Who knows? Probably the same cops."

I couldn't help but think about the time Daddy picked Peaches and me up, and we were on our way to the Varsity to get something to eat. We'd been on the highway for a few minutes when we heard sirens and red-and-blue lights invaded our car.

Daddy pulled over. "I want you girls to stay quiet. Don't move. Don't say a word. You understand?"

"Yes, sir," I'd answered for Peaches and me.

When Daddy spoke to the officer, Daddy's voice sounded less like a trombone and more like piano keys. And while the police wrote a ticket for a broken taillight, Daddy kept both of his hands on the steering wheel, even though he usually only drove with one hand.

Tangie's voice pulled me out of my memory. "Marshall always says to note badge numbers."

"Daddy says most police officers are fair, but it only takes a few unfair ones to make it hard for everybody."

"That's true. Something's gotta be done. The unfair cops can't win. For every case that makes the news, hundreds like Roderick's don't. They need people in their corner, too."

Tangie was like the grown-ups on the news who would even go to jail for what they believed in. It made me proud to have a big sister that could get so pumped up to help somebody that she didn't really even know. But I didn't want to get all emotional and tell her. What if Roderick had little sisters, too? I bet they'd want everyone to help him. Then I thought about how Frank was a soldier and was always standing up for others.

"Your dad doesn't mind you protesting, right?"

"He's cool with it, but on his schedule. With him by my side. If he's busy, I can't go. That's not how it works when you really care about something. Marshall says that's what college is about. Taking a stand. Changing things. If my daddy wasn't so stubborn, he'd sit down and talk to him."

"Maybe if he comes to the party."

"Not happening. My dad made that clear. That's why he won't let me stay here. Daddy thinks if I'm away for the summer, I'll forget about Marshall. But that's not happening, either." When she shook her head, all those beads in her hair clinked like tiny bells.

"He'll be here when you get back. You can help change things with him then," I said.

"Doubt it. Boys don't always wait for you like in movies. Dad would blow a gasket if he knew I was even thinking about going to one of those protests without him. But that's what I'm into. And I should be able to do it without my dad watching over my shoulder."

"Even if you could get hurt?"

"You sound like my dad. You can't believe everything you see on TV. Most of the protests are peaceful. Plus, what's the worst that could happen? Police arrest me? Sometimes I think I wouldn't even mind that if it meant I was standing up for something on my own."

I thought about Kevin and was glad that he seemed only interested in riding his bike as far as he could.

"You can stand up for something even when you're not a teenager, right?"

"Of course," Tangie said.

I sighed like a balloon releasing air. I wondered if I should say something. I knew that Nikki being bullied for her bike wasn't as big as what happened to Roderick Thomas, but it was wrong and it hurt Nikki's feelings.

"A girl named Lucinda borrowed Nikki's bike. But she didn't really borrow it. She bullied her. Now she's riding around on it like it's hers and won't give it back."

"That doesn't sound like Nikki."

"I know. But you don't know Lucinda. She's got Nikki

believing they're friends. Lucinda says mean things to Tammy and me, and Nikki just stands there like a gum-snapping mannequin. But when we're alone, I can tell how sad she is."

"Sad and scared?"

"Oh, scared of Lucinda?"

She turned my head around to face her. "Maybe, but scared of losing you."

"Me?"

"Yeah, think about it. You've moved. Changing schools. And now you have a big sister, too. It's a lot for her to take in. It could be her way of her saying she needs you without really saying it."

"I never thought of that," I said. "Even when I was planning the party, I sorta left her out."

"Just think about it. Let me know if you need my help." I nodded. Everything she said about Nikki's feelings clashed in my head. "Right now, we better make sure all the decorations are up."

"You're really excited about the party, even if Marshall can't come?"

"Yep. I wouldn't miss it. Having this party was such a perfect idea."

"Thank you!" I said. "Oh, can I check my e-mail again?"

"Go ahead."

I opened it, and Tangie asked, "Anything yet?"

"Just Nikki telling me what she's gonna wear."

"He'll e-mail soon as he can."

"He's probably gone to Rochester already." My shoulders slumped as I started to my room.

"Cheer up. The most important thing is that you two are staying in touch, right?"

"Yeah, I guess you're right," I said. It wasn't just the thought of staying in touch with Kevin that made me a little happier, but that Tangie was trying to make me feel better like I tried to do for Peaches.

24.

A ROCK AND A HARD PLACE

"G-baby!" Mama called me a few minutes later. I darted downstairs and helped her and Peaches put dishes away, fold napkins, and set out paper plates.

"What else can we do to help, Mama?" I asked.

"Go get Tangie. I need her to help with the appetizers."

When I got back upstairs, Tangie was in the bathroom.

"Can I check my e-mail again?" I asked. Her door was open, but I wouldn't make the mistake of being a snooper again. It was almost one o'clock. The party was supposed to start at six.

"Go ahead," she yelled over the running water.

I stepped into her room, sat down, and looked at her

screen. She'd forgotten to close out of an e-mail. I tried hard not to read it, but my eyes wouldn't let me.

> I'll be there. Just be sure you're up for it. I've been out with my roommate recruiting folks to support us. Plan to go most of the night. We're not backing down.

Tangie's shower hadn't stopped. I scrolled down and read her original e-mail.

> Just be where we said at seven. There'll be so much going on with this silly kids' party, they won't miss me for a while. This is what I want to do.

My heart dropped into my stomach.

I couldn't catch my breath. I closed the e-mail, so she wouldn't be sure if I'd read it or not, and dashed out of her room without checking my own e-mail. *Saturday. That's why Tangie had suggested Saturday.*

When I got back down to the kitchen, Mama asked, "Is Tangie coming down?"

I tried to be calm. "Umm. She's in the shower."

"Okay. Let's light a fire under these appetizers," Mama said, stirring a Crock-Pot full of meatballs.

If I told Mama what I'd read, she'd tell Frank so fast it would blow the rollers off my head. All I knew was the time Tangie planned on leaving. My feelings were hurt that she didn't really want to be at the party, but whatever she had planned could get her in even more trouble than she'd

been in before. Or worst yet, hurt. I had to come up with
a way to stop her from meeting Marshall. Then I thought
about Nikki's bike and trying to figure out a way to get it
back, without Kevin's help.

All my thoughts twirled around like a cyclone, making
it hard to stay focused.

Within the next hour, our house turned into a party factory.
Mama cut up biscuit dough, and Peaches and I wrapped
them around tiny sausages to make pigs in a blanket. Frank
brought armfuls of stuff down from the attic.

"Look at this," he said after one trip. He was holding up
a funny-looking pot.

"What is it?" Peaches asked.

"It's a fondue pot. It's for melting chocolate or cheese,
and you can dip bread or fruit in it. And wait till you
see what I'm wearing. It's going to be hip." He strutted
across the floor, his hands moving like he was pushing back
water.

"Hip!" Peaches repeated.

I smiled, but inside, my stomach felt as heavy as a
whale. Tangie was telling a big, fat lie, even bigger than the
one Nikki had told us about her bike.

Everything was moving so fast I couldn't think of
what to do. When three o'clock rolled around, Mama was
ready to shoot to Goodwill. She told me and Peaches, "Take
out the rollers, and each of you wear one of my scarves."
Mama handed me a purple one and Peaches got pink-and-
white. She tied Peaches's scarf around her hair and let me
do my own.

Tangie had come downstairs to join us in the living room. "Tangie, can you tie mine?" I asked.

"No problem."

"Do it the new way. You know, a knot in the front like Alicia Keys."

"African women have been wearing it like that for centuries. That look is too old for you, anyways," Tangie told me.

Instead, she tied it with a bow on the side. It was like those newborn-baby headbands.

"You coming shopping with us?" I asked.

"Nah, Valerie waited to the last minute to get her outfit, too. We're going to the mall."

I wondered if what she said about Valerie was real or fake.

"Why don't you want to go with us?" Peaches whined. She folded her arms and stomped her feet.

Mama gently put her hand on Peaches's chin and lifted it up. "Now, wait a minute, young lady. We're not having any tantrums." I would have given anything for Peaches to throw a real tantrum, complete with yelling at the top of her lungs, flopping around like Girl that one time Peaches took her out of the water 'cause she wanted to see if Girl had a nose. But Peaches didn't seem to have that type of energy anymore.

"I'm going shopping with you, Peaches," I said, and reached for her hands, but she put them behind her back. I hugged her anyway and hoped she couldn't feel me trembling.

If I told, I'd have to rewind all the way back to the

beginning of how Tangie used to treat me. If I thought "snoop tattler" was bad, the only thing worse could be "snoop tattler turbo." But would that compare to the sticky mess I'd be in with Mama and Frank if I didn't tell?

We headed out to the store without Tangie, but I was already between what Grandma Sugar calls "a rock and a hard place." A *very* hard place.

We got home a little after four.

Music rattled the living room windows.

"What is that?" Peaches asked.

I came back downstairs and rushed to the rear kitchen window. As soon as Peaches caught up, I flung back the curtains, and there stood Frank behind a record player as large as a suitcase. Twice as big as the one down in the basement.

"You girls created a monster," Mama said as she wiped her hands on a dishtowel. "You've heard of DJ Quik? Well, this is his twin—DJ Not-So-Quik." Mama chuckled to herself and walked over to join us. I just hoped that when Daddy and Millicent came, she still felt like laughing.

At about five o'clock Mama had Peaches and me in the living room helping her do some last-minute dusting when Frank came downstairs. He stepped in front of us and spun around.

"Figures you'd be ready," Mama said, and laughed. "Check you out."

He did another spin and flicked the wide collars of his two-piece suit.

"What kinda suit is that?" Peaches asked.

"This here is called a leisure suit. And you can't wear one unless you got the right strut." Frank did his funny walk to the kitchen, moving his arms back and forth like he was rowing a boat. Under the jacket, he wore a flowered shirt that was unbuttoned halfway to show off his thick gold chains. We followed him to the kitchen, where he said, "Meet the real 2 Chainz," and lifted the necklaces and let them fall again.

"2 Chainz, my foot. You mean somebody from *Good Times*," Mama said, and chuckled again.

"Dy-no-mite!" Frank snapped back and continued strutting. I'd never seen him so playful. Almost like Daddy.

"I'm realizing who this party is *really* for," Mama said.

Frank lit two Black Love incense sticks and put them on the counter. "Can't have a seventies party without incense." It smelled like burning wood, but Frank inhaled it like he did Mama's perfume.

"Frank, you gonna make somebody choke," Mama said.

Just then, the doorbell rang. Mama went back to the living room and opened the front door. "Hey, Cora, c'mon in," she said.

"Ready for the get down?" Frank said as he joined her and did a quick two-step.

"If you ain't that sixth Temptation, nobody talks about," Ms. Cora said. "I don't even want to imagine what my husband is conjuring up to put on."

Ms. Cora and Nikki hugged Peaches, and then Nikki and I waved, but she stuck close to her mama's side trying to act shy. I didn't pay her any attention.

"We've been praying for you, Peaches," Ms. Cora said.

Then Nikki pulled out a School Teacher Barbie and handed it to Peaches.

"Thank you!" Peaches squealed, and held it to her chest.

"I'm not staying now, Katrina," Ms. Cora said. She pushed Nikki in my direction. "Don't act funny, missy. You begged me to bring you over here to get dressed with Georgie, now go get started."

Nikki didn't even take a step, probably embarrassed that her mama just said what she did. Nikki was holding a plastic bag over one shoulder, so I couldn't see what outfit she'd decided on.

"I'll be back later, Trina, but you'll swear it's Foxy Brown," Ms. Cora said to Mama, and they both laughed.

Mama wiggled her hips. "Well, I'll be Christie Love, Cora. You know what she used to say, 'You under arrest, Sugar.'"

"Foxy Brown? You're going to be a rapper, Ms. Cora?" I asked. I only remembered Foxy Brown from Jevon's room. He had one poster of her that Ms. Cora made him take off his bedroom wall, but Nikki said he just put it inside his closet.

That made them laugh harder. "Not that Foxy Brown," she told me. "We're talking about the original. You'll see."

"Who is Christie Love?" Nikki asked.

"Who knows?" I said, and mocked the way Mama wiggled her hips.

Nikki forced a smile.

"'Bout time for you two to get dressed. We're going to show y'all a thing or two." Mama winked at Ms. Cora, then eyed Peaches and me. "Time to take those scarves off. Peaches, I'll take you to my room," Mama said.

Nikki and I dashed up the stairs. When we got to the landing, we saw that Tangie's door was closed.

"My hair is too soft to make an Afro. That's why I got these Afro puffs," Nikki said.

"It's just Afro ponytails. Big whoop," I said. "I need your help with something and it's serious." I'd laid out my vest and jeans we bought at the Goodwill on the bed and plopped down next to them. Nikki stood in front of me.

She got real quiet and looked down at her strappy sandals.

"I got something to tell you first." Her voice sounded like when you want to cry but try to fight it. I patted a place for her to sit next to me. She sat so close our arms touched, then she leaned into me until our shoulders connected. We held each other up like two rag dolls.

When she started sniffling, I got teary-eyed, too, and took her hand in mine.

"You can tell me anything." She squeezed my hand tighter.

"I called Lucinda to tell her I changed my mind about her keeping my bike until the tryouts."

"What she say?"

She sniffled again before she spoke. "She said she'd bring it to me today. I told her . . ." She unlocked her hands from mine and wiped her eyes. Then she folded her hands in her lap. "I told her that I wouldn't be home. That I'd be at your party."

"She invited herself, didn't she?" I thought about what Tangie said about Nikki feeling blue about me leaving

Sweet Apple and Mama moving us out here, and tried not to be upset right away.

"She's coming with her cousin. But she promised to bring the bike."

"And you believe her?"

Nikki nodded, her Afro puffs slightly swaying. I couldn't even get mad at her. Her hands were trembling. It was more like that time after she had to leave Sweet Apple in an ambulance when she had a severe asthma attack. All the kids kept asking her about it when she returned. She tried to pretend that riding in the ambulance had been cool, but later she told me it was the most afraid she'd ever been in her life.

"I believe her. I just didn't want you to be angry at me instead of being happy Peaches was home."

"Lucinda coming isn't the worst, Nikki. I still appreciate why you did it. But when she brings your bike back, I'll tell her that I don't even want to be on any team of hers."

"We'll never see each other then. What kind of best friends will we be?"

"The kind that spend the night and have emergency drawers." I jumped up and opened one of my drawers and tossed everything in it on my bed. "All yours."

She flicked a tear away. "Thank you," she said and smiled, but she couldn't hold it long. "What if she's lying again? Maybe she's just using me like you said before."

"Don't worry, she'll bring it." I immediately crossed my fingers, hoping she couldn't tell I was fibbing. I sat back on the bed alongside of her, then reached over and hugged her. I didn't think for two seconds that Lucinda would bring that bike to the party, or anywhere else for that matter. But I'd figure out how to make her do the right thing somehow. It wasn't really big stuff like Tangie and Marshall would do, but somebody was taking advantage of my best friend, and who knows how many other kids, and I was gonna figure out how to do something about it.

"Hey, what about you?" Nikki asked.

"What do you mean?"

"When I came in, you said you needed my help, remember?"

Nikki moved in closer, her eyes as big as gum balls. "Is it about a boy?" she asked.

"Yeah, Tangie might be leaving the party to go meet one."

"She knows you know?"

"Not really. She might suspect. But I don't think she thinks I can figure it out on my own."

Nikki nodded. "We just need a way to keep our eyes on her."

Nikki and I paced in between my twin beds. We were in an all-out thinking contest. When one of us was in deep trouble—like the time Nikki took Jevon's Beats without asking and someone stole them—we'd fall asleep thinking until one of us woke up with an idea.

A couple minutes later, Nikki snapped her fingers. "I got it."

"Already?"

"Stake her out."

"Hmm. Like police do when they're trying to catch somebody?"

"Duh, yeah!"

"Don't 'duh' me," I said, but let it go quickly. I didn't need to get into a back-and-forth with her. "That's a good idea," I admitted. "We'll take turns watching her all night."

"She won't suspect a thing."

"Well, just to be sure of that, you start off doing the staking, because she doesn't know you know."

"On it! To make sure she doesn't get out of our sight, we need Tammy on the case, too."

"Her mouth is too big," I said, and put on my vest.

"Did any grown-ups find out about the hospital stuff?" Nikki asked.

"You're right. She covered for us till the very end."

"That's Tammy."

"Okay, so we got everyone staking, but what if Tangie tries to leave?"

"Oh, that's easy. But you have to be ready for her to be mad at you until you're, like, thirty."

"I'll take that over her getting in big trouble," I said. "Tell me what is it?"

She gulped in such a huge breath that I held mine waiting for her answer.

"We'll . . . We'll grab her."

I froze solid, waiting for part two. But she just stared back at me. "And?"

"And what?"

"Wait. That's it? That's your plan?"

She rolled her eyes. "Well, it's not like I had a long time to think. That's it, unless you got something better."

"Guess you're right." Grabbing her didn't seem like the best idea, but it beat doing nothing.

I held out my hand. She grabbed it, held it tight. We have only two solid pumps, two claps, two backhand slaps, and then a thumbs-up. We hadn't done our best-friend handshake in a while.

At that moment it meant that we'd do whatever we could to stop Tangie, and, even though Nikki didn't know it, that Ms. Lucinda Hightower was in trouble now.

25.

BEYONCÉ BETTER WATCH OUT

A few minutes later, Mama and Peaches came upstairs to check out my outfit and show off theirs. My vest had a long fringe, and I wore faded jeans that were chopped up at the bottom like cut-up strips of paper. All my rollers were out, and I patted my Afro until it looked like a chocolate lollipop.

"You look hip, G-baby," Peaches said, using Frank's word.

Peaches's outfit was a dress with geometric shapes on it that matched her purse and the scarf she had tied around her head, which hung down her back. Her Afro wasn't as thick as it would have been before she was in the hospital. But Mama had tried to make it real round anyway.

"Not hipper than you," I replied.

If Peaches and I were "hip," Mama was "out of sight" in her huge Afro wig. Mama was wearing a jumpsuit that hugged every curve but was wide at the legs. At the end of her sleeves and around her neck hung a bunch of feathers.

"Everybody looks groovy, now let's get on downstairs and do what, Peaches?" I said.

"Get this party started!" she shouted.

As soon as we got downstairs, we found Frank in the living room straightening one of the rug liners. But I think he was waiting to see Mama.

"Umph! Ain't I just about the luckiest man in the world?" he crowed.

"What you mean 'just about'?" She slapped his arm. He caught her hand and twirled her around, the feathers floating behind Mama like a bird.

We weren't downstairs five minutes before the doorbell rang, and a few of Mama's friends came in with kids who knew Peaches. The little kids huddled around her for a moment, and I waited for her to emerge from them fully charged. But when they rushed to the backyard, she sorta lagged behind. Two of the girls slowed. As my heartbeat raced, I resisted the urge to go and swoop her up.

"Wait for Peaches!" one of them yelled.

"Be careful!" one mother shouted. She and the other ladies chatted on their way to the kitchen to drop off their dishes. I smelled everything from fried chicken to barbecued meatballs.

"Is Peaches *okay*, okay?" Nikki asked.

"Sorta." My voice cracked, but I didn't want Nikki to feel sorry for Peaches. She might think that I felt sorry for her when her asthma was acting up. "Mama said it may be a while before she gets all her coordination back and stuff."

"It'll happen. Look at me."

"Uggh. Tonsillitis is not meningitis."

"I didn't mean it like that. But it's still an operation, and I couldn't talk. You remember."

"Yeah, okay. I got it. Thanks. Let's focus on Tangie and you know what else."

"Lucinda?"

"Yep."

"She said that she'd stop by but would only stay for a minute."

"Long as she has your bike, it doesn't matter how long she stays. Just stand by the door and greet everybody," I suggested.

"Cool. Forget about Lucinda. Checking the door is the best way to keep Tangie in and strange boys out."

"Doubt he'd show his face here."

"Why?"

"Frank won't let him come over. He'll park around the corner or something."

"How you know all that?"

"Just do."

"When Tammy comes, we'll give her all the info. One of us needs to keep watch outside, too," Nikki said.

At that moment, Tangie waltzed down the stairs looking like one of the girls from *That '70s Show*, but prettier. The clinking of her beads blended in with the music. She was wearing a minidress with vinyl boots and earrings as big as training wheels.

"Go ahead, girl. That's how you do it!" one of Mama's friends shouted.

"You look marvelous, Tangie!" I said.

"Wow! Like a movie star," Peaches said, walking out of the kitchen with Mama.

Some song where the singer kept repeating "shake your groove thing" was playing outside. Mama walked back into the living room carrying a silver tray piled with cheese and Ritz crackers. Frank strutted over to her, set it down, and glided Mama to the middle of the living room to dance.

Peaches pointed. "Look at Frank!"

We'd never seen Frank dancing before. I guess that's how he moves when they go out to do the "whole shebang."

Mama's friends grabbed their dates and started dancing right next to her and Frank. Somehow, Nikki and I ended up on the floor with Peaches dancing next to Mama and Frank, too, and Tangie was left at the door greeting guests. I held Peaches as she swayed off beat with a few of her friends. But I still kept an eye on Tangie.

Frank kissed Mama's cheek. "Save me a dance later, beautiful. I got to go tend to the grill. Them ribs aren't going to flip themselves." He headed back outside.

I glanced at the watch I'd put on just for the party. "It's almost six thirty," I whispered to Nikki.

"We can't let her out of our sight," Nikki whispered back.

I don't know why, but I glanced at the door and expected to see Kevin.

While I was dancing with Peaches, she stopped and pointed at the door. She didn't even try to make her voice carry over the music. But her eyes shined.

"Daddy, Daddy!" I shouted for the both of us, and through the door strolled Daddy in a silky gold shirt, bell-bottom pants, and platform shoes that made him seem eight feet tall. Unlike Frank, he didn't have an Afro, but he was wearing a big, floppy hat. I scanned the room for Mama. If she could see him really trying to make us happy, maybe she wouldn't be mad at him.

"That's a funny hat, Daddy," Peaches said.

"What?" Daddy said. "This was cooler than a Kangol back in the day. Called an applejack, Jack." Daddy swooped Peaches up with one arm and drew me to his side with the other. Just behind him, Millicent waved to us. Her dress flowed down to her ankles with what looked like pieces of broken glass glued on it. She had a ponytail wrapped with gold twine, making it stand straight up on her head.

"And my guest for the evening is none other than the soul-stirring, head-turning Ms. Nina Simone," Daddy announced. Millicent pretended to hold a mic and then tossed her head back to belt out a song.

"I can't carry a note in a bucket," Millicent said. "Unlike the High Priestess of Soul."

Grandma Sugar played Nina Simone's music some-times. Even the one about Mississippi that had a curse word. "Can't shelter you from hearing every bad word, but you best not repeat 'em," Sugar would say. Later, Grandma Sugar told me that in Bogalusa she couldn't go to the same schools or even use the same restrooms as white people when she was a little girl, and Nina Simone had gone through the same thing. After that, I understood why that song used a bad word, even if I couldn't repeat it. Then I thought of Marshall standing up for his classmate and wished Tangie could be with him somewhere she wouldn't get hurt.

"You sure look groovy," Millicent said to me.

"So do you!" I hugged her. A little part of me was hugging Nina Simone, too. And before I knew it, I said, "Thanks for helping get my sister to the hospital."

"That's nothing to thank me for, Georgin—I'm sorry, Georgie. I appreciate it, though," she said.

"Where's your mama?" Daddy said.

"She's in the kitchen. Want me to get her?"

"Best not, with all she has going on. We'll see each other soon." I knew for sure that Mama could probably hear Daddy's voice. And Daddy knew that Mama always says, "If I'm not doing ten things at once, I'm not getting anything done." But I just let it go. Maybe just having them under the same roof would have to do.

"Come see my friends, Daddy," Peaches said.

I started to go with Daddy and Peaches, but Nikki pulled the fringe on my vest. We eased back closer to Tangie, who was still standing at the door and talking on her phone.

"You kinda lucky," Nikki said.

"Why?" I asked.

"You have your daddy, stepmom, mom, and stepdad all in one house at the same time. When my mama's sister tries to do that, she calls it World War Three."

"Well, it was almost that at the hospital," I said. I didn't tell Nikki that Mama may just be putting on that happy face for Peaches's sake.

There was a knock at the door. Nikki and I stared at it like the thumps were sounds we'd never heard. Tangie opened it.

"Is that my oldest grandbaby?"

"Sugar! Sugar!" I shouted.

"Well, you are too hot to trot, Ms. Tangie," Sugar said as she hugged her, then held her at arm's length. "You got it going on, girl."

"You do, too," Tangie replied.

"I do all right," Sugar said and laughed.

"There's one of my babies. Where's the other one?" Sugar asked as we hugged.

"Mama said you were already in Bogalusa," I said, taking in the scent of her Wind Song.

"I was, and I'm going back soon. But when Trina said there was a party in honor of my Peaches, you better believe I put the pedal to the metal." She wore a cream-colored dress with a short cape with tons of sequins at the end of it.

"Look at your dress, Sugar. . . . You'd win the best-dressed contest," I said.

"Yes, indeed! Diana Ross and Beyoncé better watch out." Sugar put her hand on her hips. I put my left hand on my hip, too.

"Stop acting like you got a shape, now," Nikki said.

Grandma Sugar laughed. "Don't you worry, G-baby. You'll have more hips than you know what to do with one of these days." James Brown was wailing "Papa's got a brand-new bag."

I looked at Nikki, and she rolled her eyes at me. "You still gonna be skinnier than me," she said.

"Skinny or curvy, you'll both be fine as wine," Grandma Sugar said, and snapped her fingers. "I love me some James Brown. Now where is Ms. Peaches? Where is my youngest grandbaby hiding?"

"She's outside with Daddy," I said, but as I turned around, the back door opened and Peaches scurried into the living room. Sugar met her halfway and kneeled down in front of her like she would when she said a prayer.

Peaches took both of Grandma Sugar's hands and hopped right to the middle of the living room floor as James Brown now told everybody to get on the "good foot."

"Can I have everyone's attention, please? Let's make our way down to the basement." Frank waved his long arms to the entrance to the basement. People chatted as they headed down the stairs. I waited for Tangie, then followed her. It was ten minutes after seven.

Downstairs, the strobe light was flashing, and streamers were hanging everywhere. The *Welcome Home, Peaches!* banner Tangie and I made stretched along the wall.

I had to admit that it was looking pretty spiffy, and I was feeling awful proud. So proud that it took Nikki two or three nudges of my shoulder before I could snap out of my trance.

"G-baby, look," Nikki whispered.

There, inching along the wall like stuck-up snails were Lucinda Hightower and another girl.

"That's her cousin Rhonda."

Both of them had on ripped jeans and T-shirts that showed their belly buttons. Rhonda's shirt had a glitter peach on it and Lucinda's shirt said, *How Bout No*. If I was ever gonna be jealous of Lucinda, it was that moment. Mama wouldn't think about buying me a shirt that sassy. Even Nikki had a *Bye, Felicia* shirt.

I tore my eyes from Lucinda and tried to pay attention.

"Let's make sure the guest of honor is front and center," Daddy said, and picked up Peaches.

As people chatted, Mama strolled from Frank's den, pushing a cart with a cake as large as a big-screen TV. It had Fourth of July sparklers on it, and the icing spelled out *Celebrate Life! We Love You, Peaches*.

Everyone clapped. I looked over at Lucinda. And her arms were folded like she had somewhere else to be. That made me want to go sock her. I know she saw me looking her way and acted like she didn't. Nikki was next to me clapping until she noticed Lucinda wasn't clapping and folded her arms across her chest, too.

Ms. Cora was passing out red plastic champagne glasses that Mama had bought at the dollar store. Another one of Mama's friends filled the kids' glasses with sparkling apple juice.

Mama cleared her throat and wiped her eyes.

"Take your time, baby," Grandma Sugar said.

"It can't get any more frightening than when a mother can't make her child well. But thank God and all of you for your prayers and support. Peaches is getting stronger every day. And we can't love her any more than we already do." Mama raised her glass.

"Hear, hear!" everyone cried, and tapped their glasses together like it was New Year's Eve.

Lucinda whispered in Rhonda's ear as soon as Mama stopped talking. I would have given everything in my piggy bank to hear what she said. If it was one mean thing about Peaches or anybody else, I was going to snatch her lips off.

Then suddenly, I realized: when Mama had started talking, Tangie had been standing at the bottom of the stairs. When Mama finished her speech, Tangie wasn't there anymore.

But just as I started to move, Mama stepped over from across the floor and stood in front of Daddy for the first time that evening. "The girls really appreciate you being here, George. Don't you?"

Peaches and I both nodded.

"I'm just sorry there was any question that I'd come," Daddy said.

"I was out of line," Mama said.

"Same here. Should have called you first thing. You do a good job of making sure I know what's going on with my girls."

"It was an emergency. Getting Peaches to the hospital was all that mattered."

"We good, Kat?" Daddy asked. Mama nodded, but her eyes searched the floor just like Nikki's did earlier.

Daddy kissed Mama on the cheek. Peaches's ponytail smooshed into Daddy's shoulder. It was like that kiss he'd given her after the divorce was final and he came to dinner with us for the first time since he'd moved.

"Things work themselves out, George," she said.

Mama waved to Millicent, who was talking to Sugar. When Millicent stepped over, Mama took Millicent's hand in hers. "Thank you again for everything you did to take care of Peaches," she said. "Didn't mean those things I said before."

Millicent said, "Forgotten. Just grateful Peaches is back where she belongs." Millicent pinched Peaches lightly on the cheek.

"C'mon, now. This is a celebration. No time for all this mushiness," Daddy said.

"No mushiness," Peaches repeated, and lifted her head from his shoulder.

Daddy wiggled his fingers like he does when he's revving up for a tickling frenzy. Peaches started giggling before his fingers touched her stomach. When they did, she reared her head back and laughed.

"George, careful. That medicine she's on upset her stomach."

"Medicine, schmedicine," Daddy said, but immediately stopped tickling her.

Over Peaches's giggling, Daddy asked Mama, "Where'd your old man go?"

"Where else? Out to the grill," Mama said.

Daddy kissed Peaches's cheek and said, "Let's book on out there and see if that cat's got any skills on the grill."

I left Mama and Millicent chatting like they might even become good friends. Well, maybe that's pushing it, but it was better than before. I spotted Tammy and walked toward her. My only hope now was that while I was with Mama and Daddy, that Nikki had her eyes on Tangie.

"Sorry I'm just getting here," Tammy said. "Cool party," she added. She had on a regular T-shirt and jeans, but a bandanna was tied around her head that had a peace sign on it, and she was wearing earrings with dangling silver cubes. "I didn't know Lucinda was coming."

"She's brought my bike." Nikki tried to sound happy about it.

"Let's talk about that after we find Tangie," I said. "You didn't see her when you came in, did you, Tammy?"

"Nope," she said, kicking her feet out like she was ready to Cupid Shuffle. I ran upstairs as fast as I could. When I didn't see her in the living room, I ran outside where the DJ was playing "Do the hustle. . . . Do the hustle. . . ." and everybody was dancing in line. If I didn't think it would send everyone into a panic, I would've stood right in the middle of the yard and shouted Tangie's name.

The den . . . Forgot to check the den. I flew back into the house and rushed back down the stairs. Nikki and Tammy were waiting for me at the bottom of the stairs. All I wanted to do was enjoy the party.

"Any luck?" Nikki asked.

"No, but Frank's den is down here," I said, and started off for the opposite end of the basement.

In the den, Mama had a DVD of *Soul Train* playing, and a few grown-ups were dancing. Someone was even trying to get a Soul Train line going like they did in that Tyler Perry movie.

"Let's get back upstairs," I said to Nikki and Tammy.

"It's almost eight, Georgie," Nikki said.

"She could be in her room," I said.

We snuck up to the second floor. My door was open, so was Peaches's, but Tangie's was closed tight.

We all stood around in the hall. Nikki or Tammy couldn't understand how nervous I was. My palms were sweating like I had on gloves. If we stepped in her room and she caught us, I'd be forever Snoop Tattler.

"You think we missed her down there?" Nikki asked.

"Maybe," I said, but couldn't help staring at her door.

Tammy popped her gum. "What if she left earlier? She could be anywhere in Atlanta by now."

"What help are you?" Nikki said. "Anyway, we saw her not too long ago."

"Are you up there, G-baby?" Mama yelled. "Lucinda's asking for you. Get back down here soon. If Tangie is up there, tell her Val is here."

"Okay! I'm coming, Mama," I shouted. Then I whispered to Tammy, "Stand by the stairs and holler if you hear anybody coming up."

With Nikki behind me, I knocked on Tangie's door and waited. There was no answer. Then I opened it.

26.

SOMEONE'S COMING!

Tangie's bed was made, but a pair of jeans and two T-shirts were in the middle of it.

"At least it's not what she had on," Nikki said. I admitted that made me feel a little relieved. But her drawers were opened, and clothes jumbled about. She was looking for something in a hurry. Tangie's room normally looked like one you'd see in a fancy hotel, with no wrinkles in her sheets, and no clothes tossed about.

"Wow, you never told me she was like a real gymnast," Nikki said, as she picked up one of Tangie's trophies.

"Did so. Told you she was a cheerleader, too. And put that down, please."

"Gotta check all of them, I guess," Nikki said and opened

the next two drawers, feeling underneath the clothing.

"What are you feeling for?"

"A diary. You sure don't know anything about having a big sister. In every movie I've seen, they usually have diaries. Some call 'em 'journals,' but it's the same thing. It'll tell us exactly where to find her, I bet."

I didn't stop Nikki from looking, but I was sorta hoping not to find one. "I just wanted her not to get hurt, not know all of her secrets."

Then I did it. I tapped on her computer, but it was locked.

Just then we heard Tammy. "Someone's coming! Someone's coming!"

Nikki and I shut the drawers, dashed out of the room, and closed the door, just in time. We rushed to the stairs as Grandma Sugar was walking up.

"I want to take pictures of you and Peaches, G-baby," she said. "Why are you little foxes hiding out up here?"

"We're on our way down," I said.

"And where is that Ms. Tangie? She looked put together enough to give a young Pam Grier a run for her money."

"Is Pam Grier like Foxy Brown?" I asked, trying to distract her.

"She *is* Foxy Brown." Sugar snapped her fingers like an exclamation point. "Put it like this. She was something like Ms. Beyoncé in the seventies. Always had the baddest outfits and a body you had to be born with. Still turning heads to this day. Anyway, none of y'all should be stuck up here when we're celebrating Peaches. Is Tangie in her room?"

"I saw her outside talking to one of her friends on the front porch," Tammy said quickly.

"Well, then, I'll leave her be for now. Let me get you three while I gotcha." Sugar whipped out the digital camera that Mama bought her for Christmas. Her phone could take pictures, too, but Sugar said, "I don't like to depend on one thing for too much," and never would use it for photos. She told me that when Grandpa Ike died, she didn't even know how to balance a checkbook or drive a car.

Nikki got in the middle, and Tammy and I turned to the side.

"Ahh look out now . . . Here comes the newest Charlie's Angels," Grandma Sugar said.

I hoped she couldn't tell my smile was to hide that I was worried out of my mind.

After she took a bunch of pictures, we made our way back down to the crowded living room.

"I looked in the front yard and the back. She's not here," Nikki said.

Valerie, I thought. Find Valerie. If anyone knew where Tangie went, she would.

"You may have to tell your folks, Georgie, before it gets too late," Nikki said, which made my stomach sink again. Nikki would rather wear the same outfit twice in one week than be a tattletale.

But no sooner had I turned to leave than someone poked my shoulder.

"You have the nerve to invite us to a real-life kiddie party, for a real-life kid, and then act like we're not even here."

"She's not a 'real-life' kid, that's my sister." I was off to a bad start. "And I didn't invite you."

The cousin eyed us. "And what are y'all anyway, Powderpuff Girls?"

"And, uh, where are the boys?" Lucinda added; the gloss on her lips made her words slick. From the last time I saw her, she'd gotten her hair braided in thick box braids like that old picture of Janet Jackson from one of Mama's favorite movies, *Poetic Justice*.

"This is not *that* kinda party," I said.

"We got dropped off out here for this?" Lucinda said.

"Some boys might come later," Nikki added. I just wanted to pinch her.

"Uggh. Stay if you wanna, go if you wanna," I said. "But you only supposed to be here to bring Nikki's bike back. So where is it?"

"Oh, about that," Lucinda said. "Mine still has a flat. Might need to keep that bike a little bit longer. I'm sure Nikki doesn't mind. Right, Nik?" That made me steamed. Nikki only let Jevon call her "Nik." She hated when anyone else used it.

"You said you'd bring my bike today. You promised." Nikki's voice raised a bit, then cracked. I wanted her to leave before she went into a full-out cry in front of Lucinda. She'd be embarrassed for weeks.

"I'm still thinking about my team. Might not need as many 'extras' as I thought," Lucinda said.

"That's not fair. You said if I let you hold it that you'd put them on the team."

Lucinda smirked. "You told me that this was a real party. Trust me, we're even."

"If you don't give up that bike, that's stealing," I said. I thought about my conversation with Tangie and puffed my chest out a bit. "And, you're not supposed to use the fact that you're captain of the step team to get people to do what you want. It's not right. It's . . . It's bullying."

"Stealing? Bullying? You're so dramatic," Lucinda said.

"C'mon, Nikki . . . Tangie . . . remember?" We jetted off, and Tammy stayed behind with Lucinda and Rhonda. I looked back and Tammy's face was frowning like Lucinda was on her nerves, finally.

I scoured the upstairs as calmly as I could. No Tangie. I saw Nikki coming in from outside shaking her head. I regretted every word to Lucinda. Each one kept me from finding Tangie. The only good thing was Peaches seemed to be having fun, which kept me from straight-out crying. But I thought about the trouble Tangie was in and my entire body got jittery. What was even worse was Millicent was walking right toward me. Her gold dress flowed behind her like a flag.

"I haven't seen you much this evening," Millicent said, smelling of coconut and holding a bottle of water in her hand.

I sniffed a little and pressed my lips together but didn't look at her. "Oh, I've been downstairs and upstairs," I said.

"Did you help your mama with all of this?" she asked.

"Peaches and Tangie, too." As soon as I said Tangie's name, my lips quivered.

"What's wrong?" Millicent asked, and hurried me off to

268

the hallway. She handed me the napkin that was under her bottle. I dabbed at my eyes and sucked in my breath.

"I should check on Peaches."

"She's fine. But you're not. You know, you can talk to me about anything. I won't try to take the place of your mom, but I'm here. Sit down on the stairs for a minute."

My heart was pumping faster than ever. I knew I had to make a decision. As soon as that idea started circling in my head, though, Valerie popped up. She was wearing a red jumper, a black cap, and wedged sandals that all looked old and brand-new at the same time.

"Hey. Have you seen Tangie?" she asked.

"Not in a while," I muttered.

"What's wrong?" Valerie said.

I glanced at Millicent.

Millicent lowered her voice. "Is this about Tangie?"

"What about Tangie?" Valerie asked. "How's she going to invite me to a party and not be here?"

"She was here, but . . . but . . ." And then my tears gushed.

"Just take your time and tell us what's going on." Millicent rubbed the back of her hand against my cheek.

Valerie wasn't that patient. "Stop crying and tell us what's wrong."

"Tangie is with Marshall. He's planning to be part of a late-night protest. A kid at his school got hurt by the police. Tangie said that nobody is doing anything about it. Frank said she can't go to any protests without him. And she and Marshall could go to jail!" All the facts were sorta scrambled.

"What are you talking about? If she was going to get involved, she'd have told me. Marshall said a lot of hot-heads might show up and make trouble. She wouldn't have gone without telling me," Valerie said, like it couldn't be disputed.

"I found out by accident. We have to find her. Frank's gonna ground her for life. He told her she couldn't do any protesting without him there."

"Have you told anyone else yet?" Millicent asked. Her earrings dangled like wind chimes.

"Just my friends."

Valerie took out her phone. "This is crazy. I've called her twice. It went to voicemail both times. But I figured she was just getting ready and stuff. And you're sure she's not upstairs?"

"I checked up there. I'm telling you, she's gone. Think she's just mad at her dad for making her go to Bogalusa. She doesn't even care if she gets in trouble."

I twirled the fringe on my vest. "We have to find her."

"Georgie, stop crying, please. There's got to be some misunderstanding. I was just with her today, remember? She would have said something."

"I wouldn't know if I hadn't read it."

"Well, this is the thing, Georgie," Millicent said. "If I'm going to be of any help, we need to act fast. Frank is going to miss her soon."

"We need to get in a car and search for her, Millicent," I said. "We can't wait for her to come back on her own. We can't."

If Nikki's brother didn't have a car, we wouldn't have

found Nikki. It was the same way now. We had to get wheels.

"I agree with you, Georgie. Let me go get the keys from your daddy. I'll tell him that I need to make a run to the drugstore. Trust me, as soon as you say that, men think 'personal' and don't want details."

"We'll be right here," Valerie said, looking at her phone. As soon as Millicent walked away, Valerie said. "Georgie, I hope you're right about this."

"Don't you think I hope so, too? She was just starting not to hate me and I—"

"She never hated you," Valerie cut in.

"Sure felt like it sometimes. I don't want to go back there."

"Ready, ladies?" Millicent said.

More than ever I wanted Tangie home. I'd been focusing so much on what Tangie could do for me as a big sister, I don't think I thought too much about what I could do for her as a little sister. Well, the first thing I needed to do was make sure she was safe, even if it meant she didn't speak to me for a long time. And I'd never thought Millicent would be the one to help me.

"Told your daddy that if anyone was looking for you to tell them that you were with me," Millicent said.

"Okay." We walked out the door together. The music was still going and laughter echoed throughout the house. Only a few weeks ago the thought of being with Millicent made my stomach hurt. I didn't like her just because. Now I had to admit that when I gave her a chance she treated me like a grown-up and didn't even care that I'd been mean to her. Maybe it wasn't just bullies and people who didn't like other people because of their skin color who could be unfair sometimes.

Outside, the sun was setting, and the air was humid. My Afro puffed out like a Chia Pet, but I didn't care. Even as we walked to the car, I prayed Tangie would come running up.

There was a long row of cars along our street, and I didn't know which one belonged to Daddy. He changed cars often, since he owned the dealership. When we went to Monster Golf, we were in an Escalade. This time, Daddy and Millicent were driving a Chrysler 300. As soon as we got in, Millicent started it up and turned on the air. "Okay, Valerie, you know more about Marshall then any of us. Where does he go to school?"

It wasn't like when we were looking for Nikki. I didn't have any suggestions about Tangie. If I'd thought I knew anything about her, I really didn't. I realized I wouldn't even know where to find her in the mall.

"Clark," Valerie said.

"That's our first stop," Millicent said. "Have you ever been with her to his dorm?"

Valerie was quiet, but Millicent looked at her from the rearview like Mama and Daddy would do Peaches and me. "It's getting later and later," she said.

"He has his own apartment," Valerie mumbled.

"Oooh," I said, though I didn't mean to. That was probably another reason Frank didn't like him. I couldn't imagine living in a place where there weren't any parents around, ever.

"Just tell me how to get there," Millicent said. "Better yet, do you know the address?"

"But, Millicent, I don't think they're there. I think the protest is downtown, or on campus. I'm not for sure."

"It's always best to start where he lives. I heard a blurb about a protest online, but that took place last night."

"This one is different. Don't think they have a permit. That's why she said she wasn't going," Valerie said.

"If they're doing something under the radar, that would be like finding a needle in a haystack."

I turned as far around in my seat as I could, as if that would make Valerie spit out the address. She scrolled through her texts, then she tried calling Tangie again.

"Where does he live, Valerie? Tangie talks to you about him. You gotta know," I said. She avoided my eyes.

"Now her phone is going to voicemail. Not even ringing, just straight to voicemail. His address is nine-fourteen Howell Mill Road," Valerie said.

"Don't even have to GPS it," Millicent said. "Used to have a patient who lived in that area."

"Patient?" I repeated.

"I was a home health-care nurse. It's the kind of work you have to take a break from sometimes. While I'm working with your dad part-time, I'm getting another degree so I can go into nursing administration."

As Millicent talked, I wished we weren't searching for Tangie but just riding and getting comfortable around each other like Daddy wanted us to do.

"You said nine-fourteen?" Millicent asked.

"Yes," Valerie and I answered together.

She got on the expressway, but it still took about ten minutes until we turned left off the highway and onto Howell Mill Road. "He has roommates?" Millicent asked.

"Two, I think," Valerie said.

Just then, Valerie's cell phone rang. I jumped in my seat.

"Hello? Tangie? Where are you?" Valerie said. "No. I don't think your dad knows. Just calm down. . . . Georgie told us. She was worried. We have someone to help. Where are you? Okay . . . Okay. Don't move."

"Where is she?" I shouted.

"At the McDonald's on Peachtree."

In less than five minutes, we pulled up in front of McDonald's, and I scanned the parking lot and peered into the brightly lit windows. Then, coming out the door, I saw those tiny braids with hundreds of beads swinging on her head. Her seventies dress had been replaced with jeans and a Georgia State University sweatshirt, but it was her coming out the door. I barely waited for Millicent to park before I leaped out of the car and shouted her name.

She turned her head toward me and hurried across the parking lot. Her beads sounded like hundreds of tiny cymbals as she got closer.

"Watch out for cars," Millicent shouted, and Tangie and I met nearly halfway in the lot.

This time, I didn't have to hug her first. Tangie wrapped her arms around me and rocked a little, like you do when you really like—or maybe even love—someone.

27.

CORNY KIDS' PARTY

Once we were all in the car, I wished I had sat in the back with Tangie, but I knew she really wanted to talk to Valerie. It took all I had to stay facing forward and not turn around like a nosy pest.

"I'm sorry to worry everyone," Tangie said.

Her voice was all I needed to twist around. She and Valerie had their hands locked together, and I hoped that Nikki and I would be best friends like that one day and not always the fussing kind.

"First things first," Millicent said. "Are you okay?"

"Yeah. I'm fine," she said as soft as Peaches would. "Thanks to Mar—"

I almost wanted to finish it, but I'd already done enough.

"To Marshall," Millicent said. "Is that your boyfriend?"

"Not if my dad has anything to do with it."

"What happened, Tangie?" Millicent was like Mama for a minute, knowing exactly what was in my head.

"We were just going to march along the spot in Buckhead where Roderick was harassed. Police stopped him without cause. He hadn't been drinking or anything. Marshall did such a good job of getting the word out that more people showed up than we thought, which was good. But they didn't have a permit.

"When the police told us to leave, Marshall's roommate started shouting. Others joined in. Next thing I know, Marshall's roommate was on the ground. When Marshall spoke up, they put him in cuffs, too. He told me not to say a word and get home."

"I'm sorry, Tangie" was all I could say.

Millicent shook her head. "What can start out peaceful can turn violent instantly. I'm just happy you weren't hurt."

"We just wanted to march the same route Roderick walked when he was arrested. Just to show them that they don't have a right to harass us. But some protesters started blocking traffic."

"That'll get the police involved quickly, especially in that area. Have you heard from Marshall?" Millicent asked.

"Not yet. Soon as I got to the McDonald's I called Val. I knew you knew how to get to this McDonald's."

"I couldn't have helped. My folks don't let me drive after seven," Valerie said. "My dad dropped me off."

"Yeah, I forgot. Panicked." Tangie sighed.

"Tangie," Millicent said, "I don't want you to think that

I'm okay with you keeping secrets from your dad. There has been a rash of brutality claims throughout Atlanta. Emotions are high across the city. Your dad probably wants you to exercise your rights, but you have to let him know where you are and what you're doing for your safety."

"I'm gonna tell him what happened. But do I have to do it tonight?"

"No, you don't, but you have to do it," Millicent said.

"Yes, ma'am," Tangie said.

The seat belt got the best of me and I leaned back. For the next several minutes, Tangie and Valerie barely spoke a word to each other. They were so silent that I thought maybe Valerie was mad at her. I couldn't help myself. I whipped around, and both of their faces had the glow of the phone screen. Whatever they were saying was all being done in text messages. I doubted I'd ever really know all that happened, but that was okay.

As soon as we got home, Tangie and Valerie bolted straight upstairs.

"Hey, wait . . . wait!" Mama called. "Wasn't that Tangie?" She asked me as I strolled in the room. "Why did she take off her dress? I didn't even get a pic."

"Maybe she spilled something on it," I said. "She'll be right back. She's with Valerie." I was proud at how calm I acted.

"Well, as soon as you see her, bring her straight to me."

"Okay," I said, happy Mama was dancing and enjoying herself.

"Where were you at, G-baby?" Peaches said as she

saddled up to me with one of her friends who had cake in her hair.

"Had to go out a second. You miss me?"

She nodded.

"Have you been dancing?"

"I keep falling down. Mama said it will get better. Will it?"

"I fall down, too," her friend said.

"See, Peaches. It happens to everybody." But before she answered the thought seemed to leave her and helping her friend get cake out of her hair took over.

Just as I turned to go find Nikki and Tammy, they darted up from the basement and across the room to me.

"Where have you been?" Nikki piped.

"Looking for Tangie without help from you two."

"I . . . I can call Jevon and Crystal. Maybe they can help us again."

"Too little. Too late. No need. All taken care of." I brushed my hands together like people do in the movies when something is successfully completed.

"Wait, I just saw Millicent. Were you with her? You told your dad's *new* wife?" Nikki asked. "Tangie's never, ever gonna speak to you again."

"See how much you know," I said. "She's already talking to me, so there."

"Lucinda and Rhonda called their ride. She said she can't stay any longer at this CKP."

"CKP?" I repeated.

"Corny Kids' Party."

"Then why are they still here?" I said. Nikki raised her

palms. "More importantly, when are you getting your bike? That's the only reason she was supposed to be at this CKP in the first place."

"Can you not tell the world please?" Nikki said.

"Let's go back outside," Tammy said. "All the old fogey stogeys are up here."

Nikki yanked at her Afro puffs. "I don't know what to do now. She didn't bring it like she promised." It was really hard not to feel sorry for Nikki. Lucinda would have never gotten her paws on that bike if Nikki didn't think she was helping her real friends. Since I wasn't going to be at Sweet Apple next year, I was sure Mama would let me try out for the dance team. And I didn't need Lucinda Hightower's approval. I might make it on my own if I could get my nerves under control. Tammy would make it for sure if it was all about dancing. She's the only one who could do the Chicken Noodle Soup and make it cool. But if someone like Lucinda stopped teasing her about her weight, other girls would, too.

Before I could think of anything to help Nikki that didn't involve just telling our folks, Lucinda and Rhonda walked up.

"We're going out to the back till our ride comes."

"It's like a McDonald's Playland downstairs."

"Well, it is a corny kids' party," I said. "And for your information, it's for my sister who was in the hospital. If you haven't figured that out. Duh."

Lucinda acted like that lip gloss suddenly glued her mouth shut.

Rhonda tugged at her ripped jeans. "Glad your sister is okay. Cake's the bomb. Ribs, too."

"Thanks," I said, like I had a hand in that. "We all should go out there. But you two aren't going anywhere until you tell us when Nikki is getting her bike."

"Is it your bike or what? Plus, I'm sure Nikki told you the deal. Keep in mind, I was there when you tried out for dance team at Sweet Apple," Lucinda said.

She didn't say another word, but flailed her arms around.

"She wasn't that bad," Nikki said, then shut up.

"It doesn't matter if I was. She can't keep your bike just 'cause she's bullying you."

"Is that what you're telling people, Nik?"

"Stop calling her 'Nik.' She doesn't like it. Only her brother gets to call her that, and you ain't him."

I couldn't forget the times that Nikki had spoken out for me when someone said something about my "little girl" hairstyle. Or when Mama bought me cheapo sneakers and Nikki kept a new pair of purple-and-white Nikes in her locker just for me. There was something about Lucinda that made Nikki unable to talk for herself and that's when friends had to step in. Maybe that's all Tangie and Marshall were trying to do—stand up for someone who couldn't stand up for themselves.

We all were walking toward the back door. Nikki didn't say a word and wobbled like a newborn pony.

Before we made it to the door, that Barry White voice called, "Georgie!"

Nikki and Tammy froze like their name was Georgie, too. But Lucinda and Rhonda kept strolling on out.

"Where have you been, young lady?" Frank said.

What to say? What to say? Does he know anything? What if he found out? What do I do now? Please come down now, Tangie, please.

I turned around. Frank was smiling at me, so I exhaled.

"Think someone is looking for you?" Frank nodded to the right, and now all three of us faced him.

"Hi," Kevin said.

"Hi," I said. Excitement bubbled up inside me like soda pop. "I thought you left for Rochester already."

"My dad had to put it off until next week. Something came up." His voice didn't sound disappointed. But sometimes when you have to disguise it is when you feel the worst. Hurt is right there underneath the happy sound.

"It happens," I said.

"I still wouldn't be here if it wasn't for Mr. Frank."

Frank rocked on his heels. "I made an ice run, and who should I see walking with his bike?" Frank said.

"Chain finally popped," Kevin said. "I didn't know about the bus schedule on the weekend. I was heading back home."

"You gave him a ride?" I asked Frank.

"Yep," Frank said. "And I'm his taxi back home in about an hour or two, so have fun until then."

I hugged Frank so hard he stumbled backward.

"Thank you for being so nice to my friend," I said into his chest, trying not to cough because of his smoky barbecue scent.

"I better enjoy this hug." He chuckled. "There'll be enough times when it's the last thing you'll want to do. You can ask Ms. Tangie all about that." His hand flattened my Afro, and I didn't mind at all.

When I released him, I was a little too embarrassed to look at Nikki and Tammy. To them that hug stamped *I Like Kevin* across my forehead.

"Y'all have a good time," he said to all of us, then looked at Kevin. "What time did your folks say be home, young man?"

"Ah . . . Eleven at the latest. My mom will worry after then." Kevin said the words slowly like he just wanted to hear the sound. Maybe she realized how much she'd miss him now that he was going away.

"Okay. In that case, be ready no later than ten thirty." Kevin nodded. "And there's plenty of barbecue left. Don't be shy."

"Yes, sir," Kevin said, and gave Frank a salute that he returned. As soon as Frank walked away, Nikki, Tammy, Kevin, and I huddled together.

Kevin squinted at Nikki. "Lucinda's here, so I guess you got your bike back."

"Not quite," I said.

"You need to mind your own business," Nikki snapped at Kevin.

"Really, Nikki?" I said.

It was hard for me to feel sorry for her, because she fibbed about what happened with Lucinda and she'd stolen those earrings. But Tangie had made a mistake, too. Mama's favorite play is *A Raisin in the Sun*. It says something about caring for people even more when they've made mistakes. But I knew Nikki wouldn't want to hear me jabbering about a play when Lucinda's ride would be along any second, so I kept my mouth shut.

"I say we grab your mama and daddy right now and tell them that Lucinda has your bike. That would put an end to this," I said.

"Hello? Earth to Georgie! I know you're not going to Sweet Apple next year, but I am. You want me to have a permanent seat at the loser table, huh?"

"What do you think?" I said.

"Well, that's exactly where I'll be if the second most popular girl in school, me, rats out the most popular."

Didn't know exactly how Nikki's calculations worked, but I didn't sweat it.

A song that reminded me of gym class, "Y.M.C.A.," was booming from the backyard as the four of us thought about how to get Nikki's bike.

I glanced out the window. Lucinda was chugging a soda and bobbing her head.

"Okay, I have an idea. Don't let them leave. Even if their ride comes, think of something to stall them."

"You better not go tell any grown-ups, Georgie. I gotta show my face at Sweet Apple next year, you don't. I can't be a tattletale."

"Just make sure they don't go nowhere," I said to all of them, but looked at Kevin.

"I got you," he said.

I darted off into the living room and up the stairs. Tangie was coming out of her door with Valerie.

"Hey, what's up?" Tangie said, all her freckles shining. She put her arms around my shoulders and stepped with me back into her room. "I'll see you downstairs," she said to Valerie.

"Is Marshall okay?" I asked.

"Yeah, his parents bailed him and his roommate out. If I hadn't left, I would have been taken in with them, I'm sure. Wouldn't have mattered what the cause, if my dad had to come down to a precinct to get me, I'd never see Marshall again. My dad never gonna know what a good guy he is if I get myself in trouble. For now, Marshall has to have his way of protesting and I'll have mine. And it'll probably be with my dad," she said, and nudged my shoulders.

"You're not gonna see him anymore?"

"I wouldn't say that. But it won't be until we come back from Bogalusa. Hopefully, we'll keep in touch."

"You said Kevin and I would keep in touch."

"It's a little different with older boys. We'll talk about that later."

"So you don't mind going to Bogalusa now?"

"I talked to my mom. She says I can come to Houston if I really want to, which means she doesn't want me to. She . . . she wouldn't know what to do with me there for the rest of the summer. She doesn't drive anymore since what happened. Dad said he'd match whatever I made at the diner." She raised her eyebrows. "Money for my car," she said with a sly smile.

"'You have brains in your head. You have feet in your shoes. You can steer yourself in any direction you choose,'" I said.

"Cute. Guess that's true," she said.

She didn't get that it was a line from Dr. Seuss, and I

shut up before I lost like a zillion cool points. I didn't have to work hard before my excitement left.

"You didn't come up here to ask about Marshall. What's up?"

I took a deep breath and just started telling her all about Lucinda. In about five minutes, she said, "And she's still downstairs?"

"I told them not to let her go," I said.

Tangie put her hand on my shoulder and nudged me toward the door. "Lead the way."

When we got downstairs, we linked up with Nikki, Tammy, and Kevin.

"You told her," Nikki said.

"Ah, yeah," I said.

"But if we make her mad, she won't let us be on the dance team."

"At school? How does she have say so in that?" Tangie asked.

Nikki tossed her head back. "No, at the Boys and Girls Club."

Tangie put her hands on her hips. "Are you talking about that one on Richland Road?"

"Yeah," we all mumbled.

Tangie laughed. "Hello? Georgie! Have you seen my room? What do I have more of than anything?"

"Let's go find Lucinda!" I shouted.

"That's what I'm talking about," Kevin said, and we all marched outside.

28.

STRAIGHT UP TO HEAVEN

Everyone followed Tangie, including Valerie. Kevin and I lagged behind.

"I'm kinda happy my dad didn't come today."

"Really?"

"I wanted to see you before I left. You know, to help with the bike, in case you needed me or something."

"My sister says there are lots of ways to keep in touch these days."

"That's true. Rochester won't seem so far," he said, and the spot where he kissed me tingled again. Seconds later, we were all out back interfering with Lucinda and Rhonda enjoying root beer floats, Peaches's favorite drink. People sang "Everybody's got a little light under the sun" in the background.

"Which one of you is Lucinda?"

Lucinda pointed to herself, before taking a chug.

"Heard you are cocaptain of the Georgia Peach Jam Step Team? First, the bike shouldn't have anything to do with someone making the team or not. You need to learn sportsmanship."

"You need to mind your business," Lucinda shot back.

"Georgie is my sister, Nikki is her best friend, so this is my business."

"Whatever. You probably just want to try out, too." Lucinda turned to Nikki. "Don't think that bike is worth four headaches."

"Oh, is that what you think?" Tangie said.

Tangie took a scrunchie from her wrist and put her hair in a ponytail, beads and all. Then she whipped her hoodie over her head.

"You've done it now," Valerie said as she held Tangie's phone. Peaches eased up to me just in time.

"What's happening, G-baby?" Peaches asked.

"Just watch," I said, and pulled her close.

Tangie looked over her shoulder. And before any of us could speak, she floated through the air, her body a perfect arch.

"She can fly," Kevin mouthed in awe.

She backflipped two times. Stopped. Then she did that move from that old movie, *The Matrix*, that looked like her back swept the ground. Like a stop sign, she held out the palm of her left hand, then let each finger fold down individually until a current of electricity hit her wrist, ran along her shoulders, and ended in the fingertips of her right hand.

Her clap was loud before her knees hiked up to her chest, and every time her knee went up, she'd clap underneath. I started to clap along, feeling the rhythm, but didn't want to miss a move.

"All right! All right!" she shouted.

"All right! All right!" we shouted back. She clicked her heels. And stood soldier-straight with her hands along her side. Moving her head in quick, sharp turns, she surveyed her surroundings again, and sprung her hands over her head, clicked her heels again, and took to the air. Her body curved like a capital C during each of the two backflips before landing right in front of Lucinda, nearly nose to nose.

Lucinda didn't move, and her eyes were wide.

"Dang, she's good," Rhonda said to Lucinda, though we all heard it.

"Whoa! Was that my baby?" Frank shouted as he approached us. He put his hand on Tangie's back and pulled her close. "Tee, you don't know how good it is for me to see you doing what you love. . . . You know . . ."

"You don't have to say it, Daddy, I know," Tangie said.

I felt a tickle in my throat and hoped that I didn't cry because I knew what he meant, too. Morgan. Morgan would be so happy to see her fly.

"Teach me, Tangie! Teach me," Peaches said.

"Soon. Real soon," Tangie said.

"Trina sent me out to get you girls for the pictures. Glad to see you doing your thing, baby," Frank said, and kissed her forehead.

"All of these girls will be on the Woolfolk BGC step

team next year. Just showing them a few moves," Tangie said.

"Well, who better. You were captain! Y'all come in for pics when you're done."

"Go in with Frank, Peaches. We'll be there in just a second."

After Frank and Peaches left, Tangie folded her arms and stepped closer to Lucinda, who still hadn't spoken. "Ms. Jerilyn, you know, the coach, has been after me for months to come back as her assistant. This team gives everyone a fair shot and they do not like bullies. This is what will happen: That bike you have. Get it back to Nikki ASAP. If you don't, I promise you that you won't dance one minute with that team. Are we clear?"

"Yes," Lucinda said. Her eyes looked like they could still see Tangie in the air.

"I wanted to call Ms. Jerilyn and have you banned from the team, but Georgie convinced me not to. Shouldn't you have something to say?"

"Oh," Lucinda said.

I tensed up then. Tangie was pushing it. But maybe she knew Lucinda better than I did, because Lucinda glanced at me and didn't even roll her eyes.

"Thank you," Lucinda said.

"You're welcome," I said. Uggh, where was my cool? Wasn't I supposed to say something like, "I hope this teaches you a lesson"?

"Nikki, if it's not back tomorrow morning, call Georgie." Tangie reached to Val for her phone. "I got Ms. Jerilyn's number right here. Don't give me a reason."

Tangie turned to me. "Dad said the photographer is here, we should go in." She whipped around and all the beads on her ponytail snapped like a hundred fingers right in Lucinda's face.

We walked through the door, and I went up to Peaches right away. "Think Tangie will dance again for us?" she asked, and leaned into me.

"I think she will," I said.

"Oh, okay," she said, but the zest she had before was gone.

"Where's all the excitement you had a few minutes ago? Everything okay?"

"Nothing's the matter," Peaches said, which is what she says when something is "the matter."

Before I could get to the bottom of it, Mama waved at us. "G-baby, you and Tangie get in this picture, please. I don't think I've had one picture with all my girls this entire evening."

"Why don't the four of you stand in front of that window? Those mauve drapes make a good backdrop," the photographer said. She wore jeans and a blue T-shirt with *Click Chick* written on the front with gold glitter. Since Mama called her at the last minute, she could only schedule one hour.

"Yeah, that looks good," Frank said.

"Don't you go anywhere. I want you in here next," Mama called to him.

I was glad that Tangie didn't mind Mama calling her one of her "girls." Seemed like everyone followed the photographer, because more guests crowded into the living room, including Grandma Sugar. After the photographer snapped a few shots, the front door opened, and Daddy and Millicent came back in.

"Looks like we got inside just in time." Daddy made an imaginary camera with his hands.

"Mama, can the whole blended-up family be in the picture together?" a small voice piped.

Everybody laughed.

Maybe she's just a little drained.

"Y'all heard the guest of honor. George, you and Millicent get over here," Frank said, and moved the coffee table back. "Peaches wants the 'whole blended-up family.'"

"We can do that," Daddy said to Frank, and they shook hands and bumped shoulders. Not a full hug, but something close to it. Mama and Millicent didn't do as much; smiling at each other was enough.

"That includes me, too," Sugar said, tiptoeing over and making us laugh even more.

Peaches was the smallest, so she posed in the front, then I stood next to her and wrapped my hand around her shoulder. Tangie looped one arm with mine and the other around on Peaches's shoulder. Sugar stood next to us. Mama and Frank were next to her, then Daddy and Millicent were on the other side of me.

"Can't get a better family shot than that," Ms. Cora said.

"Wouldn't happen in my house," another friend added, and laughed.

"Is that 'Disco Lady'?" Sugar asked. "That DJ is going to have to play that one again once we finish up here."

"You got it," Frank said.

"Tighten up just a bit," the photographer said.

Standing around us were Kevin, Nikki, Tammy, and Valerie, and I couldn't wait to get them all together in a picture, too. I didn't see Lucinda and Rhonda. Maybe their ride finally showed up. Nikki's lips were flapping a mile a minute. She was yapping to Kevin and Tammy one second and laughing so hard that she was holding her stomach the next.

"Here we go," the photographer said. "On the count of three."

"Just a moment!" Mama said. "Everyone say 'Bogalusa' instead of 'cheese.'"

"You got it," Click Chick said. "On the count of three, everyone. One . . . two . . . three."

"BOGALUSA!" we all shouted, and even Peaches pronounced it right this time.

"One more," the photographer said. "Pull in closer on each side. . . . A little closer . . . Everyone huddle together. Good!"

As she adjusted her camera's lens, Tangie whispered in my ear, "Thanks again for helping me, Georgie. Would have been a lot worse if I had to call Dad. You're a great li'l sister."

"No biggie," I said, hoping my eyes didn't get all teary. "Thanks for helping with Lucinda."

"I know girls like her. Insecure mostly," she said.

Insecure? Lucinda? I couldn't wrap my mind around that.

I pulled Peaches in closer. She smiled along with

everyone else, but it was sorta like Kevin's smile, with sadness lurking underneath.

"Okay. On three . . . One . . . two . . . three!"

Tangie's arm tightened around my shoulder, and she leaned in until her cheek pressed against mine. As soon as the photographer snapped a few more shots, everyone started talking and taking pictures with their phones, but I linked my hands with Peaches's and we made our way toward the living room door.

I opened it and we walked out to the porch, closing the door behind us.

"If you're tired, guest of honor or not, everyone would understand if you're ready for bed."

"It's not that."

"Then what? Bogalusa?"

"No. I heard something bad." I bit my lip to keep from pressing her. "I wasn't 'posed to hear it."

Maybe someone had said something about her being slower than everyone else now. How could I protect her in Bogalusa, if I couldn't even protect her at home? There was a break in her heart that I might not ever be able to fix.

"You can tell me," I said. It didn't seem as though Mama and Daddy had fallen into a shouting match. But when things were bad between them, they'd do it in grocery stores, movies, doctor's offices, no place was off-limits. "Was it Mama and Daddy?"

"No." She frowned and twisted her lips.

I bent down until we were eye to eye. "What then?"

She looked down, then back up at me. The puffy cheeks were slimmer now, but I planted a kiss right in the middle, just the same. "You can tell me anything, right?"

She nodded and her eyes welled with tears. "One of the grown-ups told another one that everybody was getting along 'cause I was sick. And that it wouldn't stay that way."

I almost wanted to know which one said it, but it didn't matter. I wiped her tears with my thumbs just as they fell.

"They were just talking, Peaches. That's what grown-ups do sometimes. They say things they don't really mean for us to hear."

"But is it true?"

I took her hand and led her to the steps and we sat down, the music from the backyard thumping like a heartbeat.

"Want me to be honest with you, right?" She nodded. "Well, maybe a little of it is true. Everyone is on their best behavior now, but Mama, Frank, Daddy, and even Millicent were trying before you got sick, right?"

"Mama and Daddy were mad at the hospital. They didn't think I could hear them, but I could," Peaches said.

"But they're here now, right?"

"Yeah. But they never all got together before."

I put my arms around her and pulled her close. "Grown-ups are human, too. It takes time to figure stuff out."

"Am I still sick? That's why I can't do stuff like before? Not even the Dougie or the Nae Nae?"

"You're getting stronger every day. You rather be getting stronger here than in that hospital, right? Anyway, when you are up to it, we're doing our own dance, remember?"

"Yeah. The Georgie Peaches."

"You got it! The Dougie and the Nae Nae are old anyway."

Then she leaned even closer to me. The coconut oil Mama smoothed in her hair scented each breeze.

"Tangie told me a secret."

"She did?"

"She said I could tell you if I wanted."

"Do you want to?"

"Yeah."

"What is it?"

"That you tried to help make me not be sick no more."

"We all tried to help."

"She said you were gonna give me a blood confusion."

I giggled. "It's called a blood transfusion, silly."

"You wasn't gonna be scared to give me your blood?"

"A little, but I would have done it anyway."

"'Cause you love me."

Her smile lit the night brighter than the twinkling stars. Peaches hugged me real hard, and I felt jumbled up inside. Hugging Peaches made me happy, but a part of me wanted to cry. I couldn't help thinking about how much Tangie must miss her little sister and hoped when it all got too much for her, so much that she might not even be able to talk about it with anyone, she could feel her hug from heaven.

I knew that our "blended-up" family wasn't going to always be like the party tonight. But I was Peaches's big sister, just like Tangie was mine, and I prayed that I'd always be there for both of them the best I could. Mama and Daddy hadn't said anything to me, but I knew there was something going on with Peaches that maybe could never be fixed. But I bet Tangie would give anything to have her sister with her, even if she wasn't the same as before.

I tilted my head to the east and west, and listened to the music vibrate and the voices dance around. The door opened.

Tangie called, "G-baby and Peaches, let's get a pic with my phone."

"Sure," we said together as we stood up and Peaches led me inside.

But before entering the house, I glanced up one more time.

"We'll love her . . . like sky," I whispered, and wished for the wind to whisk my words straight up to heaven.

ACKNOWLEDGMENTS

To reach this point, I followed Morrison's instructions to write the book that I'd always wanted to read, along with Baldwin's wisdom on "endurance," and Thoreau's advice to "Live the life you've imagined." I thank God for allowing me to see this day, and the Reverend Dr. Richard Douglass and Zion Hill Missionary Baptist Church for keeping our family in prayer.

I thank my editor, Laura Schreiber, for the joy in your voice when you talk about *Love Like Sky* and my agent, John Rudolph, for that one "yes." My mother, Daisy Mae Raby, and the man who became Dad, Winston Raby, for your unconditional love and letting me come back home—it made all the difference. My grandparents: Ike Shepard, for his strength; Lillie Mae Shepard, who said, "You can be anything you want to be"; and my grandmother, Idella Cook Shepard, even though we never met.

Of course, my siblings: Jerilyn P. Harris, my first and closest friend; Randall J. Raby, Winston Raby, and Isaiah Raby, who kept my lights on and the landlord at bay, with special thanks to Winston for understanding when I said I didn't have a "Plan B"; and the sibling to whom I dedicated *Love Like Sky*—a senseless act of violence took him away from us in the physical, but never in the spiritual—Samuel C. Griffin. To Nikkol and Khaylin Harris, and my g-niece, Melody: Auntie hopes you all see my love for you in this work; and my brother-in-law, Reginald B. Harris, one of the best fathers I know.

The host of family who supports me no matter where I am in the world: countless cousins, including Shannon D. Shepard; Christopher, Isaac, and Dale Williams; Patrice and Velika Harris; Lily Shepard, and Tiscur Taylor. The Elzeys, Rabys, Thomases, Bridgeses, Cherrys, Amigers, and Thompsons. My aunts and uncles: Jeanette and Haywood Thomas, Jean and Terry Williams, Janice and Cee Harris, and Curtis and Barbara Shepard. Cousins, great-aunts and uncles: the Sampsons of Bogalusa, LA, especially the late Uncle McClurie Sampson, who was a two-term councilman in Bogalusa and President Emeritus of Louisiana Municipal Black Caucus Association.

The love and support of my circle of friends is boundless. To thank each one is a book in itself, but I have to mention: Laverne Butler Dutkowsky, Patricia Elder, Valerie McGrady Blake, Erica McNealy, Angela Ray, and Eric Hodge. Thanks for every memory and for keeping me sane.

Thank you, Laura Pegram, *Kweli Journal*, for your

belief in *Love Like Sky* and your advocacy for writers of color; Marita Golden for mentoring and believing. The Hurston Wright Foundation. 2014 Yaddo artists, especially Kirk Shannon-Butts. To everyone in the Morris Brown College legacy. My alma mater, Georgia State University, especially Dr. John W. Holman. The professors and students at the University of Ghana at Legon.

Terry Kennedy and the late Jim Clark of the University of North Carolina at Greensboro, MFA program. UNCG MFAers. Everyone at Rochester's Writers & Books. Rochester Public Libraries, especially the Arnett and Phillis Wheatley branches. The Magees of Mt. Olive, Mississippi. Adeyemi O. Makinde. Michelle Denise Commander. Dr. Shirley Hanshaw. Duru and Ouanza Ahanotu. Marva Gardner. Scot Brown. A. Van Jordan. Tyehimba and Kelly Jess. John Dalton. Pastor Tacuma and Dr. Michelle Johnson, for being among the first to love G-baby and Peaches, and for preordering *Love Like Sky* for your students. Belinda Carmichael. Ashley Craig Lancaster. Kim Bowman. Diane Watkins. Robin Haten. Jackie Parks. Mrs. Odessa and the late Charlie McGrady. The Reverend Frederick Robinson, who introduced me to Coltrane. Valerie Boyd, who read my early stories. Tayari Jones for kindness and advice. Shay Youngblood, Terry McMillan, and Bernice L. McFadden for opening doors. Angela Johnson, Renee Watson, Jacqueline Woodson, Rita Williams-Garcia, and Nikki Grimes for priceless blueprints. Pat Lottier and my former coworkers at the *Atlanta Tribune: The Magazine*, including Renita Mathis and Adrienne S. Harris. Tokeya C. Graham. Kenny Jean. Jennifer Pittman. The staff, professors, and students of Lincoln University, past and present. Dr. Ann Harris. Lekan Oguntoyinbo. Greg Brownderville. Dr. Anita Lael. Kathleen Woodruff. Carol Taylor for initially reading and editing *Love Like Sky* and other manuscripts. Tracey Baptiste and Savvy Thorne. The Same Page and Go on Girl! book clubs.

Jevon T. Rice, for loving me and reading pages during the hardest time of my life.

Rochester, NY, for welcoming me back, and Atlanta, Georgia, for showing me many sides of life and giving me more friendships than I can name.

I know I'm forgetting several key people, but it's my head, not my heart—and another reason I'm thankful for other novels to come.